RUINS

BY

LAZETTE GIFFORD

Copyright 2016 Lazette Gifford
An ACOA Publication
www.aconspiracyofauthors.com
ISBN: 978-1-936507-65-8

Ruins
A Conspiracy of Authors Publication
www.aconspiracyofauthors.com
Copyright 2016, Lazette Gifford
ISBN: 978-1-936507-65-8
Cover Art Copyright 2016, Lazette Gifford

First Print Edition, September 2016

Dedication: I love the American Southwest, probably all the more so because I live in Nebraska. This book is for Russ who takes me there when he can, and to the mountains as well. I find inspiration there, and this is the most obvious result, though not the only one.

TABLE OF CONTENTS

CHAPTER ONE

Release from prison didn't end the nightmare.

The bus hit another small snowdrift snaking its way across Interstate 95, the road rough despite the snow plows Leander had seen traversing the road not long before. The huge bus gave a shuddering little bounce, while the wind caught at the side and tried to push it toward the edge of the road. Snow fell like a sheer, white curtain, obscuring much of the world around him.

Leander Constantinos, despite growing up in New York City, had never seen so much snow in his life.

He sat in the back of the bus, his coat hood pulled up over his head, seeking for anonymity. Lee looked out the back window and watched as the last white van -- some TV station emblem on the side -- took an off ramp a few miles short of Baltimore. No one else had followed him this far north into this horrible weather.

Free. Finally, truly free.

He sat against the hard seat and shivered, not so much at the cold, as at the uncertainty of his future. Freedom hadn't been a word in his vocabulary for more than five years. It had slipped away the day the police rushed into his apartment and dragged him from his bed, with his wife crying and his baby son screaming as they watched.

He closed his eyes and tried to block the moment away, but it had been the start of a long, long nightmare.

Leander watched as the world passed, white and gray, outside. He had gone, he thought, about as far North as he cared to travel.

Less than three hours later Lee found himself in the downtown Baltimore bus terminal, a building filled with restless people worried about the upcoming holidays. He left as quickly as he could and wandered down a street until he found a haven from the cold at a hotel. He hoped the weather kept people from trying to find him.

He spent a restless night, mostly sitting by the window watching it snow. He skipped food, afraid to leave the room and draw attention. A hot shower proved both heaven and unnerving -- no one standing over him, no one telling him to get moving.

The next morning, he went down to the lobby and checked out again, and then crossed to the phone bank in the corner. Lee knew he had to make a call before he could go on with life, but Leander feared what he would learn. However, without the call, he could only live in limbo, rather than heaven or hell.

He didn't trust the desk clerk, who might listen in, so he used the phone card he'd picked up at a shop by the bus terminal. Right now he didn't trust anyone, having been hounded for days since his release, everyone wanting his story.

They knew the story. All the reporters truly wanted was to see his emotions, and he wasn't ready to share them.

Lee pulled his hood up and probably looked sinister, but he didn't care. A single piece of battered luggage sat at his feet. He kicked at it while his fingers dialed a number by memory, and he listened to the other end ring; once, twice, again. His throat went dry.

Another ring.

A click.

"Hey-lo," a woman's voice said -- a familiar, friendly voice, but not Debra's.

"Hello, M-Mrs. Martin," he said. He bit his lip, silently cursing the stutter. A grown man shouldn't --

"We thought you would call." The friendliness disappeared, and the new sound cut like the icy winter wind. "Debra is here. She wants to talk to you."

His heart pounded, and his hands grew damp. Lee held the phone tighter, fearing he would drop it. He stopped kicking the poor luggage. He almost stopped breathing.

"Lee."

"Debra." It was all he could say. He hadn't ever expected to hear her voice again, not after the trial and the divorce papers. He hadn't expected to hear her now, only to learn from her mother what he should do.

"Lee, I've remarried." She spoke calmly, as though she hadn't just driven a knife straight into his heart. "I came to my mom's house as soon as I saw the news because I don't want you hunting me down at my home. We have two little girls --"

"My son," he said, panicked, remembering a two-month-old he had hardly known, and loved with all his heart. "Gavriel --"

"We have renamed him. He's Gary now, and he thinks Andy is his father, Lee. It's better this way. You don't want to ruin his life, do you?"

"Ruin?" What the hell was she saying? "They found

the guy who killed Missy Reed, D-Debra. They proved it wasn't me. I'm out of prison. I didn't d-do it. How can I ruin his life by being innocent?"

"You bring disaster, Lee." She stopped and took a ragged breath. He heard more emotion in her gasp than he had in her words. "You always bring disaster, don't you? Is that what you want for Gary?"

He heard neither regret nor anger in her voice. She didn't feel anything toward him. The realization came as a mind-numbing revelation and an end to a dream which had kept him -- mostly -- sane in prison for the last five years. He had held to her memory, even without letters, or a whisper of any compassion or belief in his innocence. They had been married and happy. He had always thought it would count for something if she learned the truth.

The silence stretched for too long while he held tighter the phone. He blinked, decisions made.

"I'm sorry I b-bothered you," he said. He meant those words, too. "I won't call again."

"Lee --"

He hung up. She knew he wouldn't call back. He had, no matter what, never broken a promise.

Leander picked up his suitcase and walked out of the building, waving away the doorman who wanted to call a taxi for him. He headed into the snowy December morning, wandering past festive displays, and avoiding the rush of shoppers dashing from one shop to the next. He heard snippets of Christmas Carols and watched through one window as young mothers stood in line with their children, waiting for a few moments and a picture with Santa.

Did Debra take Gavriel -- Gary -- and the two girls to see Santa today? Lee turned away, wondering what he had done to God to deserve this. Before the arrest, Leander Constantinos never even had a speeding ticket. He had done everything people had expected of him: gone to college to be an architect like his father wanted, married and had a child like his mother wanted, and worked hard like Debra wanted.

It kept snowing. Leander walked down the street, away from the holiday cheer.

His parents had gone back to Greece soon after the trial ended. He had no idea where his older brother had gone, but the fact he'd never written to Lee in prison seemed enough of an indication of what to expect there.

Debra had remarried.

Five years of lies had torn his world apart, and Lee found nothing left he could grasp so he could go back to what he had been and no way to repair the damage. They had found the man who had murdered Missy Stern. They'd found his basement trophy room with the knives he'd used, the locks of hair he'd saved, the pictures he'd taken of Missy and the others. The state set Leander Constantinos free with some money, his few belongings, and an apology. He had thought the nightmare ended. Everyone knew he was innocent.

Leander looked down at his left hand and the gold band he had so carefully slipped on his finger when they gave it back to him. It had felt loose, and he'd feared it would slip off. Now Lee unclenched his fist and shook the ring into his right hand. He stared at the plain, unadorned gold. He didn't look at the inscription on the inside of the band: Leander and Debra Constantinos. Forever.

Lee tossed the ring out into the snowy street and walked on.

Fate brought him back to the Greyhound Bus Depot

once more. He went inside, checked all the boards, and found one bus leaving within the next two hours and heading west, away from the snow, the lost dreams, and the lies. He had never been to the west, though he'd loved to study the history back in college before the nightmare began.

He bought a ticket to Santa Fe, New Mexico.

And he wondered if this feeling of emptiness was what it really meant to be free.□

CHAPTER TWO

Cheveyo Rey found the phone under a pile of paper on the table and grabbed it on the third ring, grateful he didn't have to maneuver the wheelchair clear across the room to look through his jacket pockets. These days he was grateful for a number of little things.

He punched the button and put it to his ear. "Hello."

"'Ello Dr. Rey, sir," a startlingly happy British-accented man said from the other end. "And 'ow are you today, sir?"

"I'm doing fine, Smithers. How can you be so ungodly happy at whatever hour of the day it is there?"

"Five in the morning, sir. And I'm being paid well to be happy. Are you ready for the call?"

"Oh yes, let's get it over with," Rey said. He pushed away the scattered papers, and pulled out the last fax from the esteemed London law firm of Wall, Smithers, and Doyle, once again reading the counter offer Catha Incorporated had made.

Damn impressive counter offer, really, but since the accident, that he had decided that he didn't want to sell. Maybe he had become reactionary, but every time he wanted to hold on to the life he'd had before someone had shoved him out in front of the lorry on a busy London street --

"Call is going through, sir," Smithers said. "The Computer program is running and synced."

"Good." His London law firm went to a lot of work to make certain people thought he still resided in London. However, once he'd been well enough to travel, Chev had gone home to New Mexico -- if not to the reservation where he grew up, at least close to it. He liked this area. He couldn't say that he felt safer here, but he did feel calmer.

"And how is life in the Wild West these days?" Smithers asked, still cheerful.

"Snowy here at Taos. Pretty, though."

"Snowing in March? There's no call for that sort of behavior. Your man Jeeves is making sure you take care of yourself, is he?"

"Morton is taking care of me, yes." He grinned despite himself. "And Patrice has finally let me sneak in the back of the museum and play with pieces of broken pottery again."

"Ah, good on her, then," Smithers said. "And your wife, Sandra?"

"Apparently having a wonderful time on the French Riviera."

"I thought she would be in New Mexico by now."

"I'll let you in on a secret: she hates it here. The month we spent in New Mexico after we married ... well, let's just say it wasn't the most pleasant time in our marriage. I should probably be in France with her now --"

"You need to be where you feel comfortable," Smithers said, his voice losing much of the infectious joy he had held a moment before. But it came back in the next moment. "And what is there not to love about New

Mexico? Fresh air, wide open spaces, horses and cowboys."

"And Indians," Chev added, brushing at his own dark braid.

Smithers laughed in agreement and then sobered with a little cough. "The CEO of Catha Inc is on the line, sir."

Things clicked. Chev heard the computer simulation created to convince the Catha people he was still in London.

"Mr. Rey?" a thin, older voice asked. Petulant -- not a good way to start this conversation. Chev had heard the tone before and knew this would not go well.

"Dr. Rey," Chev corrected him, and then leapt right into the heart of the matter. "I'm afraid, Mr. Kinmore, that I'm going to turn down your offer."

"It is a very reasonable offer!" the man said, his voice rising in anger.

"It is more than a reasonable offer. However, I am reevaluating what I want out of life, Mr. Kinmore."

"This isn't about personal enjoyment --"

"This is very much about personal enjoyment. I love importing and exporting art almost as much as I love archeology. If I sold my company to you now, what would I be doing tomorrow?" His hand brushed against the wheelchair. He could not go out to the dig. If he could, he might have sold. Now, though, he needed something still --

"I don't see that's the point at all. I can make you a lot of money --"

"I have a lot of money," Chev said.

"Well, fine then." And he hung up.

"You know, Smithers, some people just don't take no for an answer very well."

Smithers gave a little half laugh, muttered something, and then laughed again. "Well, it can't have been much of a surprise. I'm already getting a fax from their corporate headquarters threatening to sue you over ... bloody hell, I'm not sure what they intend to sue about in this case. Don't worry. We'll settle it."

"Good." Aches eased in his shoulders. He looked around the room and stopped at the wall of Hopi-Tewa pottery he had bought both from galleries and from the potters themselves. Some brown with black images and others white with black and brown images lined carefully lit glass shelves. On the third shelf stood a piece out of place with the others -- ancient, black and white Anasazi ware. He had found it himself, out on the land he inherited from his grandfather.

"Sir?"

"Sorry," Chev said, pulling himself back. "Glad to have the business over with. Now I can get back to work."

"But you will be careful," Smithers said.

"Oh yes. Very careful."

"Good. I think you did the right thing, sir. Money isn't everything, as they say. I'll call you in a few days with the final report."

"And the bill for this ungodly hour."

"Yes sir, that too." He laughed. "One last item. I have a report here from the detectives who say they've not had any progress in the attack against you."

"Tell them to keep investigating until the end of April. If nothing has turned up by then, I'll consider it closed."

"I'll pass your instructions along, sir. I believe this takes care of all our business this morning. I'll talk to you soon."

The phone clicked as Smithers hung up. Chev was

almost sorry. He wouldn't have minded a little more company tonight. He thought about calling his wife, or maybe Patrice -- but he put the phone aside instead, and shifted papers on the table. He pulled out the employment form Patrice had brought him yesterday. The applicant would be into the museum for an interview tomorrow, but several years, not covered in the paperwork, left Chev uneasy. He didn't think he'd be hiring this one.

And that reminded him of yet another battle to be fought. A stack of papers on the right side of the table came from Red Sun Associates, a company offering to buy his land down near Santa Fe for development. He'd already told them it wasn't going to happen, so the bastards had gone to the state to try and get title to the 'undeveloped and under utilized' area.

It wasn't going to happen. Chev went through the papers and began jotting down notes on his phone to send off to his Santa Fe lawyers. Lately, he'd spent far too much time with lawyers, and not enough with the land.

He shifted in the chair and tried not to think about what kept him hidden here in his home.

Morton showed up a few minutes later with a sandwich, milk, and several pills, doing his job as good as any Jeeves could have done. Morton sat them on the table, eyeing the mess as though he wanted to tidy things right now.

"Don't even think it," Chev said.

Morton barely hid his smile. "Your physical therapist will be here in half an hour, Dr. Rey."

Good reminder. Chev lost track of the days. "Thank you."

Morton nodded and slipped away, heading toward the front of the house, to be ready for the therapist's arrival.

Very proper. Sandra would approve. He'd take Morton with him to France when he went.

Chev found himself staring at the wall of pottery again. He had inherited land and money enough to move from the pueblo when he turned twenty-one. Ten years later, he'd built up a nice little trading empire, selling locally made pottery, jewelry, and carvings overseas. None of those pieces on the wall would have sold for less than $5000 dollars. The Anasazi bowl, virtually unchipped, would have gone for at least twice as much, if not a lot more.

He made money, the potters made money, and he didn't cheat anyone. All in all, it wasn't a bad way to live.

Except when he remembered the hands on his back, shoving him out into the street....

CHAPTER THREE

With his last thirty dollars in his pocket, Lee walked down the long row of the adobe storefronts on Paseo del Pueblo Norte. Tourists wandered in and out, jackets pulled tight against the brisk March air. Patches of snow still lay in the shadows, but most of last night's storm had melted away.

Lee wanted the weather to turn warmer, or else to live in a warmer building. The clapboard apartment he called home was more than he could actually afford, but he had found nothing cheaper. Lee needed a real job. People said jobs would be more plentiful when the summer tourist seasons kicked in if he could hold on that long. The snows had melted, and the ski resorts closed down early this year. Jobs had become scarce. Some had suggested he go back to Santa Fe, but he had felt uncomfortable there -- and for reasons he couldn't name. Maybe there had been too much bustle and too many ways to get into trouble. He wanted quieter places, but he didn't want to leave the southwest. He loved this area filled with symbols and glimpses of things he'd only been able to study in college.

Taos appealed to him; the blatant attempt to draw tourists was at least honest. He'd wandered through four jobs in the last two months -- all temp positions, barely enough to keep a roof over his head, never mind food. He wanted --

He wanted the job he had applied for last week, the one that led him to Desert Street, and the vast, domed building sitting slightly back from the corner. The Desert Traditions Museum had opened two months before his arrival. He had scraped together a few dollars to go in and wander around, caught up in the wonder of walking through the model of a partial pueblo, Chacoan style, complete with Kiva and T-shaped doors. Walls of the museum held displays of pottery, carvings, beads, clothing -- there hadn't been enough time to look at it all, and he'd not had spare money to come back since.

Now he stood outside the door to the building and tried not to feel like a fraud. Why should they hire him? He had no credentials -- and while those hadn't been required, according to the listing he read, the job still required some knowledge of local archaeology. He had been good at this in class, but --

Lee stopped that train of thought and shook his head. He forced himself to pull the door open and step in, and paused long enough to orientate himself. He headed right toward the door with Museum Office etched in the glass.

A woman looked up from her desk and observed him from behind thin, wire-framed glasses and a lean face framed by dark hair hinting at gray along the top. At least she had a neutral stare, which he preferred to some he had gotten in the last few months. He didn't know why so many people glared. He didn't have this life story written across his forehead, after all.

"I've come for the job interview," he said, softly and slowly. No stutter this time. He hoped the suit jacket didn't hang too badly to him. He'd lost more weight in the last few months, and his hair had started to grow longer. He thought he ought to cut it. Despite knowing this was a fool's errand, he still wanted to make a good impression.

"Ah. You're Mr. Constantinos," she said and stood, offering a hand. "I'm Patrice Barnowl, Museum Curator, Mr. Constantinos."

"Lee," he said.

She smiled as she drew a paper from the piles on her desk, and then went past him and locked the office door. "This way, Lee."

They went out another door and into a hallway lined with old-world adobe walls. The place smelled of mesquite and sage, and they passed by dozens of southwestern designs; the ubiquitous Kokopelli with his flute, which Lee had gotten quite used to, but also some unusual ones, like a Hohokam Sun Priest symbol and the upside down tripod he remembered meant Hawk Clan. Others he didn't recognize at all. He hadn't seen many of them since he left school.

Browns and blues gave the area a feeling of patience and peace, and he felt calmer, which surprised him. Whoever had designed the building had done an excellent job.

The hall opened on the left side for a few yards, showing the museum below. People wandered through the ruin as a guide explained different facets of what they saw. He hadn't taken the guided tour, but it might be fun.

The full hall closed back in around them again, and they passed by a dozen doors. The Desert Traditions Museum, although privately funded apparently was not without resources. Besides the building, the artifacts and exhibits, he saw computers still in boxes in one office, and crates of supplies in another.

They finally reached the far end of the hall, passing a man who looked suspiciously like a guard sitting on a bench outside a long, room filled with tables.

Pieces of broken pottery covered the tables; the real stuff, Lee realized, his heart pounding a little harder. He had to force himself not to reach out and touch something, just to feel it once. A dark skinned man looked up from one of those tables and nodded a greeting as they neared. It wasn't until Lee stood opposite him that he saw the wheelchair.

"This is Leander Constantinos, Dr. Rey," Patrice Barnowl said.

"Oh yes! I'm Cheveyo Rey." The stranger reached across the table. He had a good strong handshake, and one of those blended Hispanic and Native American accents Lee had gotten used to hearing around here. The name seemed familiar, too, though he didn't exactly know why. "I read your resume. I have a couple questions we need to discuss about your application. Let's go to my office."

Lee knew what the questions would involve: Explain the missing five years from the time Lee, twenty-two and getting top marks in college disappeared and suddenly turned up here, looking for a job in a field which had not been his major.

He had spent five years and two months in prison, and another three months since they set him free. He'd worked at jobs from fast food cook to bricklayer's apprentice, but none of them had allowed him the escape from the lingering shadows of the past. When he saw the ad in the paper, he had spent the afternoon at the library filling out a resume he had downloaded from the museum's website. It had been a whim. He had never expected the letter inviting him this far in.

Dr. Rey's office turned out to be the one filled with boxed computers. He wheeled himself in and looked around with a start. "Going to have to get these set up sooner or later. Find Mr. Constantinos a chair, Pat -- and one for yourself."

"Sure," she said.

"Let me help." Lee quickly followed her out, past the guard who had followed them -- Lee hadn't noticed -- and into the next office. Lee wished it had taken them longer. He wanted to delay the inevitable, but they were back in Dr. Rey's office in a couple minutes. He and the museum curator sat down. Cheveyo Rey looked up from the resume with his head tilted.

"The missing five years," Lee said before the man asked.

"Yes."

"Prison, for a crime I didn't commit." Rey's eyebrows rose as he frowned. Patrice Barnowl shifted in her chair as he reached into his jacket and pulled out a brown envelope. "I know how it sounds."

He handed the envelope to Dr. Rey who at least looked curious, and watched as the man pulled out the first of the papers which was the oldest and much read. He had hunted down all the information he could from the internet, having learned quickly that people didn't take him at his word, even in jobs where his past shouldn't have mattered. Dr. Rey read the papers and handed each on to Patrice Barnowl with a frown before he pulled out the next one. Rey had taken out the last one and read it once, and then again.

"Damn!" Rey said.

Odd reaction, and not what he expected. Rey handed

the last article to Patrice, and then stared back at him. They waited for her to finish reading. She did and sat there with all the papers in her hand before she looked at him.

"My God, this is awful, Lee," she said.

He shrugged, but it was nice to hear those words from someone, finally.

"The article said you were married," Rey said, waving a hand toward the papers.

"I was.   We divorced right after the trial. Debra remarried and took my son with her."

"Other relatives?"

"My parents went back to Greece." He wondered why Rey asked, but he didn't mind. He'd grown numb to all sorts of pain in the last few years. "They never contacted me again, and I don't know if they've heard the news. I have no idea where my brother went."

"Hell," Rey said, shaking his head.

"Yes," Lee answered. "Yes, it was."

"And still is?" Rey asked, looking into his face.

"Y-Yes."

Rey still held his look. "What is it you're looking for here, Leander Constantinos?"

"Work," Lee said and then he found himself amending the far too simple of an answer with a shake of his head. "No, that's not entirely true. I want work that means something to me. I want out of the nightmare. I want to believe I still have a future."

Rey reached into a pocket on the side of the wheelchair and pulled out a sherd and held it out for him to take. "What is this?"

He'd never actually held a piece like this before -- not a real one. Goose bumps rose on his arms as he carefully took the sherd of pottery, his fingers tracing the long curve up to a lip that belled outward at the top, and then tracing the path back down to the zigzag design in black and white. He smiled as he looked back at Dr. Rey. The visit had been worth it for this moment and the chance to touch a real piece of history. "I'd say from the shape it's an olla of some sort. The design looks like maybe San Juan Pueblo one or two phase, I think."

"Damn. That's amazing. I've never met anyone able to identify a piece without looking at reference books. Why wasn't Southwestern Studies your major?"

"My father wanted me to be an architect. I slipped in what archeology studies I could because I liked them, and could say I was studying the building styles." He reluctantly handed the sherd back.

Dr. Rey noted the reluctance as well and smiled. "The pay isn't good, Lee --"

"I don't give a damn." He leaned forward, his hands on his knees. "Let me sleep on the floor and grub for food in the trashcans. I don't care about the money. This is the first thing --"

He stopped, appalled by the outburst.

"It's all right. I want this to be more than a job for someone, Lee. I want a person with a passion for the work because I will trust him with a hell of a lot. And I need someone who can take care of himself and go places I can't get back to yet like the archeology digs out on my land. No, the wheelchair is not permanent. I have business dealings overseas, and I learned a London branch of my export business had started shipping drugs with the pottery. I was the one who called the officials in and went there to help clean up the mess. They said they had rounded up the entire group, and it had been a relatively small time operation. But a week later I was ... hit by a lorry in

London, and it was not an accident."

"Your own nightmare," Lee said, feeling an unexpected kinship. He tried to shove the emotion aside, although Dr. Rey nodded agreement.

"I own some land, Lee, and it has ruins on it. The land has been in my family since ... well, since before Cortes in one sense -- except those ancestors wouldn't have understood how you could own Mother Earth. My great-great grandfather came to New Mexico. He'd been a Don in Spain, but he was probably part Moor and left before the family went into disgrace. He traveled in the Yucatan for a while, looking for gold, and took a Mayan wife. They settled here, and by the grace of God he survived the Pueblo Rebellion in 1680. Their son married a woman from the San Juan Pueblo, and his sister married a man from Acoma. The family had a habit of marrying outside the tribe, and bringing new blood and new traditions to the lands my great-great grandfather had left to his family."

"Which brings us down to now," Patrice said, with a shake of her head. "And the current trouble."

"It's good land, wild and free," Chev said. For a moment Lee could see the longing in his eyes as his hand brushed against his leg. "But now a developer wants to build a community there, and a lot of rich people want to buy the houses he will build. I don't intend for them to live on my land, and it's already making me unpopular. You are going to be a face associated with me. So I'm hiring someone to stand out there in front of all the animosity and do it for my dreams. This may not be, all things considered, the position you really want."

He started to speak, stopped himself, and began again. "I want something I can be passionate about. I didn't know that until I held the sherd. And really, I may be better suited to the work than anyone else. I already believe in the battle for what's right, Dr. Rey."

"When can you start?"

"Yesterday. Now. Immediately."

Patrice laughed first, and then Cheveyo Rey joined in. "Good. Excellent. Wouldn't you like to know all I'm going to want from you for your $15.50 an hour?"

"The ad said $12.75."

"The ad was wrong. What I'll want is for you to go places I can't. I'm not sure how far Red Sun will go in this battle, and I'm trying to be careful. You saw Tomas out in the hall? He's a former State Patrol officer I've hired as a private guard. We have guards at the museum and guards out on the land. However, sometimes you're going to have to go places without backup, if for no other reason than we don't want to draw attention. And sometimes you'll sit in the back room with me and stare at piles of sherds, trying to put together puzzles with most of the pieces missing. All that for $16.00 an hour."

Lee laughed. It was unexpected. "I'll take the job. Can I start now?"

"Oh yes. Come on back to the tables. Patrice, it's nearly five. Can you have something whipped up at La Luna for us? Do you like Italian, Lee?"

"Yes, but you don't have to --"

"I'm hungry. I have promised my wife, who is still in Europe, that I will stay out of sight, which means having dinner brought in."

"I don't want you to feel sorry for me."

"Well, that's something we both feel, isn't it?"

He nodded. "Yes, I suppose so."

"Good. Patrice --"

She stood. "I'll have them make up several dishes and

I'll go pick them up when they call." She held the papers
out to Lee.

"I don't need them."

"Good," she said and smiled. She took the papers with
her.

Lee felt a little twinge at the thought of his past
disappearing down the hall, but he let it go and gladly
followed Cheveyo Rey back to the room filled with broken
pottery.

CHAPTER FOUR

Morton opened the side door and let them both in. "Good evening Ms. Barnowl," he said with a nod. "Will you be staying for a drink?"

"Not tonight, thank you. I think a storm blowing in, and I want to get back to my apartment." She reached down and squeezed Chev's shoulder. He looked up at her, surprised. "You did a good thing, hiring Lee tonight."

"Damn right. Did you see how well Lee did with the San Juan Pueblo III dipper? He'd have worked on it all night if we'd let him."

"You know that's not what I mean," she said. Her hand lingered for a moment. Chev wanted to reach up and touch the fingers, but he didn't. She pulled away. "Good night, Chev."

"Goodnight, Patrice." She walked back out into the windy darkness. A splatter of rain hit the walkway as he watched. "Drive carefully!"

"I will!"

Morton waited by the wheelchair until they heard the van start and pull away. Tomas had pulled up beside the side of the van and rushed up the stairs to his apartment over the four-car garage. He never put his car away -- said he might need to get to it too quickly. Tomas gave a wave as he disappeared inside.

Morton closed the door and extricated Chev's jacket from his arms. Cheveyo realized, suddenly, how tired he really felt. It had to be nearly one in the morning, but they'd had a good day.

"Your wife called, sir, and would like you to call her back. I put the number on the table by the phone."

A good day right up until that moment. He grimaced at the reaction because it was unfair to Sandra. Lately, though, their phone conversations had not gone well, and he didn't want to end the day badly. Best to get the conversation out of the way.

"Thank you, Morton. I'll call her, take a quick shower, and head for bed."

"Yes, sir."

Morton pushed him to the dining room and then headed upstairs to prepare the shower and to turn down the bed. Sometimes the man amazed him. Granted, Chev paid him a lot of money to do this work, but it still seemed odd and wondrous.

He went into the dining room and picked up the phone, looking at the number. Interesting -- a Paris exchange. He wondered why she had moved away from the coast. Probably following the other birds, fluttering around Europe.

He dialed. The phone rang and rang.

"Yes?"

"Hi Sandra!" he put some bright, cheery emotion into his voice and a little joy. "I'm glad you called!"

"It is late there, Chev. What are you doing out so late? You know --"

"I stayed at the museum, love," he answered, cutting

her short because he had heard that lecture too many times. "Some beautiful little pieces of pottery came in the other day. It was a quiet, relaxing night while I worked with a new employee and Patrice did paperwork."

"Oh." The mention of Patrice always brought a little bit of ice in her voice. He wondered if he had subconsciously done it on purpose, in hopes she'd cut the conversation short. He wanted to shower and sleep.

"Did you call for a reason?" he prodded.

"I thought you might be interested in joining me in Paris," she said. "But I suppose I'm no match for broken pottery."

"I'd be tempted," he lied. "Unfortunately, I have the trouble with Red Sun coming up. I really can't go before it's settled."

"Oh give them the damn land. It's not worth the trouble."

He looked over at the wall of pottery and counted to ten before he spoke. "The land has been in my family forever, Sandra. I'm not going to suddenly let it get bulldozed --"

"I don't know why everyone wants your damn land," she said, still sounding cross. "But never mind. What's the word from Catha?"

This conversation wasn't going to get better. Chev felt his shoulders tighten before he spoke. "I turned down their offer."

Her breath caught. "You what?"

"I turned them down. I don't want to sell the export business, Sandra. I like doing the work I do. And what would I do otherwise? I thought you'd be happy, to be honest. With the export business, I would still be traveling elsewhere. Without it, I'd tend to stay here with the museum."

"You have become obsessed with things since the accident Chev. It's not natural --"

"It was no accident."

Silence. They'd gone over this part a few too many times as well. She saw no one push him into the street. It had been a dark night, and the driver couldn't be certain if anyone else had been around. Chev had the distinct feeling she didn't believe him and had begun to suspect his insistence meant a mental problem and she'd started putting distance between them for a reason.

It cut, sometimes, in the long lonely nights.

"I need to go get ready. I have a lunch meeting with friends," she said suddenly. Her voice softened a little. "Stay safe, Chev. Promise me you will still stay out of sight and you won't let anyone know you're there."

He suddenly realized how odd a request sounded from a woman who didn't believe him about being pushed -- but maybe she really did believe him. Maybe she couldn't admit it to herself.

"Chev?"

"That's why I hired the new guy, Lee," he said. He tried to sound cheery again. "He's going to do all the running around. I'm staying careful."

"Good. I have to run. I'll talk to you soon."

"Bye!"

The phone clicked. He couldn't be certain Sandra heard the last word. Chev put the phone down and stared at the table for a while. He would not sell his land to Red Sun. He might still sell the export business -- Sandra might be right in part. He'd ask Patrice what she thought --

Oh, now there was another subversive thought; that he would turn to Patrice for answers, rather than his wife.

"Sir?"

Shower, bed. Chev turned the wheelchair around and headed toward the chairlift to take him up the stairs to the second floor. A person had to love modern technology, he thought. Otherwise, he'd have had to find some first-floor apartment in town. He loved this house. It made him feel better -- calmer -- to be here.

Patrice, at least, understood his feelings, even if his wife didn't.

CHAPTER FIVE

Lee had been working at the museum for three days and already felt as though he had put on weight. Dinner with Chev, Patrice and Tomas turned out to be a regular occurrence, and anyone still working joined in which alleviated some of his embarrassment. The food was great: Italian, Mandarin, Tex-Mex....

On the third night, when they left the offices before eight, he insisted on walking home. He'd already faced the embarrassment of having Patrice and Chev drop him off at the corner by his apartment in a rundown area of town. The weather was better tonight, and he didn't mind walking through town.

After a couple paychecks, he would change his housing. Apartments were damned expensive here in town, but he could find something better than his current place.

The night felt wonderful, with the weather brisk but clear. Some shops hadn't yet closed, and he looked in the windows, imagining things he would buy once he had money again. Lee even wandered into a bookstore, first searching through the mystery section, but then moving on to the local history shelves. He wanted to read up on some of the ancient cultures from the areas, knowing he really didn't remember as much as he should.

They had several good books, including a few by H.M. Wormington; he wondered how many people realized H.M. stood for Hannah Marie. Her book E*Prehistoric Indians of the Southwest** had been one of the first, and best, he had read.

Other people passed by him in the narrow aisles, but after a few minutes, he became aware of a woman lingering close by. When he turned, he saw her staring at the shelf and shaking her head in dismay.

He smiled. "Need help?"

"I would like something ... readable?" she said, sounding entirely uncertain. She had a heart-shaped face and short brown hair streaked with a little gold -- looked naturally sun-lightened, but he couldn't be certain. She shook her head as she ran a hand over the spines of books. "I moved to the area about a month ago. There's so much to learn!"

"Yes, there is. It's wonderful."

"You don't sound like a local either," she said and looked him over once. "Vacationing?"

"No. I moved here a few months ago, too." The question made Lee nervous, reminding him of his past, and things he didn't want to discuss. He rushed on before she could ask more. "You'd like something basic, right? Here is one covering local tribes, past and present. I glanced over it a few minutes ago, and it looks good."

She took the book, her fingers brushing slightly against his. "Thanks!"

She walked away.

His hands had started to tremble, and Lee stood in front of the books for a long time, taking short breaths and trying to get control of himself again. It had been a stupid reaction. He finally picked up one of the books by

Wormington and headed for the cash register, parting with a few dollars of his hoarded money. He'd have more in a few days, and he hadn't had to pay for food for a while, anyway.

Some of the glow of the evening had disappeared with the encounter. Lee felt stupid, reactionary, and childish, and he hoped to hell this wouldn't be his reaction to every woman he chanced to meet at bookstores.

He had met Debra at the college bookstore, and in the same sort of section, which put the strange reaction to this encounter in a better light. He knew he wasn't ready for those reminders yet.

Lee strolled the rest of the way home to the rundown apartment building. People had congregated in the driveway again, the music loud, and beer cans tossed on the gravel that took the place of a yard. He went past them with a pretended good-natured greeting, thinking again about moving out as he headed around the corner of the building to his first floor rooms.

Roaches scattered as soon as he turned on the unshielded overhead light. He grabbed the can of spray he kept by the door and laid down a thick fog while he stood at the doorway. The scent of the stuff made him half ill, but it gave him at least a feeling of protection.

Lee took a quick shower, slipped on a pair of cutoffs and sandals, and swept up dead bugs. He had taken to wearing the cutoffs to bed since there had been three police visits at the apartment building in the few weeks he'd lived here.

Lee brought a bare-bulb lamp over beside the bed, wound up the alarm clock and set it down. He propped the single pillow up against the wall and began to read. It proved to be a better distraction than listening to the people shouting out in the driveway or counting the bugs on the floor.

He saw the same woman two days later at the museum. He had looked down over the open area back by the offices and noticed her wandering through the lower floor with the book in hand, and leafing through it at each display. Lee watched, amused by her interest, and the way she bent closer to look at items in the lower displays, her face, intent and interested. She never looked up.

It's late, he thought. I'm done with my work for the day. I could go down there and walk with her. We could talk about the exhibits.

And then what? Dinner? Walk her home?

Deb had walked with him through a dozen museums, her hand in his. They'd talk about their favorite displays and pieces for days afterward, and they'd gone back as often as time and money allowed.

His hands tightened on the railing, and he froze, petrified by the idea of even the slightest social contact with this woman. This *stranger.* How could he trust her?

No, that wasn't the problem. It had nothing to do with trusting her; it had everything to do with how he now viewed the world, knowing how ephemeral moments of happiness could be, and how much they could cost. He wasn't ready to pay the price again. So he made excuses as he watched her. He hadn't been paid yet, so dinner was out; he didn't have a car, and he'd be embarrassed if they had to take hers. Besides, the weather looked like rain, so it wasn't a good night for a walk, and he had more work to do.

The last was an outright lie, but a good excuse to get away before she spotted him. Lee pulled his hands from the railing and slowly back up, afraid he would either be ill, or he would run. Stupid reactions.

Chev sat at the end of the hall, watching him. Lee froze again, a quick glance at the area below. The woman had moved on, but his heart still pounded with fear.

"Lee?"

"I ... I forgot to do something," he said and started to toward the offices. He immediately regretted the lie and stopped by Chev's wheelchair. "No, I didn't forget anything. I just -- I --"

"Are you all right?"

Lee took several deep breaths, leaning against the wall. "I'm sorry. I panicked. I'm not entirely certain why."

Chev looked up at him, craning his neck, and shook his head. "Come to my office."

"I --"

"Come on."

Chev backed the chair up, turned around, and headed toward his office. Lee followed, feeling worse than a whipped dog. He had been an idiot to do something to make Dr. Rey look again at the man he had hired and reconsider --

"Sit down." Chev waved to a chair. "I get tired of looking up at people."

Lee dropped into the chair. Chev had not rolled back behind the desk. He sat in front of Lee, his hands in his lap, fingers rubbing a scar across the back of his right hand -- a relatively new scar, from the color of it. When he looked up, and Lee saw the bleakness in his face, he resigned himself to going somewhere else --

"I had to leave London," Chev said. "I couldn't, even after they let me out of the hospital, consider going back on those streets, especially in this damned chair and feeling so helpless. I hadn't been helpless when it happened, so how could I trust my safety now? I remember seeing the big damn truck coming at me, and the sound of the brakes squealing. And that's the last thing I remember until I woke up in the hospital, twelve days later."

"I'm sorry," Lee said.

"I think you really are. I think you're sorry because you know too damn well how I feel. You were hit and left for dead, and by some miracle, you got your life back. You have reason to panic. Sandra said no one else was there, that I just stepped out into the street, and no one pushed me. Sandra is my wife. She's still in Europe." He stopped and shook his head as though to dismiss that line of conversation. "You and I know how fast all the good things can be taken away. But Lee ... I'm not the one who is going to do it to you."

"Damn." Lee leaned back, feeling tense muscles in his shoulders relax for the first time in too damn long. "I feel like I'm walking on eggshells, and I don't even know why. I've been out for months. I'm not going to do something stupid and get sent back to prison -- but I hadn't done anything before. How can I know? How can I be sure?" The words came, unstoppable, despite a part of him trying to damp down the emotions and get control again. "And you know the worst part? The people who prosecuted me didn't do it maliciously. They thought I'd killed the girl and a few others. So I can't even have a real enemy to face. All I can do is ... walk on eggshells, and try to figure out what I've done wrong."

"You did nothing wrong," Chev said, frowning.

"You think so?" Something dark welled up inside this time. Bitterness flooded through with memories of the last five years. "You don't know what I did while in prison."

"What choices were you given?"

"You don't know what it was like." His hand started to tremble. He looked at it, appalled as if the hand belonged to someone else. He could see a set of scars where someone had cut with a piece of plastic, sharpened on the cement wall, while the others held him --

But it had not been his choice. None of it. The choices he made now -- those were the ones that counted.

"Lee."

He looked up. His vision had narrowed the colors sharp, his head pounding. He swallowed, his mouth dry. The moment of prison memory had been far too real. He took deep breaths and forced calm, and it seemed to come easier this time.

"Leander?"

He almost smiled at the name. People seldom called him by it, and no one in prison had.

"Sorry. Better." He pushed both hands through his hair. "In fact, I think it helped. I think something finally broke lose."

Chev looked surprised and then smiled. Lee thought he must look better. He felt a hell of a lot better from one breath to the next. The nightmare hadn't disappeared, but it wouldn't walk like a malignant shadow following him through every moment of the day. No. He'd grown tired of panic and distrust. Time to move on.

"I'm done with the paperwork and boxed up the completed bowl, so I'm going to take Patrice's suggestion and leave while it's still light out tonight. I'm going home. Walking. Free."

Chev had started to protest. He stopped and nodded. "I'll see you tomorrow."

Lee walked back out to the overlook, but the woman

had left. Just as well. One step at a time.□

CHAPTER SIX

The intercom buzzed. Chev wondered how long he had sat there, thinking about Lee and hoping he'd done the right thing, forcing the confrontation. He rolled back and hit the button, wondering what Patrice could want this late in the afternoon --

"Yeah?" he said.

"Sandra is on the phone and wants to talk to you," Patrice said, her voice entirely too neutral.

His wife had *never* called the museum before. In fact, he'd had the feeling Sandra denied it existed, having told him he shouldn't waste his money to build it. He'd gone ahead anyway. She'd said nothing more. And never called until now.

Maybe something had gone wrong! She was in Europe. He had enemies in England --

He grabbed the phone up and hit the blinking button. "Sandra? Are you there? Is everything all right?"

"Yes, of course," she answered. Her voice sounded prim, as though annoyed that Chev had asked.

"You called the museum. You've never done that before," Chev replied, wondering why he felt like he had to apologize for being worried about her. "Never mind. Why did you call?"

"To tell you I've made a decision. I've talked with my friends, and they agree. Chev, you are no longer the poor little Indian Boy who grew up on the reservation without a father. You are a rich man who needs to break ties with the past instead of letting it suck you back in and drain your money. So either you sell the land and the museum and move away from New Mexico, or I am going to divorce you."

His heart thumped. Once. And then steadied.

"Sandra --"

"No, don't say anything Cheveyo. I'll call back in a week."

She hung up.

He looked at the phone with a half dozen things ready to say. He could call and say them, but right now the last person he wanted to talk to was his wife.

This wasn't the first time she'd made an odd ultimatum only to forget the demands when it was evident he wasn't going to comply. When she remembered the prenuptial agreements they both signed, she would doubtless forget this one as well. Her friends pushed her toward things like this --

And why did he keep making excuses for her, as though she had no mind of her own? He'd married her because she was intelligent, not some bubble-headed bleached blonde. But four years later -- with her half way around the world making demands --

Patrice came to the doorway and looked in.

"You really need to hang the phone up, Chev," she said. "You're tying up the line."

He looked at it still in his hand and carefully sat it down on the cradle. Then he looked back at Patrice. "She says to sell the land and the museum or lose her. She's given me a week."

Patrice winced, and then lifted her hand. "Sorry."

"Oh, I did more than wince. I'm tempted to call Smithers and have him start separating our accounts and limiting her access to funds. I won't. Not while I'm angry. But you know I'm not going to sell, right?"

"I never doubted it," Patrice said, frowning a little.

"I wonder why she doesn't understand me as well."

Patrice looked at him. She sighed. "We have a long history, Cheveyo Rey. If she spent time with you --" But she stopped the rest of her words and shook her head again. "I have some work to do in the office. I came back to tell you I got an email saying we're going to get part of the traveling Earl Morris Collection next spring if we can get all the paperwork in on time."

"Damn!" he said, excited again. "How many pieces?"

"They're going to drive up and look the museum over. It depends on how much security, how well built the exhibit hall is, and such. Nothing we have to worry about. Oh, and Professor Belinato says to arrange for the pick-up of the 'damn olla' as she calls it. She'll be in Santa Fe on Monday."

"You could -- or maybe we should send Lee," Chev said. He leaned back. "It wouldn't hurt to let him have some time out of the building doing some work. Don't you think?"

"I like the idea," she said and leaned against the doorframe. "You're going to want Lee to drive out to the site, too, and pick up anything they have to be shipped back here. I think Lee would really enjoy meeting them."

"Yes." He looked at her and tilted his head. "You do that very well, don't you?"

"Distract you from your anger? I have a lot of practice." She gave him a quick grin. "Give Sandra her week. And think long and hard about what you want, Chev, and how you'll deal with whatever decision you finally make."

"I'm not giving up the land to a group of tight-assed rich white men to bulldoze ruins and build another island of affluence on the outskirts of one of the poorest reservations in the state --"

She lifted her hands and laughed. "You are preaching to the choir. Don't you have some pottery to put together or something? Go be useful for a while."

She turned and walked away. Chev grinned and then rolled out and down the hall to the tables. It would help calm him to do the work he so loved. Damn, he wanted to get out to the dig again! How much longer...

He pushed the longing away with a little prayer of thanks to Spider Old Woman and her medicines -- because the doctors in London said something extraordinary had saved him not only from death but also from permanent damage and paralysis. He remembered dreaming about the cacique societies and hearing them chanting words he had almost forgotten -- Tewa language. There, on the verge of death, and half way around the world, he had felt closer to his people than he had in the years since he left the reservation to go to college. Closer, in fact, than he had when he had visited the Pueblo and his mother.

When he came out of the coma, he'd asked Sandra to get him some feathers-- turkey, magpie, eagle, oriel, summer warbler, duck. She had patted his hand and ignored the request, as she had anything else connected to his native culture. Smithers had gotten the feathers for him, which was no small feat, really, when he thought about it. Sandra had not been happy.

He was not selling his land, his culture, his museum, or his dreams. Sandra -- he tried not to remember being in bed with her, or naked in the surf along their private beach in Mexico. God, he had been in love with her...

Been in love with her?

He chased the thoughts away and picked up pieces of pottery.

Lee was waiting for them at the back door the next morning, despite the pouring rain. Chev shook his head and grinned while Patrice, lecturing Lee on what an idiot he was for standing around in the storm and at least not going next door to the coffee shop, left Chev sitting out in the rain.

Tomas finally pushed him in, and Patrice looked back, startled and started laughing as she slid out of her raincoat and hung it up.

"Well, you did always tell me I have a one-track mind," she said.

Any day that started out where he could make fun of Patrice had to be a good day. She went up front and got the checks and handed them out to everyone. Lee started to put his in his soggy pocket and changed his mind, pulling out a slightly less wet -- and very thin -- billfold.

Chev stayed with Patrice to do paperwork for the Morris Collection, thinking about all those lovely pieces of pottery. Insurance questions were not a problem. He'd pay extra if he had to, although he already had the museum highly-insured to make it look reasonable for groups like this. If they were lucky, they might get a semi-permanent selection.

Damn, he loved this work.

At noon he headed back toward his office, wondering

what Lee was up to. Probably down in the museum setting up the new flyers at each display --

He looked over the edge and found something totally unexpected. He saw Lee talking to the woman who had sent him running the day before. Not only talking but laughing. He could hear the sound all the way up in the hall.

Well damn. Good. Chev saw Lee check his watch, nod, and walk away with her. Lunch, no doubt.

Another addition to a good day. He still thought about the call from Sandra the day before, but it had stopped triggering an emotional response. He'd spent a long night -- alone -- in bed thinking about the situation. He could sell everything. He could move to Europe and take up archaeology and trading somewhere else.

And would she like that change any better? She liked the bright life and fancy clubs where they'd met. He'd told her everything about himself the first week, including his love of his native land. She hadn't understood what those words meant.

He cared for Sandra. He didn't love her enough to give up his land for her. They'd had a few good years. He'd pay her off and move on. Harsh way to think about their relationship, but she'd chosen the terms with her own demands.

Chev thought about going and telling Patrice his decision, but then he decided that telling Sandra first might be the more proper move, and right now he wanted this done properly.

He could wait a few days before he made the news public. Wait for Sandra to call back, rather than having one the law firms hunt her down. He didn't want to embarrass her. Chev didn't want to end this badly ... but he did want to end it.

The intercom beeped, surprising him again. He'd been sitting behind his desk for more than ten minutes, staring at the blank screen of his monitor.

"Yes?" he said.

"You have a call from Red Sun," Patrice said, her voice very sharp with anger. "They said your wife called and told them to get in touch with you here."

"Damn." He'd done his best to make sure the Red Sun people didn't know he had come back to New Mexico because he found them incredibly annoying and didn't want them showing up at the museum. What the hell was this with Sandra? She'd been the one who insisted no one know he had returned to New Mexico, and then she gave the information out to a competitor with the ethics of a buzzard watching for a road kill?

"I could hang up on the bastards," Patrice suggested.

"I'll talk to them."

"Sure, ruin my fun," she said and walked away. A moment later the light on his phone pulsed. He picked it up. "Good afternoon," he said in his best, neutral voice.

"Am I speaking to Mr. Rey?" the man on the other end asked -- a young sounding voice with a clipped Eastern accent -- probably Boston.

"You are speaking to *Doctor* Rey," he answered. "And you are wasting your time. I am not going to sell the land."

"That's not what your wife implied," the man answered, sounding annoyed.

"My wife is in Europe. She obviously misunderstood the situation, Mr...?"

"Stillman. Edward James Stillman, CEO of Red Sun Enterprises. I need your land, Mr. Rey, and I intend to have it, even if it means going to the state to take possession. I already have lawyers looking into what it would take to have the state exercise imminent domain. The land is underutilized, and I can show just cause --"

"You are doing your best to piss me off, aren't you?" The words finally stopped Mr. Edward James Stillman for a moment. "Did you think telling me you would get the government involved was going to frighten me into instantly selling? Well, screw you. I'm Hopi; we've dealt with the government longer than your people have been in this area. I am not going to sell the land. Go find somewhere else to build your little rich man's paradise."

And he hung up. It felt good, too. He tapped the intercom button, wondering if Patrice had seen the call end.

"Yes?"

"If Mr. Edward James Stillman -- or any other member of Red Sun -- calls again, tell them to go fuck themselves," he said cheerily. "Oh, and if my wife calls, you can tell her the same thing."

Patrice coughed, gasped, and sputtered. He laughed and went back to the work he loved.□

CHAPTER SEVEN

Lunch with a woman he barely knew turned out to be both fraught with worries and a surprisingly fun hour. They went to the Coffee House, a small café around the corner from the museum, and where Lee had grabbed sandwiches and coffee a few times over the last week. The choice saved the question of cars and money since he could afford eating here, even before cashing his first real check from the museum.

The afternoon had turned cloudy and cold. Lee thought he could feel a little ice in the air, and he lifted his face into the breeze, breathing in the cold air and the scent of the pinyon pine trees lining the walk.

Mary, though, huddled into her jacket and walked with her head bent, and her hands shoved into her pockets; she was not a cold weather person.

People crowded along the sidewalk. Tomas had said the weather could turn hotter at any moment, and those trying to avoid the vacation rush were already gathering. Lee wondered if he'd like it as well around here with so many strangers around. Right now it felt cozy -- David from security held the café door open for the two of them, and Tomas waved as he went out with what looked like lunch for Chev and Patrice.

"Do you like working at the museum?" Mary asked as they stood in a line forming up behind food counter and register.

"Yes, I do." He smiled. "It's a great group to work with. I'm considering going back to college to pick up a degree in the field. I always liked it, but now ... well, I can't really think I'd enjoy doing much else."

"You think you'll still feel the same way in ten years?" she asked. They moved a couple steps forward.

He thought about the question for a moment. "Yes, I do. I hope so, anyway. You can never guarantee the future, of course, but based on my life now, I couldn't think of anything else I'd like to do instead."

She peered over someone's shoulder and into the case. "Is the chicken salad sandwich good here?"

"My favorite. I don't know if you'll like it, but I do."

"Good enough." She gave a little shrug and finally loosened the jacket in the warmer building. They still had two people ahead of them. "I'm taking the spring and summer off from work. I'll probably go back to being office staff somewhere afterward. It's not bad work, and the pay is good. You have to be careful of where you hire on, though. You get in a place with a bad attitude, and they're likely to be pissy about giving you references, too."

"Sounds unpleasant. Oh -- only one chicken sandwich left? You know I lied about it being my favorite. The roast beef is really my favorite. Really."

"Good, cause I'm taking the chicken," she said with a bright smile. And she did.

They finally found their way to a small table in the corner, bringing back sandwiches, coffee and chips to share. They talked about living in this area, where both of them had arrived lately, and from entirely different coasts.

"I don't know if I'll stick around through the winter," Mary admitted. She carefully nibbled on a chip and looked out the window. "It's too cold for me now! Winter... Nah."

"Where will you go?" he asked.

"I'll go back to San Diego, probably." She shrugged, sipped her coffee, and shrugged again. "I needed to get away from home and family for a while. Test out my new found wings after the divorce and fly to some place different. I like it here, but it's not home."

"I like it here because it's not home," he said and looked down at the sandwich for a long moment.

"You get quiet, Lee," she said, shaking her head. "I never know what to do when men get quiet on me."

"It happen often?" he asked, hoping to steer things away from him again.

"Sometimes," she said. "I don't have lunch with men very often these days."

"Me either. With women, I mean," he hurriedly said, and then laughed at how silly he sounded. Movie dialogue.

"Divorced, too?" she said.

"Yes." He could have gone on, but he didn't. "There were good reasons."

"There usually are, really," she said. "And I'm not trying to pry. I like knowing someone here. It's odd ... I chose this place because I wanted to get away from everyone I knew. Now I don't think it's what I really wanted at all."

"It's good you had the opportunity to find out, though," he said. And he knew it applied to himself as well.

He wondered at what moment he had started feeling relaxed as he talked to Mary Powers. He had a nice lunch, and they parted at the café door, laughing. He hoped they had lunch again soon. Walking back to the museum he lifted his head again, breathing in the scent and the cold air.

He'd be staying....

CHAPTER EIGHT

C hev happened to be heading for Patrice's office when he saw Lee come back early from lunch, and alone. He looked happy, though, and Chev didn't press him for details.

Later that afternoon Chev called Lee, Tomas, and Patrice to a meeting and related the information on the situation with Red Sun. Patrice would pass the information on to other workers as they needed it. News of Red Sun going to the state government to get the land was bound to draw attention.

Chev did not add his own feelings about Sandra yet. He would talk to Smithers later tonight to get his advice on the matter and talk to his firm in Santa Fe tomorrow to have them primed and ready for Red Sun -- which reminded him of something else.

"Lee, before you go -- I'm going to need you to drive down to Santa Fe on Monday and pick up something from the college for me. Is it going to be a problem?"

"None at all, as long as I can use a company car," he said with a surprising laugh.

"You don't have a car, do you?" Chev asked.

"I have something that calls itself a car, but I leave it

parked at the apartment to save us both a lot of grief and embarrassment."

Lee was getting a sense of humor -- or maybe getting one back. Chev laughed. "It's not a problem. You'd take a company car anyway. I have a piece of pottery for you to pick up, and our insurance people insist we ship things like this in cars they have fully insured."

"Oh, good. Sure, I'd love to go."

"Great. Damn, this has been a surprisingly good day."

"Yes it has," Lee agreed and grinned.

"Let's order in Mexican," Chev said when he saw the time. Then he stopped and waved his hand toward Patrice before she started away. "No. Let's go *out* for Mexican. Sandra blew everything by calling Red Sun and telling them I'm here. I don't see any reason to hide anymore."

Patrice had stopped by the door, looked worried for a moment, and then smiled. "Yes, you're right. But Tomas comes with us."

"Of course, he does. It wouldn't be a proper dinner without him."

And they had a damn good meal, too. It felt like a celebration, but Chev didn't know what exactly they celebrated. Maybe just of life. Sometimes he didn't celebrate life enough.

CHAPTER NINE

More than a week of working at Desert Traditions had not dulled the joy of coming in each morning. Even so, despite his luck with the first sherds, Lee had come to realize how much he didn't know and had already become a familiar face at the library and bookstores after work and during lunch. He didn't mind. It gave him something to do -- something he wanted to do.

He'd run into Mary twice, and they'd had lunch again. They seemed to run in the same circles -- bookstores, libraries, and museums. She made him nervous, but he liked her company. Friends.

He had forgotten Chev intended for him to go to Santa Fe until Chev tossed him the car keys on Monday afternoon and they went out to the parking area behind the museum.

"You're taking the Jeep -- the white Rubicon," he said waving toward the car sitting by the fence. "Paul took it out and filled it up, but the gas card is in the case attached to the back of the passenger seat in case you need it."

"Hell, with one of those I should be able to get to California and back on one tank, right?" Lee said. "Santa Fe is less than 100 miles away!"

Chev laughed. "Good point. Once you pass Cuyamungue on Highway 84, and about three miles farther there's a little dirt road flanked by two pinion pines with a chain strung between them and a hawk symbol on a wooden sign. That's my land. Make sure no one has plowed down the chain while I wasn't looking, will you?"

"I will." He crossed to the car and patted the Desert Tradition's symbol on the side, The D and T surrounded by various petroglyph symbols.

"I don't know how long Professor Belinato will take to get the pottery to you. She said she'll be holding class but she also has archeology sites to cover, and I've never had much luck pinning her down. We should have gotten you a cell phone --"

"Chev, calm," Lee said. He unlocked the car and let the door stand open, heat escaping like a breeze off the desert. "I'll go down, I'll find her, I'll get the pottery and come back."

"Yeah," Chev said. He rolled back a little. "There's a briefcase in there for some paperwork she'll give you. You'll have to sign for the item she has when she hands it over. You've got plenty of time to look around. Have a good trip. Stop for lunch and be sure you get receipts. You're on company business, Lee. Don't give me that look. We need the expenses, you know. Tax stuff."

He laughed, thinking how little difference a couple tacos would make on the spreadsheets. He'd do it to keep Chev and Patrice happy, so maybe they'd let him go off on trips like this again.

Freedom ... an odd feeling as he climbed into the car and started it up. Damn nice car, in fact. He looked at the speedometer and found it registered less than five thousand miles. He'd never driven anything so new in his life.

"Go," Chev ordered with a smile.

He pulled away, then looked back, worried -- but Tomas stood at the doorway, watching. Tomas had become a shadow that he sometimes failed to see unless he looked. The man took his work very seriously, too. Lee would hate to be a person stupid enough to cause Chev trouble.

Tomas waved as he went past. Lee grinned and returned it, and then pulled out of the museum's private back lot, around the long outer wall, and finally down to Paseo del Pueblo Norte.

The bright sun beat down on the car, making sharp shadows everywhere he passed through the flat, open land near Taos. Mountains rose nearby to the right, almost bereft of snow. He passed ubiquitous adobe buildings, fancy new houses on land stripped bare, past dilapidated trailers, and shopping malls -- and finally out into the open vista filled with sagebrush and distant mesquite trees. Eroded hills with patches of red and white shown through the sagebrush, and sometimes the Rio Grande sweeping by with far more speed and force than anything else in the desert.

This proved to be an excellent day for a drive, without many people on the road. He went past the turn off to Los Alamos, thinking he'd like to go back. He'd driven up right after he first bought his car, but the feel of security around the place had frightened him in ways he hadn't expected. Tall, windowless buildings behind fences had signs that said things like cryogenics -- alien, science fiction terms. Now, though, he'd put the memory of prison farther behind him, he thought he might like to see the town again. He wanted to know more about the place's strange history. Though Bandelier, with its odd ruins, might appeal to him more.

But not today. From the Espanola turn off all the way to Santa Fe he passed increasingly urban development. He feared he would miss Chev's land. He slowed, grateful for the light traffic so the semis could go past him without trouble.

And there it was -- the dirt road and the chain across the drive. He pulled over to take a look, parking by the gate and getting out to stretch his legs, as though a drive of about sixty miles had been so horrible. Off in the distance stood a small adobe house, and he saw horses in a corral. The road went past it and off toward some hills.

Pretty land. Sagebrush, grayish green, stood in clumps while a small, spiked-leaf plant with tiny purple flowers grew up around the pinion pine gate posts. He saw a stand of cactus cushion, and some of the ubiquitous prickly pear -
-

A state patrol car had slowed down and pulled up beside him.

It was all right, it was all right. The man got out of the car, started forward, and then looked at the Jeep and grinned.

"Didn't see the DT symbol! Sorry! I try to keep an eye on the road for Chev. I'm his cousin, Popovi Da."

"I'm Lee Constantinos," Lee said, holding out his hand and hoping the palm didn't feel damp and clammy. They shook, and the man still grinned. "I wanted to get a look at the place."

"Have Chev give you a tour," he said, and then the smile faded a little. "When he's ready to. Damn people. Told him he should stick near home. If you talk to him -- well let him know I'm still watching for him."

"I'll do that," Lee said, realizing the man didn't know Chev was in the area. He wanted to tell him ... but no. No, he had no way to know if what this man said was true. "I have something to pick up in Santa Fe."

"Don't speed," Popovi said with a laugh as he went back to his own car.

A few minutes later Lee drove into the outskirts of Santa Fe. It felt as strange this time as it had the first time, as the desert suddenly gave way to an oasis of green. Trees lined the ridges all along the highway, and red-tiled roofs peeked out from beneath the canopy now and then. Gradually the Old Town came into view. This city already had such lovely buildings as the Palace of the Governors more than a decade before the Mayflower found Plymouth Rock. Until college, Lee hadn't realized how old the European settlements were in this area of the country, compared to the East Coast. It had been one of the first things to drew his attention.

Heading into the Old Town meant driving into history, and he could sense the old city of La Villa Real De La Santa Fe De San Francisco de Asis all around him. Despite the short time he'd lived in New Mexico, he'd come to love the area. He found Taos a little less imposing, though.

A quick drive through Old Town reminded him he had money. He found a café on the edge of the small streets, ate lunch -- barely remembered to get the receipt -- and then walked past the small shops and toward the St. Francis Cathedral.

He'd read Willa Cather's *Death Comes for the Archbishop* as soon as he learned it was about Jean Baptiste Lamy, the man who had built this church. He had not gone inside the week he'd spent in Santa Fe. Now he hurried across the road and up the steps.

His parents had been devout Greek Orthodox Christians. He had stopped being *devout* anything five

years ago.   Still, walking into the St. Francis Cathedral
brought a startling surge of emotion.   He wandered around
for a few minutes, found the Lady Chapel with La
Conquistadora -- the oldest venerated statue of the Virgin
Mary in the United States.   She didn't look old, but
knowing her history drew him to her.

History: he found the chronicle of his strange corner
of the world so fascinating that he couldn't imagine walking
away now.

However, a glance at his watch showed it was getting
close to three, and he did not want to miss the professor.
He'd be back.

He had no trouble finding the Santa Fe Community
College, but it gave him a very strange feeling to see all
those kids wandering everywhere. Before prison, he'd been
one of them. How could he feel so much older -- and so
different -- after just five years? His hands trembled at the
thought, and he sat in the car for a few minutes, watching
as the school security car circled twice. They did no more
than glance his way. The emblem on the side of the vehicle
made him official.

He finally got out of the car and brushed at his
clothing before he pulled out the briefcase, feeling silly and
ostentatious carrying it. He locked the car and headed for
the administration building.   In a few minutes, he was
jogging across campus to where the professor was holding
her current class.

By the time he finally found the right place, students
began streaming out of the building, and he feared he'd
missed her and messed up the first assignment Rey had sent
him on. Panic eased, though, as an older woman exited the
building, and another student addressed her as professor.
She was a small woman, dressed in jeans and a nice shirt,

with short hair going gray. He didn't want to intrude on the conversation which seemed to be about the two types of Yuma stone arrows, so he walked along with the small group. One by one the students began to break away. When they finally reached the administration building two still walked with her, and she stopped and looked at him, brown eyes narrowed in a look that could probably quell students.

Lee smiled. "I'm Lee Constantinos," he said before she could ask. "Dr. Rey sent me --"

"Oh!" She gave him a bright smile and her face colored. "Of course. I had expected Patrice, but I remember Chev's email said he might send the new guy. Come up to my office. Dorothy, Mark -- put your questions to me in writing, and I'll see what I need to answer."

The two nodded, neither looking happy as they turned away. Lee felt sorry to have taken their time and started to volunteer to wait -- but Professor Belinato caught his arm and shook her head, pulling him into the building before she spoke.

"They want me to give them easy answers Mr. Constan...?"

"Lee."

"Lee," she said and started along the hall at a brisk pace. "They want easy answers so they don't have to go look for them. I don't want this work to be easy. They need to *want* to look and to love the act of discovery."

"Oh yes. I understand."

She pushed open a door to an office and looked back at him, nodding. "You love the work, do you? Learning answers?"

"I did when I was in school. I had to ... drop out."

"Damn shame," she said and waved him inside the

crowded room. "How's Chev doing?"

"Well, I think. Patrice says he has a private nurse for physical therapy several times a week to get him back on his feet. He seems -- I haven't known him for long -- but he seems like a man who wouldn't cling to false hopes."

She stopped and stared at him. "You're right. Thank you. Chev was a student of mine several years ago, and one of the few with real fire, although he did have an agenda he wanted to push. He wanted to find -- to prove -- certain answers, and it's a bad way to go into the field. I think he outgrew that tendency, though. He started asking questions rather than looking for answers to suit him."

Lee wanted to ask more about Cheveyo Rey, but he refrained. He wanted to understand Chev, who gave him a chance to work in his favorite field, but understanding would likely come better from working with him rather than from an outside source.

Professor Belinato unlocked a cabinet and pulled out a large wooden crate with a hinged top and a padlock. She took a key from around her neck and unlocked the top, pulled up some packing material and then pulled out a lovely olla -- bands of red and cream, a line of odd creatures moving across it, and hardly chipped at all, so that the rounded jar with a narrow top looked as though it could have been made a month ago.

Belinato turned the pottery for him to see the side and smiled.

He thought his heart stopped.

Writing? Writing in a neat cursive hand; Spanish, Lee suspected.

"Ah -- it's not as old as I first..."

It took him a moment to translate the words... Christmas Day, in the year of our Lord, 1527. Alejandro de

Seville.

"This isn't possible," Lee said. He looked at her, frowning. "I assume you were given it to prove it's a hoax?"

"Basically, yes. And I can't prove it's a hoax, but I can't entirely prove it's authentic, either. However, considering where it was found -- in a ruin on Chev's land and by a group of young, but legitimate archeologists -- I'm tending more and more to think this is real."

"The Franciscan friar who was the first Spaniard to make it this far north didn't arrive until 1539, right?"

"That's always been the belief," she said. Her fingers brushed lightly over the rim of the olla. "Fray Marcos de Niza went North at the behest of the viceroy of New Spain, Antonio de Mendoza. He returned with tales of the seven cities of gold. Lies all of it, but it brought Coronado running in 1540 and started the Spanish push north. Now do you want to see what really makes this olla odd?"

"This doesn't?" Lee said, with a wave of his hand at the writing.

She turned the pot again.

It was not writing this time, not in the European sense, at least. The drawings were rather fine considering the medium. Lee recognized one glyph but not the others.

"All right the feathered snake is Quetzalcóatl, which means this is Aztec?"

"Right. These two appear to be the symbols for deer and house -- we think it might be an Aztec name, Mazatlcalli."

Spanish and Aztec together? That didn't have a good connotation in most circumstances, but here they were, obviously in the same place at the same time, and a thousand miles from where they should have been, and at best a decade too early.

"If this is legitimate --"

"I've found a reference to an Alejandro de Seville with Cortez. He was among the two hundred and seventy men left behind by Cortez in June 1520 when he escaped from the Aztecs at Tenochtitlan. Those he left were in a garrison in another part of the city, and Cortez apparently didn't think any of them were worth risking his life to try and save when he ran."

"And one may have survived? And came here with an Aztec?"

"Who knows for certain? This could be a hoax. But I did all the checking I could for Chev over the last few months, and I have all the data I could find. The pottery matches other material from the time, and we got lucky. I found a partial thumbprint on this one and on another dated piece from the same kiln."

He felt his heart do a double beat this time.

"This is incredible," he whispered. He let his fingers brush where Professor Belinato had touched the surface. "It doesn't really change history, but it does give it a strange new depth, doesn't it?"

"This is a riddle to work out," she said and began, obviously with some reluctance, to pack the olla up again. "Historians and archeologists both love puzzles, you know. This has been shown to very few people so far. We're trying to keep the existence a secret in hopes that something else is found to corroborate the find."

"This has to be priceless if it's real."

"Exactly. There has never been another piece like it. And now I'm going to give the olla to you to take back to Desert Traditions."

"I'm not sure I'm as happy about having it in my hands

as I should be," he said.

"Oh, believe me, I know the feeling," she said with a laugh as she locked the lid down and handed him the key. "I've had this in my care for three months now. The first day it seemed wondrous with possibilities. Then I thought about Chev's enemies, and how they might enjoy destroying something so important to him."

"Yes, exactly. Thank you for reinforcing my paranoia."

She laughed and patted him on the arm. "I have all the information on the olla in triplicate -- one set for me, another in a safe deposit box, and the last set will go with you."

He signed for the olla, put the paperwork in his briefcase and then gathered the box up by the handle. Professor Belinato walked him to the Jeep and looked far too pleased to see him -- and the box -- leaving.

There would be no sightseeing on the way home. He put the box on the floor in the back and laid the passenger side seat down to make certain it didn't go flying. Then he drove carefully out of the college lot and headed straight toward the freeway.

An automatic glance at the fuel gauge won a little grimace of frustration. The needle hovered around a quarter of a tank or less. Lee started to turn toward a gas station.

That couldn't be right. The tank had been more than half full when he pulled into the college's parking lot. A glance at the rearview mirror showed a large white pickup -- two men -- following close behind and preparing to turn in the gas station as well.

He turned in, eyeing the possibilities -- but he'd never get to the olla out and reach the safety of the building in time. Heading back to the college seemed a far wiser move.

Ease in, around to a gas pump, pretend you don't notice the big white pickup pulling in behind you....

Lee waited until they had practically stopped before he hit the gas and shot forward, bouncing over the curb and back out into the street, where he nearly collided with a battered van. The driver swerved and blocked the way back toward the college. Lee went up over the opposite curb, swung to the right, and hit the gas again, heading for the next block.

He'd lost the pickup for the moment, but they would know where he intended to go, running for the closest safety. He had to be tricky.

Lee turned down a street and purposely away from the college. Down an alley, across another street -- no sign of the truck. He picked up speed, praying the cops spotted him, but after five blocks he gave up any such hope.

He had to dump the box somewhere and get away from this area, and back near the college, as fast as he could so they didn't know he'd been this far out. Seven blocks -- it was the best he could do. He found an alley behind a row of small businesses and saw junk piled up behind a store -- pallets, boxes, and other packing debris. It didn't look as though it had disturbed in some time. He prayed to God no one took it into his head to clean it up before he got back!

Lee hit the brakes, leapt out, yanking the box with him. He shoved it down behind a trash bin and threw a couple cardboard boxes and some bundles of paper over the top.

Lee ran back, jumped in the car hitting the gas almost before he got the door closed, and headed back toward the college. He couldn't let them know he had gone this way, so Lee floored the gas pedal and raced back almost an equal distance in the opposite direction, and then slowed as he came closer to the college.

Spotted. Damn. He had almost believed it had been some kind of mistake, a faulty gauge, his rampant paranoia springing full force -- but he saw the truck the driver saw him as well and spun in his direction. The tire's squealed.

He wasn't going to reach the college and help. He barely had time to turn before they rammed him from behind. He tried for a store parking lot, but they shoved up against his bumper and pushed him past. People stared in amazement. Someone grabbed a cell phone. Good.

They weren't going to let him stop in any place with a crowd. Maybe just as well. He didn't want to drag anyone else into this trouble with him. Lee hit the gas, pulled away from the truck, dashing for the freeway.

The Jeep coughed and nearly died going up the ramp, but it caught again on the curve as the last of the fuel sloshed across the tank. He put his foot down on the gas and shot out into the traffic, startling more people, but making some distance.

The pickup followed. Hell, where were the damned cops now that he really wanted to see one for the first time in a lot of years?

The engine coughed again, sputtered -- and he knew he wouldn't get more than a few yards. He wanted to pull out into the middle of traffic and let the car die there, but traffic cut him off, the truck came up behind and quite easily maneuvered him off onto the shoulder.

Hell. Try running? No way off the Interstate. He briefly considered charging across the traffic, but even as slow as it was, he didn't think it was a good idea.

He got out of the car and into the open where the people passing by could clearly see him. He wanted witnesses. The two men came from the pickup, one up on the driver's side where he stood, and the other circling around the Jeep. Tall, bulky men with Stetsons and Raybans, almost identical western style shirts, and jeans.

The man coming up beside him caught his arm in a visor-like grip and snarled, while he looked over the top of the Jeep. "Is it there, then?" he said with a surprisingly thick British accent that sounded comical from this cowboy.

The other man had yanked the door open and spent far more time looking through the Jeep than it deserved. Except for the briefcase, there was nothing else in it.

"Not fucking here," he said. Texas drawl there. Odd pair.

"Wipe that smirk off your face, you stupid bastard, and tell us what you did with the bloody box. We saw you put it in the car."

"What makes you think I'd tell you?" Lee asked, leaning against the car. He felt remarkably calm, as though he had gone far beyond the fears that had plagued him before he actually faced danger.

And this was dangerous, beyond a doubt.

"I could punt you out into the traffic, couldn't I?"

"Yes. Of course, you'd have a hard time getting away. And you still wouldn't have the box."

"Let's get him in the truck," Texas said. "We've already drawn far more attention than the boss will like."

Brit, his large hand still tight around Lee's arm, dragged him to the back of the Jeep and around to the passenger side of the truck. He did not want to climb in, but as he balked something hit him across the back of the head....

CHAPTER TEN

The intercom buzzer went off. Chev jabbed at it, reaching for his coffee cup. "Yes?"

"Chev something --" Patrice stopped. "I'm coming back there."

The line went dead.

The sound in her voice turned everything to a moment of ice. Chev sat the cup down and rolled away from the desk as he listened to her hurrying down the hall, almost at a run. Tomas, who had been sitting outside the door reading, suddenly stood. Chev could see the guard at the corner of the door, looking worried as well.

By the time Patrice appeared his blood pressure had to have gone up to dangerous levels. He felt dizzy and ill when he looked up at her.

"Tell me it's not Lee," he whispered.

"They found the Jeep on the freeway in Santa Fe. There had been a report of a large white pickup pursuing it. There's no sign of Lee, and no blood, at least."

"Oh hell. Damn them! We need to get down to Santa Fe."

"I'm going to get the van," Patrice said, her voice shaking with anger. "I told the others to close up tonight and told the guards to be wary tonight."

She started to go past toward the back door, but surprisingly Tomas caught her arm. "I'll get the van," he said. "You get him to the back door. If they made a move on Lee, they could be after any of Chev's friends. We have to be careful."

Chev nodded. He wanted to tell Tomas he shouldn't go alone either, but the guard had already darted away. Besides, he had a gun -- and Chev knew he'd use the weapon if he had to.

Neither he nor Patrice said anything as she stepped up behind and the wheelchair and pushed him toward the back door. She stopped there, the door open the width of her foot, which she put in the way to make certain it didn't close again. He could hear Tomas starting the car.

"I never thought something like this would happen," Chev said, shaking his head.

"This is not one of those things you can consider." She looked down at Chev, and the anger in her face softened a little. "You did nothing wrong."

"I shouldn't have sent him out. I shouldn't have -- I knew I had enemies. I knew --"

"You know better, Cheveyo," she said and almost put a hand on his shoulder, but pulled back. "You aren't the one in the wrong here."

"If something has happened to Lee --"

"You'll spend every cent you have to find out who did it and make sure they are brought to justice, one way or another," she replied, and he nodded, grim-faced and angry. "But let's get to Santa Fe and find out what's happened. Let's not think the worst."

Tomas brought the van up and got out, surprising Chev, who assumed he would drive them. The stocky, short-haired Hispanic looked at Patrice with a frown and then down at Chev.

"You two go straight to the Santa Fe police. I'm going to do some checking with the State Patrol. I'll go with you if you think you need me, Chev --"

"No. Patrice can hold back any ten madmen," he said and felt a little better for the joke. "Go and find out what you can."

Tomas gave a single nod and jogged to his own car. It made Chev feel better, in fact, to have other people working more angles. Tomas didn't drive away until they did, and then he followed for a few miles, making certain no one followed them. Tomas honked and turned back about five miles out of town.

He and Patrice said nothing at all. He didn't know what Patrice might be thinking, but he concentrated on remaining calm. The day had grown late, clouds lining the mountains, and lightning flashing now and then in the distance. The night would come quickly, which would make looking for Lee more difficult.

Patrice drove straight to the Santa Fe Police Headquarters on Camino Entrada. Chev didn't like the buildings, most of them without any cultural flavor. He looked at his hands and said nothing as Patrice got them to the right building and brought his wheelchair around.

The day felt hot and sullen, mimicking his mood.

Patrice talked to the woman at the desk, and in a moment a young man came out and introduced himself as Detective Perez. He led the two back to a small office where paperwork sat stacked on his desk. He sat down, even-eyed with Chev, and indicated the chair where Patrice could sit.

Chev could see questions and assessments in the man's

eyes. Best to get all of it settled right away and go on to the real problem.

"I'm Dr. Cheveyo Rey of the Desert Traditions Museum in Taos. This is Patrice Barnowl, the museum's curator. Leander Constantine is my employee. Have you learned anything about his disappearance yet?"

"Desert Traditions," Perez repeated. His attitude changed, and Chev suspected he didn't often deal with professional class people, and the two of them worried him on some level. "That was the emblem on the side of the Jeep. Was he on museum business?"

"Yes. Lee had come to Santa Fe to pick up a box from the college."

"Box?"

"A piece of pottery," Chev said, starting to get a little annoyed with the lack of cooperation and the one-way conversation, though he reined his anger in, knowing it was misplaced. "It was a potentially important piece of pottery."

"We found nothing in the vehicle," he said, shaking his head with a little show of regret, as though the pottery might matter to him. Chev thought better of the man. "Here's all we have so far, Dr. Rey. Someone punched a hole in the gas tank while it was parked at the college. Four different people reported a confrontational exchange between the Jeep and a large new white pickup with no plates. Is it possible someone would go to this kind of trouble to get hold of this piece of pottery?"

"It's possible," Chev said. "But it is possible this is trouble followed me from London, where someone tried to kill me a few months ago. You can get all the information on the case from the Taos police, and a far better report than I can give you. That time is jumbled for me, and this isn't helping."

Perez started to say something, but he stopped and nodded.

"All right. So we have two possible motives -- the pottery and your enemies. Could there be a third? Did your employee have any enemies of his own that you know about?"

"I assume you ran a check on his name when I gave it to you," Patrice said.

"Yes. We had a half dozen Leander Constantine's show up, and without...." He stopped and looked back at Chev and then to Patrice. "He's the one released from prison."

"Yes," she said. "And Lee knew about the trouble with Chev in London. We didn't send him off without warning, but none of us expected anything like this. Not here, and not going after Lee instead of Chev."

Perez finally leaned back in his chair and shook his head. "This is a real mess."

"Yes, it is," Chev agreed.

"I'm inclined, under the circumstances, to think this is your trouble and not his. Fill me in on what's going on, and I'll get the rest from Taos as we need it."

Chev shifted uncomfortably, but he began the tale -- as simple and straightforward as he could manage. He gave the man the number of his London law firm and saw the moment when Perez suddenly realized Chev had a lot of money, which probably made the idea of someone trying to kill him more likely. Chev also gave Perez the numbers to other people the detective should contact for answers. He thought about Sandra and decided not to bother. He'd have to hunt her down first, and right now he didn't want to think too much about her.

Was this Sandra's fault? Had she told others, besides the Red Sun people, where to find him? He didn't want to think it. He didn't want to blame anyone but whoever took Lee.

Perez had finished taking notes. "I'm going to send for some comp records and faxes. I'll be right back."

Alone with Patrice, Chev looked at her and shook his head with growing despair. "It's not worth this."

"We don't know what any of this is, Chev. It could be Lee's trouble following him. But whatever the reason for this problem, I'll be damned if I want those bastards to win."

"I want to find Lee."

"I'm going to believe we will," Patrice said. "Because believing anything else will not help."

Chev stared at the wall for a moment and then nodded. "We're going to go see Grandfather after we're done here."

"Yes," Patrice said. "Good."

Did she believe in the old ways? They never talked about their life before, growing up on the reservation. They'd both gone on to other work and left the old world -- mostly -- behind.

Or was she glad to see him turn his attention away from anger? It didn't matter, especially since he'd never decided entirely what he believed. Right now, though, he would examine every possibility to get Lee back.

Perez returned a moment later. "I don't have a lot to go on," he admitted, settling back in the worn chair. "We're looking for the white pickup. If we can find out where they bought gas for it, we might be able to trace at least part of their path. We're talking to everyone who came forward as a witness. Beyond that, we have to hope something falls together."

"You have the number to my office and my cell phone," Chev said. He started to roll back and stopped "I might be out of range for a while tonight. Reception on the rez is lousy some nights, especially in a storm. I'm going to go out there to see my grandfather. He's a shaman."

"Shaman." Perez looked startled. "You're an educated man --"

"Educated in ways old and new," Chev replied. "And desperate enough to try anything."

Perez apparently understood. "Be careful."

"We will," Patrice said as she stood. She looked anxious to get going. "We'll be very careful."□

CHAPTER ELEVEN

Thunder rolled loud and close.

People were carrying him.

"The bastard's coming around," England said. "This looks like a good spot."

"Yeah."

He opened his eyes in time to realize he was flying.

Hit hard against rocks and tumbled, and the world went dark again.

Rain.

Rivulets of icy water ran down Lee's face, cold enough to make him shiver. He opened his eyes to darkness, tried to lift his hand, but everything hurt to move --

Lightning radiated out in silver lines of fire, so bright he tried to shield his eyes. For a heartbeat, he saw the desert before him and then gone again into the dark night. He could feel the hard edges of rocks at his back, but sand beneath his -- damn! -- bare feet. Moving his head made him so ill he laid there gasping in as much rain as air, and hoping he didn't pass out again.

The storm blew over him with frightening intensity. He'd never been out in the open in a storm like this, and part of him wanted to dig down into the ground and find cover. He stayed still, trying not to shiver, and trying to get some sense of what to do.

He couldn't stay here. He had to get back to Chev and Patrice. Night had fallen. They'd be worried by now, and the last thing he wanted as to cause those two any grief.

He maneuvered to his knees, his legs sinking into the wet sand. A dried weed of some sort scratched his hand as he moved, and he paused a moment, waiting for the lightning so he could see something, and maybe get an idea of his surroundings.

Feeling returned to his numbed shoulders, and it was not a good feeling, either. He stayed as still as he could manage for a few breaths and then slowly turned his head. Sore, but not worse. He feared he might have cracked a rib or two from the pain in his chest, but he could move.

The storm had lessened, the lightning moving out of his direct sight. Rain fell in a light mist, and he could feel a cold breeze picking up. The storm at least wetted the sand and kept it down. He didn't think he wanted to be out here in a dust storm.

He didn't want to be out here at all. But like most of his life in the last few years, people didn't seem to take what he wanted very seriously.

Lee stood, his hands automatically checking his pockets, and finding them completely empty. Dizziness made him ill, and he almost went back down, but he leaned back against the rocks at his back. He looked up. The rock wall behind him wasn't very high -- maybe twenty feet to the top. The two had been up there when they threw him. He doubted they'd walked very far carrying him, so the best chance of getting back to civilization had to be up there as well.

Besides, he could hear water running close by. This was probably a dry creek bed of some sort, and with the storm, it might fill up quickly.

He started to climb, cursing as his fingers scraped against damp rock and his toes jabbed into small crevices, trying to find purchase in the soft wet stone. Lee briefly considered walking along the creek and looking for an easier way, but he feared he would not find this spot, which was the only reference he had for where England and Tex had been.

Not far to climb, but he slipped twice and twisted his ankle -- didn't need any more injuries!

Up.

Lee hadn't realized he'd reached the top until he found himself looking at a wide flat area. Scrambling up the last of those wet boulders proved to be the hardest part. He had nothing he could grab at the top, and kept sliding backward before his feet could find a crevice. Frustration nearly sent him tumbling all the way back down.

He finally sprawled over the top edge and stayed there a long time. He might have passed out because he had the vague feeling of time having passed. The storm had gone by then, and when he finally sat up, he found a bright gibbous moon hanging low over the desert.

Beautiful: stark, with the stands of creosote black against the lighter ground, and a mixture of sagebrush and mesquite. The scene took his breath away; while he thought he ought to get moving, he stared in wonder, and it made him feel better. Maybe he'd needed to rest because he'd felt stronger afterward. Although when he stood, he felt every ache in his body.

And he didn't know which way to go. He stood on slightly higher ground that stretched out in all directions.

Lee looked back over the edge of the cliff he had so laboriously climbed and could still see no sign of life. If there had been any footprints, the storm had washed them away. He supposed he wouldn't have seen them in this dark anyway.

Go right, go left, or stay.

He turned to the right and began walking.

The mesa finally dropped away again. Lee thought there ought to be a road because Tex and England wouldn't have carried him far, so he followed along the edge until he at least found what looked like a trail. His feet hurt. He must have stepped on every single rock.

Shapes, indistinct and dangerous, gathered in the dark night. He brushed against creosote and rice grass, but he also learned that a small, squat cactus could look like more boulders. His right hand ached, a few cactus spines still embedded in the palm. Barrel cactus, maybe. The spines had been very long.

He didn't rest over the next few hours. Rage, fear and a sense of self-preservation kept him moving, first across the treacherous boulder lined path, and then off into the flatter, open desert.

He looked up at the sky, wondering if he remembered stars and constellations well enough to navigate by them. Maybe not, since he couldn't pick out one from the other -- though he had never seen them so clearly before! Bright stars, glowing like fire. He could also see the edge of the clouds moving off, lightning in the distance now. A jet flew high over head, almost dead on in the direction he'd been walking. He took it as a good sign and kept going.

A few steps later he had the worse scare of the entire nightmare journey. His foot came down on a small rock that shifted in the sand and sent him sprawling. He cursed as he hit, new pain shooting through his ankle. And something moved, close by, sand shifting, shifting ... and then a rattle.

His heart pounded so hard for a moment he couldn't hear anything else. His initial reaction was to leap up and run, but his survival instinct cut in and he held very, very still. If the snake decided he was a good, warm place to curl up on, he didn't know what he'd do.

Something brushed against his foot, over the ankle -- a warm, soft undulating movement. He held his breath and willed the leg not to tremble. He felt cold, his clothing still wet from the rain and hoped the snake found it uncomfortable as well.

The creature paused, half on one side, half on the other. Could he kick it off? No, it would fly toward his head. He had to wait. Just wait.

The rattler moved on, and he could hear the sound in the wet sand for a couple minutes. The snake had not gone far.

He got to his knees and scrambled away as fast as he could, afraid there were others, afraid he would put his hand right down on one. He moved until he ran out of breath, and sat, his knees pulled up to his chin, despite the pain in his chest. And he stayed there, shaking, for a long time. The night had gone silent and cold. He could see no sign of civilization, and for all he knew, he had died and gone to hell. He would have expected hell to be a prison cell, but this worked as well.

Going crazy.

No. Not now. Not having survived so much else.

He stood again, his legs rubbery, and he almost fell -- but Lee willed himself up and kept moving. And then, somewhere far, far ahead he saw the flash of lights on the lower ground. And again -- and Lee realized he saw a road, although so far away he couldn't measure the miles.

Lee found his emotions taking a roller-coaster ride and he wept. Oddly, Lee felt better for it. Maybe he could allow himself to cry here away from everyone who would make judgments. Maybe he could do it because seeing car lights, he knew he could not be irredeemably lost.

Several deep breaths later, and with his emotions in order -- and his bout of philosophy and self-analysis past -- he began to limp toward the road. He knew he'd never make it tonight -- but he kept walking. He had a goal now.

CHAPTER TWELVE

Patrice drove slowly over the rutted dirt road leading up into the hills and the pueblo. Chev wanted to complain about the slow pace, but he said nothing. She drove carefully as a kindness to him, but even the little bumps jolted knitting bones and sent tremors of agony through his back and legs.

And he didn't know how to feel about this sudden urge to go running back to the mystic past, to the place before he went to college ... to the place where he had followed Grandfather everywhere.

"This is cra-zy," he said as they hit another bump.

Patrice glanced at him and shook her head. "No, it isn't. Your grandfather has an uncanny ability to know things. We'd be stupid not go to him now."

"That's what I keep t-telling myself. Don't slow. I want to get there and back out yet tonight."

Patrice had started to slow, but then she eased back down on the gas and picked up a little speed beyond what she'd been driving before. "We'll find him," she said barely above the sound of the engine and the rough road. "We'll find Lee."

"I hope so."

"You need more faith. More belief."

"I left that behind long ago, you know."

"No, you didn't. You still believe in the hawk, don't you?"

He frowned but then nodded because he couldn't lie to her. "Yes."

"What more do you need? Besides, that wasn't really what I was thinking. I thought you should have more belief in Lee."

"I do. But I also know the people we're up against, and I know what they're capable of doing. Hell. There's grandfather."

Patrice had already started to slow down. The old man sat on a boulder beside the road, and the car lights bounced off him, a ghostly apparition for a brief moment. Someone who wasn't used to Grandfather might have been frightened enough to crash. Chev, though, wasn't particularly surprised to find him down here on the dirt road, several miles from the pueblo.

The old man slipped off the boulder with ease and walked toward them with the gait of a fifteen-year-old, rather than someone who had topped eighty. Chev shifted, uneasy and uncomfortable, and started to open the door.

"No, do not get out," Grandfather said, pushing the car door shut. "You are not ready to walk, Little Hawk. Don't be embarrassed. You have done nothing wrong."

Chev looked at him, startled by the words before he felt something heavy lift within his soul. He had, somehow, expected blame for the having strayed so far from the reservation, and for having gotten involved with people who had no feel for life. He had thought Grandfather would disapprove of everything he had done.

"I have a museum now in Taos," he said.

"I know. They say it is very good, and you have aligned the building with the Right Path, and you show the willing outsiders that their ways are not the only ways. It's good work, Hawk. I am working on a gift for such a worthy place."

It was unexpected. Chev's heart swelled, and his throat closed. "Thank you."

Grandfather patted his arm. "You came because there is another trouble, though."

"Someone has taken one of my employees. We hope he's still alive --"

"He is."

Odd. Chev immediately believed grandfather and felt a rush of relief spread over him. "We need to find him. This is my fault. I don't want --"

Fingers tightened on his arm. "This is not your fault."

"I never should have --"

"You do not control the world. I would think you knew that by now."

"But I sent Lee."

"Yes, but you did not send the others. And this Lee was a lost soul before he came to you. You gave him direction, didn't you?"

"How did you --"

"Oh, I can see you, grandchild. I watch you, though not well enough. It is I who failed, you know."

"No!"

The old man tilted his head, a ghost of a smile on his dark face. "We shall work together to make this right, and save this young man from the land. I can sense him out there, alone and uncertain. Angry and afraid at turns. He is out of balance with the desert, but not so much as some outsiders would be. Still, he needs saving before the darkness hiding in his soul overwhelms his good sense."

"Darkness?"

"He has a sense of the dark, of the wrong. And he fears it because it lives in him."

"He was in prison for many years, Grandfather," Patrice said softly, leaning over Chev to look out the window. "And for something he didn't do. We thought... we hoped to give him something better."

"You have. Now it's time to save his body as well as his soul."

"Where can we find him?" Chev asked.

Grandfather took a single step away from the car, turned to the wind, and chanted softly. Such things, Chev knew, were not part of the world where he now lived. But he closed his eyes and breathed in the same wind, with the taste of sagebrush and sand. Chev could almost... almost see where Grandfather looked, out across the desert and the dark. There... something... a shape or a feel out of place with the nature and life around it.

"There," Grandfather said. "You see him."

He waved off toward the west.

Chev opened his eyes again, feeling oddly out of place here. "Thank you," Chev said.

"Go. He needs saving, your friend. And while you save him, I shall look into the hearts of your enemies and learn what darkness they fear. Go."

Grandfather walked away. Patrice took a deep breath and began backing the car up. "I'm not sure if it helped or not," she confessed as she turned the car around, inching back and forth on the narrow path.

"I saw him. I can find Lee. I don't think it's going to be easy, but at least I know what direction we need to go."

He saw her turn, startled, and then the dull lights of

the dashboard showed a flash of a smile which looked as much predatory as it did friendly. "Good. Let's go get him."

Chev leaned back in the seat, muscles relaxing this time as they bounced across the road. Chev would go get Lee and then... and then get on with other things. He'd had enough of this game. Time to change the rules.

CHAPTER THIRTEEN

L ee had sat down. He didn't know when it had happened. He his head pounded, and his legs hurt, and he wanted to rest for a moment.

His legs cramped, and his mouth felt so dry it hurt to move his tongue and lips. He didn't want to get back up.

The dawn came quickly, a bright light spreading to his right. He hadn't realized he'd been walking southward, though he should have known it from the movement of the moon or the stars.

The sudden bright intensity nearly blinded him, but he squinted hoping to see something that would give him hope.

Nothing. Desert, creosote, sand as far as he could see and nothing helpful. He couldn't say why he had dared hope for anything better. He wanted....

Time to get up and move again. Sitting here would not help. Lee started to stand but went right back down breathlessly mumbling a curse that hurt his lips to speak. He wanted to stand. He wanted --

Wanted to run. He wanted out of the nightmare his life had become. If he made it out of this he would leave Taos --

And run where? How far?

No. Lee liked his work here. Why would he let these bastards ruin his life and put Chev and Patrice through more hell? No.

So he had to get up and start walking. His legs protested, and his feet felt like fire where the sand rubbed against them, but he moved. After a few steps, he no longer felt as though he would fall over. Balance seemed precarious still, but not impossible. He walked and at least had a chance to avoid stumbling into small cacti and stones in the light of day.

Little creatures scurried away in the morning light. They would find shelter before the heat of the sun baked the land. He looked around, squinting again. No cover for him.

He walked, watching the ground, hoping he was moving in a straight line. Now that it was light he could pick out something straight ahead and keep on a path toward it. Anything relatively close worked best since he found if he chose anything too far away, his mind wandered, or he'd forget which of the bushes he'd aimed at.

A small piece of dark stone caught his eye; out of place against the sand, and oddly shaped. He bent carefully and picked it up.

Arrowhead. He laughed, the sound dry and a bit painful, but real. He had made his first find as an archaeologist. He wondered what had brought the person who lost it out here. Hunting? The stone still looked sharp, though it had been worn down a bit in places, likely by the sand.

A good luck piece. Lee started to put it in his pocket -- and stopped. Sharp? Just ahead was a stand of prickly pear cacti, and one ha a couple fruit still attached, though both had been nibbled by birds. Two lizards darted away when he neared. For the next half hour or so, Lee used his arrowhead to carefully cut away a large piece of the pear. He then spent as much time cutting away the skin, poking his fingers far too often with the spines. The flesh oozed liquid onto his fingers. He licked them experimentally. Sweet taste. He broke off a piece and stuffed it into his mouth, chewing carefully in case any of the spines had broken off. Then he sucked on the mashed, pulp.

He pushed the rest, and the arrowhead, into his pocket, chose his next target and started walking again.

Amazing the things you could see, watching the ground. Plants with lovely flowers -- it had been a wet spring, here in the desert. Lee crossed the paths of small rodents and birds, tiny paw prints and the marks of talons running rampant in amusing little circles. A little later he found the sliding path of a snake, and then prints of what appeared to be a large lizard. He didn't want to run into it.

An old dirt road crossed his path, and he wondered if he should take it instead. It didn't look used, though. Sagebrush had started to grow up in the ruts. It wasn't going to lead him to anything helpful, and he still had hope of the distant road he had seen in the night. Now and then he even saw a flash of light against metal.

A few steps farther and he found a cluster of peyote, the small gray cactus topped with silky, light pink flowers. It was an ugly cactus, except for the flower. He walked on, not in the least bit drawn to the idea of hallucinating when he needed all his already scattered thoughts to survive.

Stopped. Looked back. Returned despite himself.

The peyote was not in a cluster -- it was in a perfect little circle and had obviously been tended by human hands. Humans had been here. Lee thought he could sit and wait for them.

For how long? It wasn't as though cacti needed daily care. Looking around, he could find absolutely no sign of the last time anyone had come this way. No footprints, no tire tracks. Nothing.

But humans had been here. Although not helpful at the moment, the sign of civilization lifted his spirits at last. He began limping back away again.

Not long afterward he found a swarm of flies and beetles crawling over what looked like horse shit. He couldn't see any other pieces nearby, but it was still another good sign. He kept going, though each step became more of a limp. He chewed on another piece of cactus, wondering what Chev and Patrice were doing now. They must be worried about what had happened to him.

The thought brought another wave of righteous indignation, and more strength to keep going.

The desert couldn't go on forever....

CHAPTER FOURTEEN

Despite feeling like they had headed in the right direction, Cheveyo had not yet found Lee. Noon had come and gone, the outside temp growing dangerously higher. He and Patrice had traveled up and down the highway, taken a few back roads, and filled the gas tank twice at the same small town station, which drew some stares.

"Lunch," Patrice insisted and pulled into a small café in Corona.

"I don't want --"

"The car needs a rest," Patrice said, tapping the heat gauge. "And we need to think this out better."

He wanted to argue, but she didn't give him another chance. Patrice got out of the van, pulled the wheelchair out of the back, and came around to his side of the car. He wanted to sit there like a sullen child, but -- damn it had gotten too hot inside already. And besides, being sullen wouldn't help.

So he slid down into the chair with her help. Someone coming out of the café held the door open, and he managed to politely thank her. The single waitress led them to a table where he could slide in out of the way.

By then he realized the cool, dark interior of the café felt relaxing. Neither he nor Patrice had slept the night before, and the weight of the crisis had started to catch up with them. Chev stared at the menu as though he had never seen one before; as though the words were in some strange language. He looked at Patrice with a whisper of panic when the waitress returned, unable to make any sort of decision.

"Two cokes," Patrice said. "Two chef's salads, ranch and French dressing. Anything else, Chev?"

"No," he said, knowing he sounded tired and grateful. "That should do it."

The waitress nodded, dark hair falling over her eyes, frowning slightly as though she didn't trust people who were a bit unusual. She went back toward the kitchen, threading her way through the tables, past truckers, and ranchers who sometimes talked too loudly.

Chev's cell phone rang, startling him. He grabbed at it, hoping --

"Cheveyo Rey," he said, answering it, almost breathless with hope.

"This is Edward James Stillman, Mr. Rey --"

"It's Doctor Rey, you stupid bastard." Chev saw Patrice's eyes go wide. "I am not selling you my land. There is no reason for you to call me again."

"I thought, under the circumstances, after hearing about the trouble with your employee, you might reconsider. Surely a man in your situation would find it far more comfortable in a place of --"

"Don't call me again. And you'll be hearing from my lawyers at any time now. You are not going to get my land."

"I'm not going to give up."

Chev hung up. For a moment he dared not speak. He wasn't often this angry, and he laid his hands carefully on the table and counted to ten before he looked back at Patrice. "Word is out on Lee," he said. "Red Sun seemed to think it would be a good time to talk to me about the land, and remind me that being in a wheelchair had to make this more difficult than I should face."

"Damn those people," she said and nodded thanks as the woman brought them their drinks. "I don't understand those people."

"He's starting to sound desperate," Chev said. "Maybe he found out from the state he couldn't get my land. Hell, I don't know. I don't even really care much. At this point, if I could trade the land for Lee, I'd do it."

"I know," she said and sipped her drink for a moment. She looked tired, and flustered, and Chev could see anger in the wrinkles around her eyes.

"Maybe we should go back to the museum," he said. "I can't say we're doing any good out here. Damn, Patrice. I should never have --"

She unexpectedly reached over and put a hand on his, startling him. Years and years ago, when he had lived on the reservation, she had been his older, forbidden lover. Those seven years difference had seemed insurmountable at seventeen. Now....

They had grown far past the youthful forbidden fire of their first relationship. Chev welcomed her touch, the whispering of understanding and kindness. He wished he hadn't been stupid in Europe -- not the accident, but the marriage that drove the final spike between Patrice and him. He wanted to tell her... but now was not the time. They needed to concentrate on finding Lee.

"You and I believe Lee is alive," Patrice said. "Don't

shake your head. We both know it's illogical, and we both know there is far more to the world than what people can call up on a computer or even see with their own eyes. We'll find him."

Chev wanted to argue, but he couldn't decide why. Maybe he wanted to save himself from belief and disappointment. The meeting with Grandfather, in the dark of night, seemed unreal now. He lived in the world of computers and GPS, not dreams and visions.

Yet, even as he thought it, the feeling he'd had when talking to Grandfather came back. He knew Lee's direction. He had to take the time and to find patience. To find balance.

The waitress brought the salads, some of the ubiquitous tortillas on the side. Chev had never realized the custom was mostly local to the Southwest until he left the area for the first time. Chev began to nibble at the food and then found himself eating with more enthusiasm. So did Patrice.

He had nearly finished when he saw a state patrol car zip past the café window. A heartbeat later he heard breaks and saw it unexpectedly back up. The front passenger door swept open, and someone darted to the building --

Detective Perez from Santa Fe stepped in, pulling his sunglasses off as his eyes narrowed. Chev had already put down his fork when Perez spotted them.

"I don't know how the hell you two happened to be in this area right now, but I recognized the emblem on your car. Get a move on. The pilot of a small plane, out looking for wild horses, spotted him. He's about fifteen miles out."

Chev threw a fifty down on the table, and Patrice grabbed the wheelchair and pushed. Perez held the door open.

"What are you doing out here?" Patrice asked. "Long ways from Santa Fe."

"The call came straight to me since it looked like my missing person case. No state patrol in this area, so I caught a ride out with Officer Peltin. Can you keep up with us? We're going to be doing some traveling --"

"Go," Patrice said. "We'll keep up. It's damn hot out there. The sooner we get him, the better."

Perez started back to the state patrol car, the man in the driver's seat glancing their way. Another state patrol car pulled up behind them -- and a moment later the driver leapt out. Perez looked startled, and a little worried.

"Chev!"

"Popovi!" Chev reached up and grabbed the man's hand in a solid grasp. "Damn glad to see you!"

"When the hell did you get back to the US? Why didn't you tell anyone? And hell! Patrice! I didn't know you and he --"

"I work as the museum's curator," she said.

"Oh, yeah." He finally let go of Chev's hand. "I heard the call about your guy maybe being found. I met him out by your land. Nice guy. Let's go get him before the day gets any hotter."

"Good plan," Chev said. He grabbed the van's doorframe and pulled himself to his feet and got in, stupidly glad Popovi didn't try to help him. "And I didn't let anyone know I was back because of stupid God damned trouble like this. I never expected it to strike someone else."

"Hey, we'll get him," Popovi said. He helped Patrice get the chair into the back. "Not far to go, from all I heard."

People had come out and stared at the cars, probably thinking Chev and Patrice were some wanted criminals. He didn't care. She climbed into the van and started it.

Perez had turned around and headed back to the other car. Popovi climbed into his, and in the next moment the lead patrol car pulled out, lights and siren going this time.

"I told you," Patrice said as she

"Yeah, you did. I'm sure it's him. I'm glad we hadn't gone back." Chev relaxed and let the bumps and leaps the van made pass through him. He watched the car ahead. They would get to Lee soon. He could see a small plane circling back and forth over the highway.

"Make certain we find out the pilot's name," Chev said, waving toward the plane. "And what his dreams are."

Patrice looked at him and smiled brightly. "Yeah. I like that idea."

The patrol car ahead had picked up speed. Patrice pushed down on the gas pedal, and they kept up.

CHAPTER FIFTEEN

A shadow had passed over him, heading away. Lee didn't look up, although he thought he should. No matter. He watched the sand, trying to look at his own shadow, to avoid the glare that had begun to make his eyes hurt. Walk on and on. He thought it got turned around a couple times, reset himself by the sun, and headed on.

The shadow passed over him again, and he heard the sound of the engine. Lee looked up in surprise and shock and fell at the same time. His eyes blurred, the world looked suddenly covered in a haze. He swatted at a fly, the buzzing....

The buzzing was a plane, sweeping low over him, circling, sweeping back. The pilot had seen him. Lee forced his arm up and waved. The plane dipped a wing and flew away.

The feeling of relief, knowing civilization had found him, left him almost too weak to move. He wept again, though not for long, and with a strange detachment besides. He'd gone through hell in prison. He'd never cried then. How could this trouble so overturn his emotions? Why now?

Because he had hoped for vindication and a new life, and instead --

Instead, some bastards who wanted to get to Chev had used him as a tool to break his new friend. Lee tried to get angry at those thoughts, but the emotion wouldn't come. Instead, he closed his eyes and let the heat bake him. There would be help coming. He could rest now, and wait.

But ... he couldn't. He had to keep walking, at least for himself. How long would it take for the person in the plane to get help back to him? And what -- what if the person really wasn't going for help? What if he had been the people who had left him here? Waiting for them would be stupid.

Lee struggled back to his feet, dropped to his knees again, and then got back to his feet once more with a surge of anger. He was not going to fail this time.

Walking proved to be far harder. Perhaps his body had already started to give up, thinking he had been saved before his mind called him back to reality. Maybe the rest of his body hadn't quite gotten the message yet. Which way had he been walking? Which way? No matter.

He started to walk, and then realized he was following his own trail back into the desert. *I will not go back.* So he turned around, moving slowly so he didn't fall on his ass again, and started walking in the opposite direction. Not much farther. Walk. Walk.

Did he hear cars?

He looked up as golden dust, caught in the wind: bright and beautiful, swirling before him. He stopped to watch, swaying a little, finding it hard to stand still. He felt in his pocket. No more cactus and his mouth felt horribly dry. He should have taken the peyote. This would have been beautiful...

Sat down.

And people converged on him. He saw two uniforms. Police.

"I didn't kill her," he said, his voice dry, the words painful. He looked around for Debra and his son. They had to believe him. "I didn't kill her!"

"Lee."

Not all police. Patrice knelt before him, grabbed at his shoulders. He stared at her. She didn't belong to this nightmare. She represented every hope he'd dared to hold in this new land.

"I didn't --" he whispered, panic when he looked up at the police again. One of them glared.

"We know," Patrice said. "Everyone knows."

"Here. Give Lee a little water." One of the policemen dropped down on his heals. He seemed familiar. "See if you can get him to take these salt tablets. Then we'll get him in the car and back to the road. We need to get him to the hospital in Santa Fe."

Water? He had never wanted something so much in his life. Patrice pushed a canteen to his mouth. The water slipped over his tongue and was so icy cold that he shivered. Wonderful. He wanted more, but she pulled the canteen away and he couldn't lift his arms to stop her.

"Here," the man on his heels said, holding something out. "Take these salt tablets. You understand?"

"Tablets," he said, his voice a little better this time, though his throat hurt to talk. "Water?"

"With the tablets," the cop said.

It seemed reasonable enough. A little water, a tablet, a little more water, another one. By then his mind had started to clear of the haze that had held him most of the day.

"Lee?" Patrice said.

"This has been a hell of a couple days," he admitted.

She looked so relieved it surprised him what a few words could produce. Her fingers tightened on his shoulder, and he didn't wince despite the sunburn through the thin, light blue shirt he'd worn. "Who brought you out here? Why?"

"I have no fucking idea," he admitted. He managed to rub his hand across the back of his head, but his fingers were sunburned, and the hair felt like sandpaper against a wound. "I don't know who they were. Big white truck. Sunglasses. One sounded like a Texan, the other one was British. Both dressed like they'd walked out of some New York director's idea of the Wild West. Acted it, too. Macho bastards."

Another man leaned down and grinned. "I'm Detective Perez from Santa Fe. Damn glad we found you, Lee."

"Are you?" he said, a little surprised.

"Here, a little more water," Patrice said. Lee thought she might be trembling.

Lee gratefully sipped the water. He knew they'd be moving soon. Perez had gotten a cloth damp and laid it against Lee's forehead. It helped, but he felt damned tired suddenly.

"He's coherent," Perez said. "There's some sign of heat exhaustion, but not heat stroke. Looks like some cactus spines in his hand -- and his feet are pretty badly cut up. Bad sunburn --"

"Got thrown down some damned hard rocks, too," Lee added, opening his eyes.

Perez had been talking into a cell phone, and he grinned at Lee. "Yeah, that was him. Yeah. Bruises on his arm, but he doesn't seem to have trouble breathing, so I don't think there's anything broken. Lee -- any bites? Bugs or animals?"

"I don't think so," he said. "Can we get the hell out of this damn sun and away from the sand for a while?"

"Sounds like a good idea," Perez said. He handed the phone to Patrice, but she did not close it down. Lee looked at it suspiciously, but he really didn't care --

Perez caught hold of him by the arm and pulled him up. He hissed with the sudden pain, but he was still more than happy to get up out of the sand. The police car wasn't far away --

But the world went very dark.

CHAPTER SIXTEEN

C hev turned in his seat, ignoring the pull of muscles in his back, and tried to see where they had folded down the back seats of the van.

"How's he look?" Patrice asked.

"Still out of it," he said, grabbing the arm of the seat and peering over the top. Not any worse than some of the therapy exercises, he mused.

"Not surprising," Patrice said. "He's had a long couple days. Relax, Chev. He's back. He was coherent and joking. He's had a rough couple days, but he's going to be fine."

Chev stared at the sleeping -- or possibly comatose -- figure stretched out in the back of the van. Chev's wheelchair had been transferred to the patrol car leading the way back to Santa Fe. They thought Lee might feel more comfortable stretched out in the van rather than curled up in the backseat of the police car. Chev felt better having his friend closer, anyway. The last two days had been hell on him, too, and he'd started to feel the weight of the lack of sleep and the emotional intensity now.

Chev took friendship very seriously. No one except Patrice understood. She had known him a long time, though --

"Turn around," Patrice said. "We're going to be taking some turns now. The last thing we need is for you to make yourself worse."

He wanted to snap at her, but he didn't. He carefully turned and settled into the seat, making certain the belt snugged tightly. They had already reached the outskirts of Santa Fe, the desert giving way to an odd swatch of green that always seemed so out of place to him. Traffic had picked up, and he hadn't noticed -- and some cars didn't bother to get out of the way of police cars with lights and sirens. Chev curbed his urge to send curses in several languages. Someone thought they could cut the van off, but Popovi, in the second patrol car, dissuaded people of the idea.

They reached the hospital without any trouble, despite the traffic. Attendants had Lee out of the van and whisked away before Chev could get out. Although anxious to follow, he stopped long enough to thank Perez, Peltin, and his cousin. Perez stayed with them, Popovi said he'd come by the house soon. Peltin walked back to his car and drove away with hardly more than a nod -- a man who did his job, and moved on.

Patrice pushed him through the door into the cooler interior. He shivered at the change, and at the rush of people all around. Though he had been unconscious after his own accident, he still felt an odd sense of déjà vu. The scents and the sounds started a rush of panic, leaving him cold with sweat. Chev had to take several deep breaths before he got control, and he feared if he didn't do something to distract himself, he would be ill.

"We're going to need some info on the man brought in -- name, family, insurance and such," a woman said, coming toward them.

Thank God for Patrice who handled everything very well. It made him feel unexpectedly safer. Perez kept close by as well, watching over them. He wondered, suddenly, if they were in danger.

"I'm going to call the museum," Chev suddenly said and pulled out his cell phone. "And the Taos police, to make certain the rest of the workers are guarded."

Patrice looked at him and nodded before she went back to filling out forms. Perez lounged nearby, and Chev rolled back by the man, in case they needed questions answered.

He talked to Julio, a day guard at the museum, and learned there had been a minor bit of trouble, including a broken glass case, but they'd suffered only a small chip out an artifact inside. The police were still there, and Chev handed the phone over to Perez so that they could do cop-speak to each other. It helped to pass the time to listen to them. He tried not to fret.

Over the next hour, various people came out of emergency saying Lee would be fine, but Chev knew he wasn't going to believe it until he could talk to Lee himself. Until he could see Lee ... walk away.

There it was. The one thing Chev had been stopping himself from thinking and the one fear he carried with him every day -- that the doctors lied to him, and he would never walk again. And now they lied about Lee, too.

"Hey," Perez said. He put a hand on Chev's shoulder and held the phone out with the other, the conversation done. Chev took the phone and dropped it back into his pocket. "You all right?"

"Worn out. Tired of it all," Chev admitted. He looked out the glass doors toward the bright street and the green grass that hid the sand. "I want to go back to excavating. I loved the work."

"But you're good at running the museum, aren't you?"

"Good enough. I have money to throw at it, and that helps."

"Has to take more than money for this sort of thing," Perez said, sitting down in a nearby chair. "I got the feeling you had a fire for this work, as well."

"Yeah, that too," he admitted. "If I didn't, I would have sold out long before now. But you have to wonder when you should give up. I knew there was a danger, Perez. I didn't believe they would go for anyone but me."

"They didn't try to kill him, not outright. They put him in a place we wouldn't have too much trouble finding him. I think it was a warning."

"Maybe," he said and shifted uncomfortably. A couple days out on rough roads left aches and pains he didn't want to think about right now. "It doesn't make this any better. I don't know if I can put anyone else in danger. I don't know if it's worth it."

"I would guess maybe they should have a say in it."

Chev frowned, but the man did not look away. "We're talking about some old pots and broken pottery --"

"Bullshit," Perez said, startling Chev. "We're talking about history, knowledge, and the right to protect what we can from greed. And don't tell me that you don't think so."

Patrice laughed unexpectedly behind him. "It's nice to see someone slap Chev down now and then," she said. "He can get damned pompous and self-righteous, usually at the entirely wrong time."

"I do not!"

"And did I mention childish?" she added, dropping into a seat by Perez -- and just out of reach. "Word is excellent on Lee, Chev. I had a bit of a disagreement over the insurance since he hasn't worked for us for long enough to be covered, but I settled that with a call to your bank."

"Good," Chev said. He looked back at the desk where a woman glanced toward them with obvious envy. Cheveyo Rey was not poor. Sometimes he forgot how that affected others.

"They're taking Lee up to a room. I insisted on a private room. They don't think he'll be here more a couple days, though."

"Really?" he said, despite himself.

"Really. He's going to be out of it for the rest of the night, and they suggest we go get some rest somewhere. I want a hotel room, a shower, and a damn good dinner. Any chance you can join us, Detective Perez?"

"For the shower or the dinner?"

Chev started to protest Perez's answer and swallowed the reaction very quickly with a reminder that his wife's name was Sandra, not Patrice. He had no right to get bothered by a joke.

What did his reaction say, though? Nothing that surprised him.

He'd missed part of the conversation, a little laughter, but he came back to it with -- he hoped -- no notice from the others that he'd been so sidetracked.

"I will be sticking close to you two over the next couple days," Perez said. "It's my orders while we try to get this mess cleared up. Dinner would be great. It's been a damn long day."

"Yes, it has," Chev agreed. "Patrice, go ahead and book us a Casita at the Santa Fe Hilton, if one is open, and if not take one of their better rooms. And I'm open to any place for dinner. Do they have my cell phone number here, in case Lee needs anything?"

"They have it," she said.

"We're leaving an officer here as well," Perez added. "He's already on his way, should be here at any moment."

"You're taking this seriously," Chev said.

"This is possible trouble we can circumvent by a little precaution," Perez said. "So, until your group is out of town, it's what we're going to try and do."

"Thank you," Chev said and this time, he really meant it.

CHAPTER SEVENTEEN

The drawn curtains dulled the sun's rays to a soft, welcoming light and didn't hurt his eyes. Walls of beige, curtains of blue -- the room had a far nicer feel than his tenement apartment.

Cool and soft sheets eased his burning skin -- movement felt painful, though not as bad as he expected. He reached for the glass of ice and water on the table beside him, remembering sipping from it, although most everything else was fuzzy. He had trouble wrapping his bandaged hand around the glass....

Hospital, he suddenly realized as he sipped and that brought a nice, safe feeling he hadn't expected it.

Lee sipped the water, which helped and found the control to the bed so he sat up a little. How long had he slept? He thought the light looked like morning in the slotted lines on the floor, but it might be sunset. If he sat here long enough, he should be able to tell.

Must have slept for a while, but he awoke to find the light still bright. Must have been dawn. Nurses came and went, checked him over, smiled, and left again. He felt relaxed and napped between the visits of nurses, interns, and doctors.

The phone rang. Lee fumbled, picking it up, and felt odd and awkward. "Hello?"

"Lee? This is Mary. I didn't wake you did I?"

"Oh. No, I was awake. I couldn't figure out who would be calling me," Lee said with a little laugh. He heard her sigh of relief. "How did you find me?"

"You've been all over the news up here in Taos," she said. "I heard about you being kidnapped -- no it should be abducted, shouldn't it? Well, never mind. I heard about what happened, and I started hanging around the museum hoping for word. How are you? I meant to ask that! God, I sound like I'm blonde, don't I?"

He laughed. "I'm doing fine. Why did you call?"

"Just to let you know that I was thinking about you, and I'm glad you're all right. You've gone through hell, Lee. You realize that the papers pretty much printed your entire life story, right?"

"Oh hell."

"Don't let it worry you. It at least explains why I sometimes spooked you. I was starting to get worried about my approach, you know."

He laughed again. Maybe they'd given him drugs. "I'm sorry. I've been trying to get a feel for life again. I don't think I'm doing particularly well."

"Will I see you when you get back?" she asked.

"You bet. Dinner on Friday?"

"I'd like that."

"Good. I'll see you then." He looked up to see someone in a police uniform of some sort look into the room and back out again. Guards? Well, he guessed he should feel safer for having them there, but his mouth had gone dry.

"I'll see you on Friday, Lee. Get some rest."

"I will. Talk to you soon, Mary."

"Bye." She hung up. He sat the phone back down, feeling odd. People knew about him. The realization didn't seem to matter as much to him now that he had another life. He closed his eyes and rested again for a while.

He opened his eyes and had not expected anyone else to be in the room with him. He looked around at Patrice and Chev with a start and then gave a little laugh. "I'm jumpy."

He laughed again, which apparently surprised Chev, who looked far too intent. Lee could imagine much of what had gone through his friend's mind about this entire incident. He didn't like it. He didn't want these people to win.

"How are you doing, Lee?" Patrice asked.

"Better than I was," he said. He moved a little and grimaced at the feel of burnt skin against the soft sheets. "Glad to be here. Where am I?"

Chev laughed this time. It was a good start.

"We got you to the hospital in Santa Fe," Patrice said. "That was last night. Perez should be here pretty soon, and he'll have some questions for you."

"Perez was one of the cops out in the desert?" Lee ventured.

"Right," Patrice said, and then smiled as she looked toward the doorway. "And here he is now."

The door had opened. Perez turned out to be shorter than Lee had expected, but then he had been sitting down the last time he saw the man, and really didn't remember much afterward. Probably just as well.

"You are awake. Good. Ready for a few more questions?"

"Sure," he replied, but reached for the water. Patrice handed it to him. His fingers were still swollen, and he felt pretty much like a slug. Perez settled in the chair by the bed and pulled out a notepad and pen. The sight almost chilled Lee, remembering sitting in his living room, with other police...

"Lee?" Chev said.

"It's all right. I'm still a little rattled. What questions?"

"Tell me everything you can about the men," Perez said. "That's a good place to start."

Lee hadn't seen much of them -- but that wasn't true. He hadn't *wanted* to see them. However, they were there in his mind, and he might as well share them with someone who might find a use for the information.

So he went through an inventory of what he remembered from the accents -- which got a hiss out anger out of Chev -- to the car they drove. Perez's questions prompted a few more memories. Little details emerged, but he didn't think they would be much help. Perez took notes, nodded, and took more notes. Chev frowned, and Patrice looked ready to find these guys and have it out with them all on her own.

"Bottom line is we think they took you out and dropped you somewhere as a warning to Cheveyo," Perez said, with a nod toward the man. "If they'd been serious, you would be dead. As it is, you were not so far out you couldn't make it back. A nasty trick, and it could have backfired -- but it probably wouldn't have mattered much to them, and if you had died I doubt they would have cared."

"Yes sir, I see," Lee said, leaning back and frowning a little. His face felt tight and hot, and his body ached, but this could have ended far worse.

"Getting the pottery was probably an unexpected boon," Chev said with a little shrug. "I'll be interested if it turns up on any market."

"Damn! They got it?" Lee said.

"I'm afraid so. It wasn't in the car --"

"Oh shit," Lee said and then he laughed, startling them. "I hid it."

"It's nowhere in the --"

"I hid it in an alley. Oh hell. Find me clothes. We have to go hunt --"

"Lee," Chev started to say.

"We have to go. They know the olla wasn't in the car, so they've had time to look. If they haven't found it, we need to get there first!"

"Tell me the location," Perez said. "I'll go find it."

"If I could, I would. But I was driving like a maniac, trying to get clear of them. I don't remember the exact place, but I'll know it when I see it." No one moved. He waved at them in exasperation. "Get me some damn clothes! We can still win this one, people, and I sure as hell would love to have that feeling right now!"

"I'll go call his doctor," Perez said. "But he looks sane and wise to me."

"Patrice, go downstairs to the gift shop and buy him a large, loose tee-shirt," Chev said.

She nodded and stood, looking back at Lee as though she still considering how to argue him out of it.

"Patrice -- nothing with cats or flowers, okay?" Lee said.

She laughed as she and Perez hurried out. Lee began to leverage himself toward the edge of the bed, grimacing at the movement, and cursing under his breath. He couldn't decide if he wanted to find those men and pound them with baseball bats, or never see them again.

"Lee, if they've found it, I don't give a damn."

Lee stopped and looked at him. "I know. But if they haven't -- hell, Chev. This would be great!"

"I don't like what happened to you. I'm thinking about shutting everything down."

"No."

"Lee --"

"Don't do it. We are not ready to give up, Chev. I want these bastards now. Where are my pants?"

"I don't need martyrs."

"Good. I don't want to be one."

"Lee --"

"Look," he said, and carefully pushed hair back again. His fingers were starting to move better. "I've gone through hell for no reason at all when they sent me to prison. I want to -- to do something right, Chev. So let's go and see if we can't win this round after all. If we don't, well hell. That's life. But there's no reason to throw away the chance. Where the hell are my pants?"

Perez and a doctor stepped back into the room. The young black doctor frowned when he saw Lee sitting on the edge of the bed. Lee met the look with far more resolve than he thought he had.

"I was going to release you in the morning," the man said. "This can't wait until then?"

"No," Lee said, forestalling anything the others said. "But I'll come back as soon as we've run this little errand. Will that keep everyone here from lecturing me anymore?"

Chev smiled, clearly starting to fall under the spell of this possibility. Lee really hoped -- but he wasn't going to be horribly disappointed if they didn't find the olla. He'd had far worse disappointments in life.

"My pants?" he said again.

"Here," the doctor said, pulling open a closet. "I'm getting a wheelchair. You need to stay off your feet as much as possible for a few days to let those cuts and scrapes heal. You will come back?"

"Right away," Chev said. "You have my word, too."

"Good." The doctor crossed and dropped the clothing beside Lee. He could see the tag now. Dr. Tedson. "You're going to miss dinner. Get something to eat while you're out. I have more medication for you, and you can't take it on an empty stomach."

"I know a really great hole in the wall Mexican place," Perez said. "Not far from here. We'll hit it on the way back if the rest of you agree."

"Sounds great to me," Lee said. He picked up the clothes Tedson handed to him, forcing his stiff fingers to move. The right hand was wrapped in bandages. Cacti spines, he remembered. He was already starting to feel worn, just from sitting up and arguing with these people, but he was not going to let it slow him down.

He headed into the bathroom, grateful for a little bit of privacy while he dressed. It turned out not to be too difficult.

Tedson came back with the wheelchair, and Patrice arrived with the tee-shirt, which luckily had a great Kokopelli design on it. It felt light on his shoulders, too, though the little movement of the cotton against his burnt skin proved unpleasant.

No one argued as Perez pushed Lee's wheelchair out of the room, Chev, and Patrice right behind him. And by the time they reached the door he had started to feel the adrenaline again and knew that would carry him through this little adventure. Patrice got the van and got Chev in the back seat while Lee made himself as comfortable as possible in the front where he could better direct them. Perez rode with them instead of taking his police car.

"I'm sticking with you three," Perez said, settling by Chev. "Traffic this time of day is brutal. I don't want to get cut off and not catch up with you again. If Lee is right about this, then there could be people out there looking for the pottery -- people who won't be happy to see you three in the area. Or they may think you're the perfect people to follow to get what they're after."

"We don't mind having you along," Patrice said. She pulled the van out to the corner and stopped. "Which way, Lee?"

"Head for the college. I'll have to find my way from there."

They didn't have far to go, but the traffic slowed them. Lee kept his eyes open, searching for familiar faces in the other cars since he doubted his abductors would still be driving around in the white pick-up. He would have enjoyed seeing them arrested.

"There's where we found your vehicle," Perez said, leaning forward and pointing across the freeway at a little flutter of yellow 'crime scene' police tape on one of the posts.

"Remember that spot and the entrance ramp there. I'd gotten rid of the olla by then. It gives us one part of the parameter for the search. I never crossed under the freeway."

Perez nodded and sat back. "Two more exits to the college."

Patrice took the second off ramp, driving slowly once they hit the street. Nothing looked familiar until Lee spotted the gas station packed with kids from the college.

He felt a little shiver looking at them again, remembering when his life had been that simple.

"Start here," he said, with a wave toward the lot. "Turn left."

"The spot where the car was found is toward the right," Perez said.

"I know, but I tried to get as far from the pickup as I could, so I could get rid of the pottery."

Patrice turned, went for a block, and paused. Lee sent her up and down streets, retreating and retracing their steps. He feared the others would start protesting soon, and it didn't help his state of mind. Then he saw an alley -- not really anything he recognized, but it seemed right.

They turned down it, the van brushing along overgrown bushes at one side. It still didn't look right until he could see the next block.

"I think that's it," he said, waving his hand toward the pile of rubbish ahead of them. "I got out and shoved it under some stuff that looked like it hadn't been moved in months."

"Wonder why this hasn't been ticketed," Perez said as Patrice brought them to a stop.

Lee got out before anyone protested, Perez following close behind. However, the minute he started sifting through the debris, he knew something was wrong. He looked up, shaking his head.

"Damn," Perez said. "Not here?"

"Not the right place," Lee corrected. "This is all cloth and old mattresses. The place I was at had wood and paper. But it can't be far."

"Lee," Patrice said, standing on the edge of the driver's side doorframe and shaking his head. "This is pretty far from where they found the Jeep."

"I drove like a madman to get here and raced back before they realized how far I'd gone," he said, leaning with a hand against the wall. The sun had started to set, but it still felt too damned hot today.

"You need to rest," Patrice said. "Maybe --"

"No," he said. "It's close."

"You're not looking well, Lee," Perez said. "I think --"

"I think that's it," Lee said. He pointed a block away, at another pile of rubble.

"Lee --" Patrice said again.

He shook his head and walked away. Perez went with him, mumbling something about stubborn people, while Patrice and Cheveyo followed in the car. He crossed the next street feeling certain he had it right this time when he looked at the building up to the edge of the alley, the pile of wooden pallets by the side. He prayed to God it hadn't been obvious to anyone else.

He grinned as he and Perez reached the spot. "This is it. Doesn't look like anything's been moved. "

Dropping down to his knees -- because he couldn't have leaned over and stayed to his feet -- he pulled away the newspaper, cloth, and broken crates he'd thrown over the box.

And there it was. Perez had knelt with him and looked at it with his eyes gone wide and a silly grin on his face. However, he stopped Lee when he reached.

"No. Let me call in someone to make sure this hasn't been tampered with," he said. "Let's not do something stupid now."

Lee didn't think the box had been touched. He wanted to argue, but he nodded. "As long as I get to sit here and be around when they pull it out. I want to see it again."

Perez nodded. He had pulled out a cell phone. Lee sat

there looking at the box for awhile and then decided he would much rather be sitting in the van, with the AC on.

A few minutes later police cars arrived, blocking off both ends of the alley. Dogs sniffed around the area, men tapped, examined, and poked at the box. In the end, someone came to Perez and nodded. He looked grim, and for one fleeting moment, Lee believed they had lost after all.

Then Perez came to the window and tapped on it, grinning. "Come on out, Lee. I think you'll want to get it back out, right?"

He nearly hit the cop with the door since he shoved it open so fast. Patrice came with him this time, and Chev watched from the back seat with the door open. Lee pulled the wooden box out quickly, brushed the top off and with Perez's help, got it back to the van where he sat it on the chair beside Chev.

"I don't have a key," Lee said.

"I do." Che pulled out the key ring and found the one he wanted. He handed it back to Lee, who started to protest. "Open the damned thing," Chev ordered with a laugh.

He had trouble holding the key in sunburnt and swollen fingers, but eventually the lock clicked, and he lifted the lid back.

"Look at that," Perez said, peering down into the box. He seemed impressed, although he couldn't see the writing and had no idea what this olla might mean to history. "I had no hope we'd find it again. Damn good work, Lee." He slapped him on the shoulder and then began to profusely apologize when Lee almost went down.

Lee started laughing. So did the others; Chev and Patrice and the half dozen cops who had stayed for the show. Lee carefully closed the box again.

"Well, what do you say we have our meal and then get Mr. Constantinos back to the hospital," Patrice suggested. "After we have a proper celebration."

No one argued this time.

CHAPTER EIGHTEEN

Perez placed the box in the middle of the table. The waiter eyed it suspiciously while he asked for their drink orders. Chev grinned. He wanted fine wine or at least a beer, but remembering Lee had medication to take, decided not to tempt him, and ordered lemonade instead. The others had cokes. They ordered too much food, they ate, and Lee looked as though he had a hell of a good time. They probably overfed him, and got him back to the hospital too late -- the nurses certainly seemed huffy and complained about state patrol people looking for Lee. Apparently, the nurses hadn't realized he was coming back and sent the state patrol officer away, but when Perez called around, he couldn't find out what they could have wanted.

When they left the hospital, Chev felt sorry Lee had to stay -- but he had no regrets about how this day had turned out in the end. He hadn't felt that way in quite a while.

"We put a guard on Lee," Perez said, standing by the car. "He was down having coffee when we showed up, but I sent him up to the room."

"Do you really think there's a danger?" Chev asked as he pulled himself up into the van.

"No, I really don't think so. So far, these people have

been very secretive of what they do. As long as you're in a public place, I'm not worried."

"Good. God, I shouldn't have eaten so much. It's going to be months before I can jog again and run this food off."

Perez gave him a startled look and then grinned. Chev forgot sometimes people made assumptions when they saw him, sans any sort of cast and in a wheelchair. It was odd, just the same, to see how happy the revelation seemed to make Perez.

Patrice drove them straight to the hotel. She couldn't book a casita, but maybe that was all right -- he appreciated having solid hotel walls around them, and several floors of protection before anyone could get this far.

Patrice rolled him into the suite with the adjoining doors, and right then he wished there had never been any doors between them.

"Patrice," he said, his hand catching hold of hers at the doorway.

"No," she said, and pulled away, although reluctantly, he thought. "We made promises when I came to work for you, Chev. I can't brush them aside for a night, even one like this."

"I know. I'm sorry."

She stepped away, and then came back to put a hand on his shoulder. He looked up at her, surprised. "I'm glad you ... asked. I'm glad to know it's not just me."

Then she headed into the other suite and closed the door behind her.

Well, hell. He rolled himself back toward the bed and stopped there. After a moment he pulled his billfold out of his pants and opened it, flipping through torn plastic pockets -- time to replace it again -- until he found the pictures Sandra and him.

They didn't look right together. It had nothing to do with racial differences. It was everything from the clothing they wore to the way he smiled while she looked haughty and proud.

Why did he feel relief knowing she was in Europe, and he was here with Patrice? It was not a matter of safety. It was distance. Did he love his wife? Had he ever really loved her, or had it been a mad fling that should never have gone as far as it did? She wanted to marry him. He'd been happy to. He thought it sweet, and old-fashioned.

Hell, hell, hell.

Chev had thought he loved her until Patrice came back into his life. It was not Sandra he wanted to hold tonight. It was not Sandra that he would have called on to help him find Lee. He cared for Sandra, but he wished Patrice....

Hell.

He wheeled toward the bathroom, with its special, wheel-chair accessible tub and shower. He struggled out of clothing and finally spent a long, long time in a nice cool shower.

And laughed, because, on the other side of the wall, he could hear Patrice doing the same thing.

They let Lee out of the hospital the next day, laden down with orders, prescriptions for antibiotics to fight infection, and more orders. Chev listened as they warned him to stay off his feet for the rest of the week -since apparently, the little walking he'd done the night before had been a bad idea. Dr. Tedson also ordered him not to get himself left out in the desert anytime soon.

Patrice seemed very much amused to be in charge of two men in wheelchairs, enough so that Perez made jokes about Patrice's fantasy life. Patrice bowed her head and blushed, daring a glance at Cheveyo. He had to look away as well.

"If you have to come back to town during this mess, get in touch with me," Perez said. "I won't guarantee I can drop everything to come and keep you company again, but I sure as hell would like to try."

"Come to the museum," Chev said, reaching out the window to take his hand. "And we'll have dinner."

"The state patrol have word we're ready to move?" Patrice asked.

"They're ready. Don't get cut off from them. Let me know how things go." Perez finally stepped back and gave the car door a slap. Patrice eased forward, out into the street again. She looked nervous, with far too many glances at the rearview mirror.

"Straight back home," Cheveyo said. He looked over his shoulder. "Lee, I'd like you to spend a few days at my place until I'm sure you're back on your feet, so to speak."

Lee started to argue and changed his mind. "Yeah, if I stayed off at my place, you'd worry -- especially if you saw it. I plan to move soon."

Chev turned to Patrice and started to make the same demand of her, but she looked at him and shook her head before he spoke. "I don't think it's such a good idea."

"Patrice, I swear to God -- new Gods, old Gods, yours and mine, that --" he glanced back at Lee who had a mildly amused and mostly curious look. "-- that I'll not make it difficult for you. But damn -- I'll worry if I don't know that you're safe. You want calls at three every morning when I can't sleep?"

"I can't come into Sandra's home."

"It's *my* home. She hates the place. You have

noticed she hasn't exactly come running to stay there, right?"

"I did think it odd that she abandoned you," Patrice said.

Oh, and he heard so many things unsaid in her simple sentence. He hadn't ever looked at it from her angle, and how the situation must appear to Patrice, who had made sure she could help him in any way he needed, who drove him everywhere, who was everything....

"Shit," Chev said. He threw himself back against the seat, feeling sullen. Too damn many messes. "Come and stay at the house. It's my home."

"Or I get calls at 3 am?" she said.

"I promise it."

She laughed. He grinned and dared a glance back at Lee, who lifted his hands -- one still wrapped in bandages. "I'm just along for the ride."

"Lee," Patrice said. "Hell. Chev and I knew each other -- in the biblical sense -- years before he went off to college. I shouldn't have gone to work for him."

"Why? Because you aren't good at the job? Or because you shouldn't be here when Chev needs you most? Where do you think he'd be if you hadn't taken the job?"

"Probably with Sandra, on a beach somewhere safe."

"Safe from what?" Chev demanded. "This happened while I was with Sandra, remember? Or do you think I'd just be safe from you?"

"We made a deal," she said.

"Yes, we did. Neither of us has broken it."

"True. I'll come to the house. At least it'll save me a lot of driving."

Chev nodded, feeling a considerable weight lifted from him. He hadn't realized how nearly panicked he had been the last few days until the feeling finally eased. And what about the other workers? Should he get them all to safe houses? Should he close the damn museum?

"Don't get silent on me, Cheveyo Rey," Patrice said. "I never trust you when you're silent."

"Weighing things," he said. He shrugged. "Lives against the land dreams against history."

"Not just your dreams, you know," Lee said from the back.

"But my work to make them real. And if I pulled out -_"

"I'd walk away and never come back," Patrice said.

He couldn't breathe for a moment. His heart pounded with a kind of fear he'd never felt before, even when he thought someone was trying to kill him. The thought of losing Patrice --

"Hell, hell."

"I mean it," she said, with a glance his way. "If you walked away, you wouldn't be the person I ... love."

"That's not fair, Patrice!"

"The truth seldom is." They had reached the highway now, heading north. He hadn't noticed. "But we're both going to have to live with truths only you and I -- and Lee -- know."

"You can trust me," Lee said.

"Beyond a doubt," Chev said. "As soon as you're on your feet -- literally, on your feet, we'll head out to the site. It's time you see it and meet the people out there. It's time, I think, we start moving ahead again. Time to ratchet everything up a few notches and remember what's important here. We have a damned important archeology site out there. Keeping it a secret is no better than letting them bulldoze it under."

"You let people know too soon, and there's going to be treasure hunters and amateurs out there wrecking everything they can find," Patrice warned.

"Better them than the ones who are out there wrecking things out of spite."

"Yeah, I know. All right. So what's the next step? What do we do now?"

"I'm going to go out to the site, check in with the people there, and see what they think. I need to talk to the lawyers again, too. It's time to go on the offensive, at least in this part, and to stop running scared from the rest. It's not going to help."

"Good," Patrice replied, but he saw her worried glance his way. "Chev -- I don't want you to be in danger."

"But either we do something or I let go. And if I let go, you let go of me. So this is the only other choice."

"Damn."

"I woke up, Patrice. Woke up to a lot of things. I don't love Sandra."

"I know."

"I'll settle that in good time."

She nodded and asked nothing more of him.

CHAPTER NINETEEN

L
ee had rested for most of the trip and maybe even slept. He came awake when they pulled into the driveway of Chev's home.

Cheveyo Rey's house turned out to be a massive log cabin style building on a lovely forest-edge estate. They drove slowly up the long drive, and Lee suddenly had the first real feeling that Chev was rich. He'd known it before, but this brought the realization home, so to speak.

A butler let them in.

"Good to see you home, sir," he said, opening the door. "And with guests."

"Lee and Patrice will be staying here for a while. I should have called ahead --"

"It's no trouble."

"This is Morton," Chev said, waving a hand toward the man. "He takes care of things here."

Lee suspected there was at least a cook as well, but otherwise, the place looked empty. Not like the family had gone away, but like they didn't live here at all.

Lee wondered if his reaction came from having heard Chev and Patrice in the car. He wasn't sure he should have been party to their conversation. He had more than a few problems of his own, and listening in on the tale of their thwarted love affair had been uncomfortable. He didn't want to think about --

But it was there, mingling with all his own lost dreams. He wondered if he should feel sorry for Sandra, who would lose Chev.

She should have been here with him. Lee couldn't help but feel Chev's wife had cut the ties. As long as Sandra was still part of the equation, Patrice and Cheveyo would do nothing inappropriate since they had made that vow -- a vow which seemed more important than Sandra took her wedding vow. Lee thought they ought to be together. He hoped they were some day.

The place was set up for someone with a wheelchair, though nothing permanent. The took the lift up the stairs, Chev first and he went up second.

Chev showed him to a large room, with a private bathroom, TV, DVD -- it looked so much like a hotel room that he asked where they hid the menu for room service. Patrice made a quiet chuckling sound while Chev looked bothered more than amused.

"I like my friends to be comfortable," he said.

"So, all your friends are traveling salesmen who mostly live in hotels, right?"

Chev shook his head. "We could take you back home, you know... but I don't think you really want to go there do you? Are you hungry? I can have something sent up --"

Which started Lee laughing. "I'm not hungry. I'm worn out as hell, though."

"Get some rest," Patrice said and pulled Chev back out of the room. "Come down later if you get hungry. We'll be around."

He nodded, grateful they didn't bother him. He finally

settled on the bed and stretched out, to relax for a little while.

A knock on the door woke him again. He looked around, startled, worried --

"Lee?"

"Yeah."

Patrice opened the door. She looked at him, her eyes wide. "We have to go to the police station."

"What's wrong?" He thought about Chev, about the museum, about any number of things that could have gone wrong.

Thomas looked over Patrice's shoulder at Lee, grim-faced and angry. "They found a woman dead in your apartment about an hour ago, Lee. And anonymous phone call --"

Lee didn't know what either of them said afterwards. He started to walk out of the room. Patrice maneuvered him into the wheelchair.

Tomas took Chev out into the van. Chev was already on his cell phone. A police car sat in the driveway -- had they come for him? He shivered at the sight, afraid.

Patrice helped him into the back seat, and Tomas climbed in, urging him to move over. They drove back to town, and he thought Chev might be cursing as he talked on his cell phone, but nothing anyone said made sense. The police car followed them. He wondered why they hadn't put him in there. Why they hadn't arrested him. That was how the nightmare worked.

At the door to the police station he finally went from numb to panicked in one breath. He tried to roll back, but Tomas, who had been walking beside him, caught the chair and then held him down in it. Chev and Patrice had already started into the building, but they both stopped and looked back when he made a sound of protest.

"Hey." Tomas kept a hand on his shoulder. "It's all right. We know you didn't kill her. You were in Santa Fe, and you were with people the entire time -- it's already confirmed and cleared by the police. There was a question for a few minutes because someone from the state patrol said you'd checked out of the hospital the day before, but we got that cleared up. You didn't kill her."

"That didn't matter the last time," he replied and wished he hadn't spoken at all. The words probably made him sound like some sort of lunatic.

They went into the building, all four of them, and Chev still on the phone with his lawyer. Patrice told Lee this was only a precaution, but it didn't help, either.

He hadn't expected to find Perez here when they had left him behind in Santa Fe.

"I got the call at the office," he said. He put a hand on Lee's shoulder. "So I came straight up to explain you had been with me yesterday when you weren't in the hospital, but they said they'd cleared you already."

"Oh." For some reason hearing the news he'd been cleared from Perez finally sunk in, and he believed it this time. "What happened? How did she die?"

"Stabbed," another officer said. His nametag, which seemed uncommonly clear while everything else blurred, said Lowell. The tall, lean man led them to a small room filled with file cabinets, stacks of paper, and a couple desks covered with more papers. Tomas stepped out to the doorway, and Patrice stood with him, but they looked like pit bulls about bite anyone who looked at them wrong.

"Okay." Lowell sat behind the desk. He looked at Lee and shook his head. "I'm sorry we had to have you come here for this, but since it was your apartment, we had to keep everything official. And since it appears you knew the woman --"

"Knew her? Someone from the building where I lived?" he asked. He tried to remember any of them.

"No. A report said you'd had coffee with her --"

"Oh God. Mary. Mary Powers." He felt very ill again. What the hell had happened? How could she be dead in his apartment? "She called me at the hospital yesterday. Said she'd heard what had happened to me --"

Chev put his phone down, but he didn't hang it up. "Why do I get the feeling someone tried to frame Lee for this murder?"

"That's our impression as well. Someone who thought you had left the hospital yesterday is our guess," Perez replied. He sat on the edge of the desk, and Lowell seemed happy enough to let him handle Lee. Lee appreciated it, in fact. Perez had become a friend, not just another cop, and he could deal with that right now, though his heart had begun to beat too fast. "I was on the cell phone on the way up. There were a couple coincidental things that made you look like a suspect. One was the first thing you said when they found you in the desert."

He shook his head, confused. "I don't remember."

"I didn't kill her," Patrice whispered behind him.

"Oh." The words had been from another nightmare. Or maybe this was still the same one.

"Yes. The statement turned up in a report by Peltin," Perez said. "The second was your apparent release from the hospital yesterday, and people assuming you had come here, and then disappeared again. Once we cleared everything up, and the coroner set the date --"

"They killed her because she called me. Because she knew me," he said. He felt ice take hold of him now. He'd felt hot up until that moment. Now he shivered and the room seemed to blur --

"Get him some water," Perez ordered. He put a hand on Lee's shoulder. "Stay sitting down. You'd pass out if you stood."

He had been about to stand. He'd been about to run, in fact. Lee didn't know where to, but right now he wanted to get away, far away, never look back --

Patrice leaned down with a paper cup of water in hand. Lee shook his head.

"Drink it," she ordered.

Patrice's order annoyed him. He glared up at her and then felt a moment of embarrassment. For some reason, the anger helped. Fear and guilt suddenly gave way to a fury that bordered on rage. He fought i back down as well and took the glass, sipping the water for a moment. When he looked up again, Perez finally lifted his hand from Lee's shoulder and nodded.

"You realize everything we're saying here is guess work," Perez said, "but we think this is all tied in with Chev's trouble from London. We believe the men who kidnapped you were here in town yesterday. We've had vague reports matching their description."

"If they didn't kill Lee, why did they murder the woman?" Patrice asked softly, as though afraid to bring up that subject again.

"Because we found Lee?" Chev asked. Then he shook his head in negation. Anger shown in his eyes as well. "But why not implicate me in a murder rather than him?"

"Because they want to scare you," Patrice said. "Who knows what these people are thinking. You ruined their drug smuggling operation. Maybe they intend to destroy you."

"I should sell --"

"No," Lee said and startled them all. "No. If you sell than what happened to Mary means they win. I don't want it to happen. I don't think you do, either."

"I'm sorry this happened, Lee. I really am," Chev said.

"I know. But let's start putting the blame where it belongs. I'm going to help you in any way I can, and that means keeping the business going."

Chev looked ready to argue. He changed his mind in the next few heartbeats. Lee could see the change in his face and the moment he went from panicked with the fear of what would happen to others, to the fact others were doing to them for their own ugly reasons.

"I want these people," Chev said, looking at Lowell.

"We both do. We all do. Let's see what we can put together to stop them."

Lee answered the police's questions about Mary. Every time he thought past what Lowell and Perez asked, something drove into his guts like a hot knife. He did his best to keep his emotions in check, and he did everything he could to help the police find out who killed her.

If he hadn't talked to her -- the people who did this knew about his background, no doubt. He should have been more careful. He shouldn't have --

But that was no better than Chev blaming himself.

They drove back to Chev's home in silence, Tomas sitting by him again and still looking angry. Lee did his best to stay calm. He went back to his room, sitting on the bed for a long, long time.

It didn't help. Lee stumbled over to the bathroom, took a quick shower, and made his way back to the bed. He slept all the rest of that day and into the next, waking slightly a couple times -- once to see Patrice at the door, but he waved her away and rolled back over and slept some more. It seemed as though he hadn't slept in years. When he finally came down -- using the wheelchair to keep everyone calm -- he found it late in the morning of the next day. He hadn't left the room for nearly twenty-four hours.

"You look better," Chev said. He sat behind a desk, sorting through papers. Not his favorite work, if Lee could read that expression right. "Tedson warned us that you needed the sleep, but another few hours and I planned to come up and drag you out of bed myself."

"Sorry," Lee said. He brushed his hands through his damp hair. The shower had helped, but he felt shaky enough that the wheelchair was probably a good idea after all.

"Patrice will be back for lunch," Chev said and unceremoniously shoved the papers aside. "About half an hour. Can you wait that long, or would you like lunch now? I can have Billings make something --"

"I'm in no hurry for food," Lee said and suspected even lunch would be a trial. He tilted his head and met Chev's look. "Why do I suddenly make you nervous?"

Chev put his hands on the desk and stared at them for a moment. His fingers brushed over the scar again. He said nothing for a moment, and Lee would have let it go, though he hoped Chev resolved the problem soon.

"I could tell you I'm upset about putting you in danger," Chev said and looked up. "You'd believe that, right?"

"Yes, but I'd know it wasn't everything."

"Yes." A deep breath. "Lee, Patrice and I said some things in the van -- things we maybe shouldn't have said at all."

"Things you should have said long before this," Lee

corrected. He startled Chev, and he pressed on because he didn't want to see both his friends make stupid mistakes. "Don't make excuses, Chev. Don't find reasons to let go. It's not worth the sacrifice."

"I'm married to another woman," he said and waved a hand toward the wall.

Lee looked at a picture of a small, blonde woman with perfect hair, who stood with her arm wrapped around Chev's waist. Odd to see him standing.

"Nice pictures. She's pretty. But a wife would be here with you. Patrice is here."

"I didn't want Sandra here. It's not safe," Chev protested, but his voice stayed soft.

"Why are you lying to yourself? Did you suggest that she stay away? Or did your wife not offer to show up?"

"Lee," he said, and he looked like he was getting angry now.

Lee lifted a hand. "I won't say any more about you and your wife and Patrice. But I spent five damn long, hard years in prison dreaming about my wife and son, and wanting to be with them again, to have my life back. I never believed they would find the actual killer, you know. I'd already let go of all those dreams before I was released. But I held on to one and for a brief moment when I heard her voice on the phone--"

Lee stopped and shook his head, remembering that cold, dreary winter day.

"I'm sorry. I really am."

"I had what I loved most in the world taken away from me. Stolen. I don't want to see you throw it away."

"Hell. Damn." Chev looked, suddenly, as though someone had hit him.

"I'm sorry."

Chev blinked several times as though trying to get the world, or his life, back in focus. Then he looked at the pictures on the wall. He said nothing.

Patrice arrived, glad to see Lee up, and without any of the looks of worry or remorse Chev had shown. They sat at lunch in a large, formal dining room that somehow intimidated Lee more than anything else from this ostentatious home. The food tasted good though, and he hoped he didn't embarrass himself by slurping his soup, or cutting the roast beef with the wrong knife. All in all, he would have preferred lunch at Taco Bell, though.

The days passed quietly. The police called now and then, and he resigned himself to speaking with them. The worst day came when Lowell arrived to tell him Mary's family had claimed the body and it would be shipped back to California for the funeral.

Lowell left half an hour later. Chev arranged to pay for everything, and no one argued this time. "It's something I can do," he said, with a shrug. "It doesn't count for much, really, in the end."

"Lee?" Patrice asked, looking at him.

"I hadn't thought about how they would bury here somewhere else. Mary really liked it here," he said and shook his head. "But this wasn't her home. She'd talked about going back to California before winter hit. She hadn't liked how cold it was, even in April."

"Do you want to go to the funeral?" Chev asked.

He thought about it for a moment and shook his head. "No. I'd be a stranger, and a reminder, and maybe a focus for anger. Mary deserves better."

Lowell came out twice more during the week to fill them in on details -- few as they were. Tomas kept in contact with the state patrol.

And they did work. Patrice brought paperwork and pottery pieces to the house. The dining room table looked less formal each day, and the meals started to reflect the change. Billings, the cook, didn't seem to mind. In fact, Lee got the strange feeling the few house staff -- Billings the cook, and Margay, the housekeeper, and Morton -- were quite pleased to have the odd people staying there.

They passed through the quiet days, something Lee realized they had all three needed; healing and calm, while they prepared to go back into battle.

Lee asked himself if it was wise to stay in Taos, but then he asked himself where he would go, instead. How far would he run, how well could he hide? Cheveyo would help him get a new start if he really wanted out, and would do it gladly and with no animosity at all.

But that was not what Lee wanted to do.

So, on a very bright morning a week after they came home to Taos, he was on his feet and ready to go to work. Cheveyo Rey nodded, and they went out to the van and headed back to the museum.□

CHAPTER TWENTY

C hev had put off calling his wife, although he couldn't quite decide why. He'd made up his mind about their future, including everything from *not* selling the land to the divorce. The fact Sandra hadn't called made him think that she already knew his answer and hoped to avoid talking about her outrageous demands yet again.

Not this time.

If Sandra told him she was sorry for everything she'd said, would it make a difference now? Yes. He wouldn't think as badly about her, but it wouldn't change the outcome.

However, before he could pick up the phone, an email dropped into the box. He tried to tell himself that he wasn't looking for a way out of calling her as he popped the program open.

And then, for a short while, he forgot about her entirely.

The email came from PotterDay101 which meant it was an email from the people at the main dig site on his land. Because they were slightly out of wireless range, someone had to hike out until they found a node to get messages out. And they only did that --

He opened the email.

Hey dude, hope you're doing well. We're having a great vacation! Wish you could join us. You wouldn't believe the stuff we've seen lately!

Talk to you soon,

Dave Potter

Chev read the words again, looking for some sign of trouble. He found none. All the clues -- the codes they had worked out to keep the site quiet from opportunistic amateur pot hunters -- pointed toward some important find.

His pulse started pounding with excitement. Chev wanted to go out and see what they'd dug up, and he forgot -- at least for a moment -- about the wheelchair.

"Chev? What's wrong?"

He looked up, startled to find Patrice at the doorway to his office.

"Come in," he said, waving her over.

"Did you call Sandra?"

"Sandra?" he said, as though he had forgotten whom she even was. He waved his hand. "No, not yet. I'll get to it. I got an email from Potter."

"Oh!" She crossed the room and leaned down over his shoulder. He became acutely aware of the jasmine scent of her perfume, and then the touch of her fingers on his shoulder. "That sounds good. Why don't I trust it?"

"You too? I thought it was just me. We need to get out there, Patrice. I want to know what they found."

"I could go --" She stopped. Chev couldn't see her face, but he knew she had gone still for a moment. "We can go out. Tomorrow."

He looked back at her, wondering at the words, the change of attitude. "You've been trying to keep me quiet, calm --"

"And from the moment Lee disappeared, I knew the mistake I had been making. I wasn't trying to keep you quiet -- I was keeping you away from everything as if that was somehow protecting you. You aren't helpless. I know you're about ready to get out of the wheelchair, and if I don't start getting control of myself now, I'll go crazy when you start walking away without me."

"I won't--"

"Even if things go the way we think with Sandra -- providing you ever actually call her -- you and I are not going to be joined at the hip. And this -- this email -- is what it's all about, Chev. We both want to get out there and see what they've found. Let's take Lee as well. Tomorrow."

"Tomorrow," he said, with an emphatic nod of agreement. "Talk to Tomas and arrange things. How is Lee doing?"

"He's working away on a dipper that appears to be in about five hundred pieces. The man must be a wiz at jigsaw puzzles."

He laughed, looked at the email, and then purposely closed the window because it was not going to change, and he had already memorized the words. Patrice went to the door, and looked back --

"I'm calling Sandra now," Chev warned. "You'll want to be far out of range for this one. If I don't survive ... well, you know where the treasure is buried."

She had started to look worried but ended up laughing. "Good luck."

Patrice walked away, though perhaps skipped would have been a better term. He smiled and put his hand on the phone.

Maybe he'd wait until they got back.

No. It wouldn't be any better when the three of them returned from the site, and Chev didn't want to have to think about handling this all the time he was out there. He dialed Smithers first, wincing when he realized the time in London.

"'ello," a voice said sleepily.

"Sorry, Smithers. I wasn't thinking --"

"Oh, Dr. Rey, sir. Not a problem. Always a pleasure to 'ear from you."

"Have you located my wife?"

"Yes, sir. I have a number right 'ere," Smithers said and suppressed a yawn. "Let me get me other phone and I'll text it to you. She's still in Paris, and staying with friends at a private apartment."

The message came in. "Thanks. I'll need you to go to the bank in the morning and close down Sandra's access to all but her personal account. Put a deposit of $10,000 US in that account."

"Yes, sir," he said. "This is, then, is it?"

"I'm afraid so. I'm not going to sell my land, she's not going to come here, and I really don't see a point where we can make a compromise on the situation."

"I agree," he said and sounded as though he worried about stepping over the line. "Since you were married in London, I believe I have all the paperwork here to start the divorce proceedings, if that's your decision, sir."

"I would appreciate it if you could get things moving. Thank you."

"Pleasure to serve, sir. Everything else is all right,

then, is it?"

"Well, except for my enemies killing a local woman and trying to get my new employee blamed for it --"

"Oh yes. I heard about the matter from your cowboy law firm down in Santa Fe. We have hired more detectives to find out who is behind this."

"Good. Thank you." He stopped and sighed. "As much as I would prefer talking to you, Smithers, I think I better be the one to break the news to Sandra."

"Ah. Yes. And Patrice is going to guard your back, is she?"

"From Sandra or from my other enemies?"

"Yes."

He laughed, said goodbye to Smithers, and dialed the number before he could find another reason to back out again. His poor French finally got him through several sleepy people.

"Chev, is that you?" Sandra said, sounding annoyed.

"Yes, it is."

"Well, it's about time you called me, though I can't say your choice of hour is very good --"

"Sandra, I've started divorce proceedings. In the morning there will be $10,000 put in your account to tide you over --"

Her breath caught. Did he hear the sound of someone else in the room? The idea didn't surprise or upset him. He'd already cut the ties.

"You can't -- You can't abandon me like this!" Sandra's voice grew shrill and loud. "Ten thousand? My God, I spend that much in a month --"

"Well I suggest you stop doing so," he said, cutting into her increasingly hysterical outbreak.

"How can you do this, you bastard!"

"It was a long decision, but in the end, you made this a lot easier on me. I am not giving up my land, Sandra. Not for you, not for Red Sun -- and thank you so much for letting them know I'm here. Since they knew, I realized there was no reason to keep hiding."

"You've gone out?" she said, her voice unexpectedly filled with worry.

"Not a lot, but I'm not hiding. Sandra, the work is being done to end our marriage. We'll be divorced as soon as the matter can be legally accomplished. That's the bottom line."

"I'll fight --"

"You had better hunt down those prenuptial agreements we signed, Sandy," he said. "Go on with the life you want. I intend to do the --"

She slammed the phone down.

He looked at the receiver in his hand, and carefully sat it down with a shake of his head. What had she expected? He tried to think back over the time they had been together; the relatively short time, when it came down to it. They'd been married for a year and a half, and even when they were both in Europe, half the time she'd been running around with her friends while he did work.

Easy money. Chev realized that was all he'd really been to her. He did not want to be bitter. He didn't want to be angry. Mark it up to an expensive mistake and move on.

He had plenty to move on to when it came down to it. He pulled up the email once more and wondered about what the archeologists had found out at the site.

Chev felt a surge of joy at having his life back in his own hands. Patrice had been right about one thing: he wasn't going to be in this wheelchair much longer.

Since they weren't going to be at the museum tomorrow, he needed to look into any work that needed to be done. He had a horrendous stack of paperwork for insurance forms, both for the museum and for his employees. The insurance company had gotten a little worried after the incident with Lee, although they didn't have to cover it since he hadn't been working long enough for the insurance to kick in yet. Chev had paid the bills himself.

He doubted Lee realized it, and Chev wasn't going to tell him, either. Money, at the moment, was the least of his troubles.

He had been reaching for the pile of papers when the truth of the trite little line struck him in full force. He had grown up poor. Money problems had disappeared years ago, and he'd gotten complacent about the ease of his life. Odd. What would happen if Sandra somehow won all his assets in a court case?

He'd never give her the land. In the end, he could give up everything, including this museum, as long as he still had that land. Maybe that thought made him insane, or maybe not. The land defined him.

The realization didn't make him any less angry when Patrice came to say that four teens had vandalized some of the museum's displays. He almost stood and stopped himself before Patrice could warn him.

"Security caught all four of them," she said with a snarl of her own. "Tomas has already called the police and -- yeah, that would be them now." They could hear sirens. He hadn't expected them to come rushing to the museum but then considering the trouble they'd had lately, maybe the local police were jumpy.

Officer Lowell came into the museum as Patrice and

Chev came around the corner and down into the lobby. They had the group of teens off to the right of the entry, three of them looking sullen, and one smart enough to be worried.

Tomas came out to meet the group. "A couple of them had phones, so I let them all call their parents. This wasn't a random bit of teen fun, Chev. That kid in the corner, Randy Souther, told me that two guys gave them each $100 to come in here and mess things up. One of them had an English accent and wore cowboy clothes."

"Shit." Chev craned his neck around. "Where's Lee!"

"Still up with the sherds putting together that dipper --"

"I heard the sirens," Lee said from behind them. "And I heard what Tomas said. They're here in town?"

"Looks like it," Tomas said. "That could be good. Taos isn't too large so they might find the two."

Lowell spoke to one of the others, who hurried back out, and then went past to the teens, and the others followed. Chev wanted Lee close to them, and he wanted this finished right now.

"You four have now been implicated in a murder --"

"Oh yeah, right," one of the teens said, leaning back against the wall, with his arms folded across his chest. "You can't scare us with crap like that."

Lowell looked at him, his voice steady. "The men who gave you the money are prime suspects in the murder of Mary Powers. The fact that you have taken funds from them makes you suspect as well."

The boy glanced at one of his companions. "Stupid bastard. If you hadn't told them --"

"We would have found $100 bills in each of your billfolds, and with the suspects' fingerprints on them. It's actually a damn good thing he had confessed before you found out about the connection because it actually makes you less suspect."

The boy blinked, at least. "I'm not saying anything else until my parents get here."

That seemed wise.

Parents arrived in ones and twos over the next half hour. Chev and the rest of the museum staff, including Tomas, stayed out of the way and let Lowell and his people handle this particular round of trouble while they went to look at the display cases.

"When the people with the Earl Morris collection hear about this, we might lose our chance to show it," Patrice said with a shake of her head.

"I'll put it in writing that I'll hire someone to stand beside the collection at all times," Chev said. "Or I'll pay one of their people to stay with it if they prefer."

"That suggestion might work," Patrice said.

"Go call them now and tell them what happened before they hear about this from someone else," Chev said. She started to protest. "We need this done today, Patrice."

That won a little smile. Patrice nodded and went up to her office.

"The officer said you run this place." A tall, heavy-set man with a diamond ring and silk tie crossed to stand over Chev. "How much damage was done? I'll write you a check, and we'll call it good."

Chev and Lee had been working at one of the four broken glass cases, sorting out the shattered pottery and pulling shards of glass from some ancient cloth. Chev looked up at the man, and Lee started to stand, and then decided not to.

"You can't write a check to cover this kind of destruction," Chev said.

"Oh, come on -- a man like you -- you can buy more of this ... stuff if you have the money --"

Chev thought he might stand up and slug the man, but he decided on a better course. "This is my love, not my business. My import and export business has been listed in several places as one of the top ten new International Companies for the past five years. I turned down an offer for a quarter of a billion dollars to buy that company from me. So tell me, how much money do you think you can offer me to buy your kid out of trouble?"

"I --" The man took a step back.

"Sometimes money doesn't work. Sometimes they're too stupid. I'm not dropping the charges."

"You'll hear from my lawyer."

"No, one of my several sets of lawyers will hear from your lawyer. Officer Lowell will be taking your son down to the police station now. I'm sure you'll want to get there."

The police had started herding the kids away, parents following. Some of them looked as though they understood their kid had done something wrong, but the others looked annoyed. The diamond-ringed father followed, but not without a last glance back at Chev.

Lee stood and leaned against the wall, keeping some weight off his left leg. He still limped a little, but he looked much better, finally. This time, though, he frowned.

"Lee?"

"Stupid kids," Lee said, waving a hand back toward the departing group. "But still -- they don't send people to prison for something like this, do they?"

Chev hadn't considered how the situation might affect

his friend. He dialed back his own anger. "The kids will get probation, at worst. But you know you can't let the stupid ones keep getting away with things by counting on their parent's buy-outs, don't you?"

"Yeah, I know." He shook his head. "I was never that stupid."

"I doubt you had parents who tried to buy you out of trouble. The kid isn't going to suffer for this, Lee. He'll be lucky if he learns a lesson at all. From the attitude I saw there, it's as likely his parents will buy him a new car to make up for having failed to get him out of trouble so he had to suffer for a few hours. The others might learn from this incident, but I suspect it's going to take something far more serious -- something they can't buy him out of -- before the boy finds out he's gone too far."

"Why do the parents do it?" Lee wondered.

"Because it makes them look powerful. Well, with luck he'll go off east to college, and we won't have to deal with him for a few years. Let's get this up to the table and see if we can put anything back together. As soon as I get done with the damn paperwork on the insurance for this mess, I'll come down the hall and help you out."

"Ha. Is that your subtle way of telling me to get back to work?"

"Hey, unless you want to stay and do the paperwork?"

Lee quickly gathered up the boxes they had put the pieces in and headed for the pottery room. Chev laughed, and Lee gave a backhanded wave to him before he disappeared.

Good worker. A shame Lee had to come to the museum during a mess like this.

"Chev," Patrice said, coming behind him and starting to push him away before he could speak. "I talked to

Tomas. He thinks it might be wise if we head out to the site sometime after midnight. He's going to stay here in town and give some misdirection -- and maybe they can draw the two guys out while we're away."

"I don't want --"

"Anyone in danger. Anyone hurt," she finished for him. "But we're all in danger until they catch the guys. I think we should let Tomas have a go at this one. This is his kind of work."

"So what do we do?" he asked as they headed up the incline and toward his office.

"Work late, have a later dinner, and head for home somewhere around midnight. Morton will park the pickup down behind the stand of trees at the end of the driveway. We'll transfer to it, Tomas will take the van on up to the house, and we'll sneak out as quickly and quietly as we can."

"Sounds like a plan." Chev looked at her as he slid in behind his desk. "If I was ten years younger, and someone hadn't already died, I'd think this was kind of fun."

"Yeah, I know. I'm going to go tell Lee the plan. At least he finally gets to go out and see the dig."

"True. And I'm looking forward to it. I wonder what the hell they found."

She smiled. "Me, too."

He had a damn hard time concentrating on the paperwork. He called his Santa Fe Lawyers and filled them in on everything from the trouble at the museum to his upcoming divorce. He had, in fact, almost forgotten to mention the divorce, which amused Flowers.

An email from Sandra's lawyer arrived an hour later. He opened it and read enough to find out whom it was from and what it was about, and then forwarded it to both Smithers and Flowers.

He added a note to Smithers to see if Scotland Yard might be more cooperative now that a murder had been tied to the case. Something had to break loose. They had come all the way to America to continue the harassment, after all. There had to be a trail of some sort.

He wanted the trouble finished -- and he wanted to win, and let those stupid bastards know they shouldn't have used his company to smuggle drugs. He didn't believe this was a coincidence, but it might be.

He wanted answers, one way or another. Though what he really wanted to get out to the site, and back to the work he truly loved.☐

CHAPTER TWENTY-ONE

C hev threw himself into the paperwork, burying himself so well that Patrice surprised him by showing up at his door, her jacket already on, and Lee at her side.

"I want dinner before we leave," she said. "Is there anything you absolutely still have to do before we can go?"

Chev looked at the reports he'd been updating, bookmarked his spot, saved everything, and closed the computer down. "I'm ready. More than ready. You should have rousted me half an hour ago."

"I made reservations at La Luna for 9:30. We'll get there in time. If everything else goes right, we'll be home -- be at your house just before midnight."

He tried not to smile at her blunder, especially since it apparently bothered her so much. Lee, wisely, kept completely out of this conversation.

They had an excellent dinner, and spoke mostly about the trouble at the museum and never saying anything at all about the site -- not with the few people in the restaurant to hear. Chev had started by rushing through the food, but slowed and savored it instead. He wondered if anyone watched. It seemed likely English and Texas had bought others with their hundred dollar bills, but they would not have stayed around town afterward -- which brought them back to the trouble at the museum.

"I checked a few hours ago and made certain all the kids were out on bail," Tomas said.

"Good," Chev said, nodding. He saw Lee look startled. "I want them to know they're in trouble, but I don't want stupid kids sitting in jail with who knows what they might drag in. The juvie section can get pretty bad."

Lee nodded and said nothing more as he went back to his food. Patrice looked pleased. They stayed well past closing, but Chev tipped the place well for the honor.

"Patrice and I will get the van," Tomas said by the door. "I'm going to give it a good check before we start it up, so don't worry if it takes a couple minutes."

Chev could see, even in the dark, the way Patrice looked back at them, worried, as she left with Tomas.

"Did I mention I really hate this clandestine crap?" Chev asked as he shifted in the wheelchair. A cool, mesquite-scented breeze blew past them. "But if it gets us out of Taos without a showdown, I'll be happy enough."

"We're all crazy, you know?" Lee said, leaning against the back of the wheelchair and keeping watch. "If I weren't so damn scared, this would remind me of the nights my friends and I would sneak out at night and break the windows of abandoned buildings. That's as far as my bad boy days went."

"We used to go shoot highway signs, me and my 'brave' friends." Cheveyo shook his head, glancing back at the restaurant where people cleared away the last signs of their presence. "Stupid waste of time, but we didn't have much else to do on the rez. One of my friends had a car, and it broke down more often than it worked. Most of the time we went out to the highway on horseback to shoot at the signs."

Lee gave a little laugh and stopped. "Sorry."

"It's pretty damn funny when you think about it," Chev said. "And those poor highway patrol officers, though we never gave them a reason to shoot at us like they did. They never caught us. We rode with the wind in those days. Nothing could touch us."

Lee said nothing. They both listened for the sound of the van. He wanted Patrice and Tomas to come back. Talking about the good old days wasn't helping.

"I'm the only one who got out, you know," Chev said.

"Pardon?"

"Out of all of my friends, the only one who got off the reservation and made a future for myself. Oh, I had help. My grandfather died and left me money. But if I'd had been any less ambition, I'd have thrown it all away on booze and drugs. It's easy to fall into those traps when you can't see anything beyond the reservation."

"Like being in prison: You don't see anything beyond the walls."

"Yeah, I imagine so. It had to be worse for you, Lee. I knew I could walk away if I put my mind to it."

"True," Lee replied, his voice gone soft again. Chev wasn't sure he wanted to know how bad it had been -- but he wondered if Lee didn't need to talk it out a little. He'd noticed the shadows in his eyes, and the way he backed off every time they came near the wound. "I don't know how I survived as long as I did, Chev. And came out with so few scars."

"Few that people can see, anyway."

"That obvious, are they?"

"No, not really. Maybe they would be to someone

who knew you before -- but I'm making guesses. Maybe I shouldn't."

"You know, I really can't remember what I was like before I went to prison. I mean, I remember someone who got married, went to college, had a son ... but it doesn't seem like it could have been me."

"Half my friends are dead," Chev said. "Really. Drunk, car accidents, fights, stupidity. I saw it start happening when I was in my teens -- and you know, it was really hard not to go with them. It was a way out."

"What stopped you?"

"Grandfather, mostly. Not the one who died -- my Hopi grandfather. You'll meet him soon. Don't fidget. You'll like him."

"People make me nervous. I expect them to look at me and see lies. Nothing but lies."

"You've never lied to me."

"No, I haven't. But it doesn't mean there aren't lies there. Never mind. I don't know what I'm saying."

"You're saying you don't know what's real anymore."

Silence for half a minute before Lee nodded. "Yeah. I think that's it exactly. And there's the van."

"Okay. You sure you want to go with us, Lee? It's going to be a long couple days out there."

"I've been looking forward to it."

"Yeah, me too. I wish I could get out of this chair. Damn, I hate feeling so helpless. And trapped."

"Don't push too soon."

"You sound like Patrice."

"Oh, not that bad."

Chev laughed, and leaned back, forcing himself to relax. They were in for a long drive out to the site. There would be wonders to see, and time for him to hold history in his hands once more, newly dug from the earth. It didn't matter if he couldn't walk yet. He was going anyway, and no one could stop him.

CHAPTER TWENTY-TWO

Lee held his breath as Patrice eased the truck carefully away from the driveway, coasting down the slight hill with the lights and engine off until they had taken the first curve, heading south. She flicked on the lights with a sigh of relief, kicked the engine over, and glanced at her two companions. Chev sat beside her and Lee by the door. Lee almost felt as though he intruded except for the smile she gave him.

"I'm glad we're heading out of town. Keep an eye out for anyone following us, Lee. And make sure the tarp stays down over the wheelchair. That might give us away."

"Okay." He glanced into the side mirror. A couple semi's passed them in the first few minutes, but he saw little other traffic.

Chev and Patrice talked about work and the site, both relaxing the farther they got from Taos. Traffic picked up near Santa Fe, though, and 5something else occurred to him. "Isn't it going to be pretty obvious when we turn off onto your land, Chev?" he asked.

"Yeah. My cousin is keeping watch tonight, to make certain no one follows us in, but they'll know someone went in here. As it happens, those boxes in the back of the truck are the regular supplies for the ranch, and someone else will drive the truck back out as soon as it's unloaded.

"Odd time of night for a delivery, though," he said.

"Actually, we do the deliveries after midnight all the time," Chev said. He grinned. "We have it set up with the grocery store to bring the stuff out after hours. And yes, I did it on purpose specifically so that people could go in and out without too much notice. I sat it up that way from the start."

"Why? Before there was trouble? Oh, never mind. Archeology dig."

"Right," Chev said with a nod. "The Southwest is full of people looking for sites to raid. So we were paranoid from the start."

"Which helps now," Patrice added. "There's the turn off to the reservation. We could go in that way instead."

"Nah. We do have the food to deliver. Everything looks good so far. Let's keep acting as legit as we can."

The road to Chev's land wouldn't be too far ahead. Patrice began to slow, letting traffic go around them again. No one seemed to hold back on purpose.

"Both of you get down as far as you can. For God's sake, don't hurt your back, Chev."

Chev and Lee slid down, trying to get below the line of sight for the windows, which was not easy. The darkness helped, at least. Patrice stopped at the chain, grabbed a cowboy hat from behind the seat and pulled it on. She got out of the truck and slammed the door shut so the light went out. They could hear her dart over the gravel, and Lee could tell Chev held his breath right then.

Lee hadn't considered she'd have to get out to open the gate. He found himself silently saying a prayer, his heart thudding almost painfully as a car went by, and then another. They heard the chain fall to the ground, and her quick steps back to the truck. She pulled the door open and climbed in, shifting the truck back into gear and heading down the road with a quick stomp on the gas.

"You can get up," she said, slowing again. "Should I stop and hook the gate back up?"

"No. Tim will head back out with the truck as soon as they unload," Chev answered as he pulled himself back up. "Damn, Patrice, I hadn't considered that you'd be out there --"

"I timed it so the only car behind us would go past before I got out."

"You should have told me to go do it," Lee said.

"We did fine. I looked like the regular guy making a delivery. Let's not get worried about things that went right."

"Good point," Chev agreed. He looked relaxed, in fact, so Lee tried to do the same. The truck bounced down the dirt road as Patrice tried to line the truck wheels up with the ruts, which wasn't working very well. "We're about half an hour from the ranch house. We switch vehicles there to a smaller truck we keep on the site."

"You were ready for trouble from the start," Lee realized, glancing around at the empty land.

"Not of this type, but yes. We're bound to be found sooner or later, especially if I let the news of the olla out," Chev said. "I'm trying to gain us as much time as possible. I want to find something more to confirm the authenticity of the olla before someone else gets in and destroys the evidence."

"Do you think you will find more?" Lee asked.

"I don't know. I hope so. I got an email from the site. They found something, and I hope it's going to help out with the olla problem. Whatever they found, they were excited enough to get to a cell node to send me the info."

"Out of range, huh?"

"Yeah. I think you'd get a better connection if you were standing on the moon." He shook his head, and leaned forward, staring out into the dark. "I don't know why I'm so attached to this place."

"Probably for better reasons than I am," Lee said. "But I'd hate to see you give it up, too."

Chev nodded. It couldn't be a comfortable ride, but he didn't complain as they drove down across a dry creek bed and back up the other side to a long flat stretch of land, and then down and around a curve and up again -- it seemed like a long ways from nowhere to this ranch. Lee wondered if he could live at a place like this. He had never really thought about living alone, so far from everything.

"There's the house," Patrice finally said. They'd come down an incline and around a curve. "And they're ready for us."

Lee could see lights in the windows and movement as the door opened. Chev leaned forward, and then back again, as though everything looked normal. Lee tried to base his own feelings on the reactions of his companions, but right now everything seemed wrong in the dark, empty night. Stark bushes moved as they passed, and boulders looked like crouching men. He could see no line between the wilds and the yard of the house. Nature swept right up to the front door.

"How do they get power out here?" Lee asked.

"Generators and solar power, mostly," Chev said. "Usually, they're a sunrise to sundown operation -- some sheep, a few horses. Popay went in earlier today and said we'd be out, so they're expecting us."

Patrice pulled to the side of the long, low building, and

under a slight canopy. As she killed the engine, he could hear sheep bleating nearby.

"Heya," someone said, coming from a side door. A tall man, lean and quick. Lee couldn't see his face with the lights of the house behind him. "Tim is getting dressed. You remember the applesauce this time?"

"Yup," Patrice said as she climbed out. "An entire case of it."

"You are an angel in disguise. I'd ask you to marry me, but Chev would have a knife at my throat before I got the words out."

"Oh, I'd likely go for something lower than the throat," Chev said, sliding to the door after Lee got out.

The man made a startled leap from the side of the truck, cursed in two or three languages, and then laughed. "Damn! I didn't know you were there, Chev!"

"I kind of guessed that part."

"Not fair, you know, you getting all the women."

"Well, Sandra's getting cut free, so you can always go for her."

"*I'm* not that stupid."

Chev snorted and didn't argue. He sat at the edge of the truck seat while Patrice brought around the wheelchair, and the unnamed man, Tim and Lee unloaded the supplies. A couple items went into the back of a smaller, dark-colored the other side of the covering. It didn't take long until they were ready to go again. Tim jumped in the truck they'd brought in and headed out almost immediately.

Patrice took the driver's seat, Lee squeezed in beside Chev. This one was smaller and a tighter fit. They'd tied the wheelchair to the back.

"Okay, Mike -- give us a shove!" Patrice said as she put the car in gear.

"Shove?" Lee said, looking back where the man moved and leaned against the truck, rocking it a little.

"There's a drop down the other side of the house," she said. "We keep it mostly clear so we can slide down and back to the road, and coast for a long ways. I hate doing this in the dark, though. We don't dare turn on the lights until we're a few miles away, and even then it's better if we don't."

"Bright moon at least," Chev said.

They were suddenly moving. Lee felt his breath catch and adrenaline soar. Damn these people were crazy!

"Hold on," Patrice said. She had both hands on the steering wheel and leaned forward.

They went down the hill at a good clip, but she must have taken the road many times before. She turned them gently to the right and expertly navigated the slope and out onto the road below. They coasted for quite a ways down into another arroyo before she finally kicked the engine on. She did not turn on the lights, but every time she touched the brakes, the world seemed to glow red around them. Lee wondered if that wasn't just as obvious.

Driving at night without lights wasn't as horribly frightening as he had expected, though. They could see a long distance with the illumination of the nearly full moon, and they obviously didn't have to worry about any other traffic. Looking up out of the open window, he could see stars that seemed to go on forever.

They drove an hour or more, not moving very fast, and the road winding around mesas and past dried creek beds. Patrice and Chev talked about things, but Lee mostly watched the landscape.

"Time to leave the road," Patrice warned suddenly.

"Here?" Lee asked. He could see no sign of another

road through the brush and sage plants covering the desert.

"Almost," she said and began to slow down even more. "This is where it gets tricky. We have put enough distance as well as a couple mesas, between the ranch and us so no one will see our trail of dust when the sun rises."

"Well, this should be an adventure."

"It's going to be more than an hour in the dark," Patrice said. She was starting to break. He still couldn't see a road. "This is it."

She turned. The truck bumped over rocks and debris, and in a moment Lee realized they traveled down into an arroyo.

"I assume you checked the weather?" Chev suddenly said.

"No storms in the area tonight," Patrice replied, but she still glanced upward and then back down at the dark path ahead. They didn't travel quickly, edging around boulders, sand traps. Patrice followed the center of the arroyo, and she seemed to know the way, but the creek bottom must change with each rain.

"This is crazy," Lee said.

"There is a road that leads all the way up to the area of the site but it's far too obvious," Chev said. "There's a way in from the rez, too -- but it's dangerous for other reasons. Desperate people live there. Some of them would sell us out."

"How far like this?" Lee asked.

"About another mile," Patrice said. She shifted gears and took the car up over a pile of sand and rock. The tires spun for a moment, but caught, and they came bouncing down the other side. "Chev?"

"Fine. I wouldn't risk myself with this if I thought it was going to do more harm."

"Yeah, I know. You're not nearly as stupid as you look," Patrice said.

"Thank you."

Lee grinned and stared out the window. Twice he saw shadows move on the arroyo's cliff above them; deer or antelope once, and possibly a coyote the next time. Too small for a wolf, he thought, though the shadows played games.

Patrice brought the truck to a slow stop and leaned back with a sigh of relief. "We'll wait here for first light," she said. Her watch face lit as she held it up toward her face. "Less than an hour, now. Another turn or two and we'll head back up to the road."

"Road? We're going to take an actual road again?" Lee said. "Thank God."

"What kind of Indiana Jones adventurer are you?" Chev said with a little laugh.

"One who likes that kind of adventure in a theater."

"Wise man," Patrice said. "The road isn't great, but it's better than what we've had in here."

"How long on it?"

"About two hours," Chev answered. "We'll be back on my land then -- we've been skirting in and out of the reservation for a good part of this trip, and taking the long way around the edges of my land, rather than across it. Pretty soon we'll be into the mountains."

Chev sounded surprisingly cheery for someone who must have gone through a very painful ride, and hadn't slept in quite a long time. On the other hand, he didn't have any paperwork to worry about, either, and Lee suspected that helped his mood quite a bit.

"How do the people out there get around?" Lee asked. "I knew this was gong to be out in the middle of nowhere, but I hadn't considered all the implications."

"There's a group of five people there. They have horses and Jeeps, and someone rides to the ranch about every ten days to let Tim and Mike know they're all right and to pick up supplies. But it's dangerous. Someone, eventually, is going to track down the site. We have to be ready by then."

"You own a damn lot of land out here, don't you?"

"One of the largest, privately owned stretches of land in New Mexico. Maybe in the US. But that's because -- until recently -- no one wanted it. It is desolate, but the dig site sits near a natural hot spring. There are a lot of ruins on flatlands around the ranch house, but New Mexico is littered with ruins, and most of the ones on my land are not particularly impressive when you put them up against Salmon, Aztec and the like. Less spectacular than what we found in the hills, but still well worth saving."

"I'm probably stupid, but why do they want your land so badly? There's plenty of other land around here."

"Most of the rest is reservation land in this area, and some of it is government land," Patrice said. "And, according to the prelim reports they filed, Chev's land is right along the line that would be perfect for a new highway from Santa Fe --"

Lee made a sound of disgust. "Just what we need. More highways."

"Yes it is, according to the rich," Chev said. He leaned back, this time, stretched a little. Odd that he didn't consider himself one of the rich, although he quite obviously qualified. "They don't want to live with the plebs in Santa Fe, but by God, they better have quick access to any little bauble they might require. It's stupid, really. It's useless."

"And they want Chev's land because he had the nerve to tell them no," Patrice added. "These are people who take 'no' as a personal insult and an attack on their business ability. They misjudged Chev. They thought because he wasn't making 'improvements' on the land himself, he wasn't a business man."

"Different mind sets," Lee said.

"Very different," Chev agreed. "I have, I suppose, insulted their pride. I'm going to do a hell of a lot more before I'm done."

Lee nodded and leaned back again, settling in and resting. The calm here could be addictive, he thought, listening to nature through the half-opened windows. No sounds of civilization at all. He hadn't really felt this comfortable when he'd found himself out in the desert alone, and injured, but with his friends, heading for better places -- yeah, he could like it out here.

Patrice and Chev understood about the silence, he realized. They didn't try to fill it with noise -- useless talk, or music. They waited. He must have slept for a while.

"There's the light, Patrice," Chev finally said. He shifted a little. "Let's go."

She started the car. It sounded like a tank, echoing off the walls of the dry creek bed around them. They moved forward again, around a curve, past a pile of broken trees -- must have been a hell of a storm, to have dragged them all the way from the mountains to here. He couldn't see stands of trees anywhere near by. Suddenly being in this narrow confine seemed insane.

They found the road, a track of white hard-packed dirt crossing the arroyo. It wouldn't have been drivable if there had been more than a little water in the creek. Patrice turned, and the truck climbed upward again into the pale yellowish dawn. The dirt road stretched out across the sagebrush desert, a straight line to the mountains.

Patrice picked up speed, and then slowed down with a curse, as jackrabbits darted in front of them every few yards. A couple stopped in the middle of the road and stood up on hind legs, watching them approach.

"Maybe I should get out and clear the path," Lee said with a laugh. "I think we could go faster if I walked ahead and chased them off."

"I keep reminding myself that this is their land," Patrice said. "One with nature and all that crap. But you know if they weren't so damn stringy and tough, we'd be taking a few dozen to the camp for rabbit stew."

"Could make some nice mittens, though," Chev said with a laugh.

A couple more stood up in the road. Lee suspected if they'd had hands, the creatures would have been giving them the finger, and it made him laugh. And going slow at least gave him a chance to see more of the country. He began to realize how far they were from civilization -- which reminded him again about his most recent trip out to the desert.

I'm not alone, I'm not alone. And they didn't abandon me the last time anyway.

"Lee?"

"You know, Chev -- you don't miss much at all," he said, and tried not to sound annoyed since he knew the feeling came from embarrassment. "I'm fine. I was thinking about my last trip out to the desert. Did I thank you two for finding me?"

"We had help," Chev said. "It's obvious I couldn't have done it on my own."

"Bullshit," Lee said, and Chev looked startled this time.

Patrice cursed more rabbits and slowed to a crawl but kept out of the conversation. "You and I both know you will do whatever you have to in any situation. The fact you had help was good. I don't think you and Patrice really needed it."

"That's a lot of faith you have in me," Chev said. He looked down at his hands, his finger rubbing against that scar again.

"Yes, it is. I think it's because you have so much faith in me."

"I -- grandfather."

Patrice had already slowed the truck again. A man sat in the sand as though he was part of the desert, waiting for a car to come by on a road which probably didn't see a vehicle more than two or three times a year.

The hair on Lee's arm began to tingle and rise and the unnatural feel of the unexpected meeting. As the truck stopped, dust from their passage covered the figure, but when it cleared, he had already stood and strode toward them -- an old man with the walk of someone far younger. Silver hair hung to his shoulders, and a smile showed on a face with lines that didn't seem to have anything to do with age.

"Heya, grandfather!" Patrice greeted him happily as she got out of the car, as though this meeting was somehow perfectly natural.

Chev looked at Lee and laughed. "Roll down the window. It's all right. It's grandfather. H e... shows up places. He doesn't bite. Not in this form, anyway."

"Shit. Don't say stuff like that." But he rolled the window down.

Patrice had come around to their side of the truck and greeted the man like friends gathered on a street corner in town. It looked incongruous out here in the middle of the damn desert, with nothing but brush and rabbits around.

Grandfather leaned against the door, looking inside the window. "Heya, Chev, Lee. The tan looks good on you, Lee."

Lee laughed. He hoped it didn't sound hysterical.

"What brings you out here, Grandfather?" Chev said.

"Thought you'd like to know, the vultures have their bulldozers gathered up in Sanista Canyon. Don't worry, though. They spend more time fixing them than driving the monsters. Can't seem to get them to work right."

"Grandfather --"

He shrugged and pulled something out the leather shoulder bag he carried. "You can give these back to them if you want."

Spark plugs, wires. Chev took them for a moment, then shook his head and handed them back out. "I don't want them. Police find those on us, and we're in for trouble. Get rid of them somewhere else."

Grandfather grimaced. "You're no help, Hawk."

"I'm not the one out vandalizing other people's vehicles."

"Well, not this time. But you know where I learned how to do this, don't you, grandson."

Patrice laughed again. Lee grinned -- this very strange man had a wicked sense of humor. He couldn't quite bring himself to relax yet, but he did find Grandfather intriguing.

"Is there anything else?" Patrice asked.

"A plane lately," Grandfather said. He shielded his eyes and looked up. "Making passes, looking for tracks. They'd be wiser to come in on the ground -- or maybe not. They know they are not wanted here. They can't see much from the air, but they have started looking in the foothills.

I went to the camp and warned your friends. They have everything under cover. No problems there. But you'll want to get there and off the road soon."

"I'd love to," Chev said. "Keep the jack rabbits out of the way so we can make some time."

Grandfather nodded. "Okay."

Lee swallowed.

"See you later," the man said, and waved them away.

Patrice nodded, put a hand on the man's shoulder and nodded her thanks. Grandfather stuffed the sparkplugs and wires back into his bag and stepped away as Patrice climbed back in and started the car.

"See you later, Grandfather!" Chev shouted

He gave a negligent wave of his hand. Patrice drove away.

Chev looked back at Lee. "I suppose that did seem odd."

"Odd. Yes. And where the hell are the jack rabbits?"

The road had cleared of the creatures for the first time since the sun came up. Lee looked into the rearview mirror. Grandfather waved.

"I'm not tied to the old ways, you understand," Chev said. He leaned back and looked relaxed again. "But every time I see grandfather, I brush up against them and feel closer to the world. I don't know how he does what he does, Lee. But he knew we'd be here today. The Old Ones walk with him, and he's our tie to the land."

"And to the damn jack rabbits," Patrice added with a laugh.

"And those," Cheveyo agreed. "I'm grateful he's willing to help me."

"It's a sure sign that you're on the right path," Patrice added.

Lee thought he looked better for the statement. They also made good time without the furry obstacles crossing in front of them. The road seemed remarkably smooth, as well. Lee wondered if there might be an unnatural reason for that as well. He didn't ask.

The day grew hot very quickly, and the breeze from the open window felt good, although white dust soon covered them, sticking to damp skin. Lee could see the hills ahead. The land had been rising for some time, and they often sped across the top of buttes before dropping back down into another dry creek bed. The road had become little more than two tracks in the dirt now. He couldn't imagine who would have come out this way to make the trail to begin with.

"Anything else out here?" he asked.

"There's a ghost town -- a few shabby buildings that never amounted to much. I think the mine was a scam," Patrice explained. "The town never had more than three hundred people, and it died out at the turn of the century. I think a fever took out about half the population, and the rest finally left. It's about five miles from our site. I never could figure out why they didn't build closer to the springs. They had no natural water source where they were."

"Greed," Chev said. "They couldn't trust themselves to be far from the gold, even though the mine hadn't given them enough income to survive on. People are strange. Especially white people."

"Hey," Lee protested.

Patrice and Chev laughed. They had finally reached the foothills and a line of trees. Lee felt far less conspicuous now.

"Being out here is like heading into the past," Patrice said. "Taking a car up to the site never feels quite right.

Like we're intruding."

"We are," Chev said and then shrugged. "If the land did not want us here, we would never have found the site, Patrice."

"What, we take you two out of the city, and you both go all mystic on me?" Lee asked.

Chev snorted, but he nodded as well. "I guess so. There are days when it's hard to live in two worlds. There are days when I wish I could be Grandfather."

"You'd go mad," Patrice said. "You were never meant for his role. Grandfather knew it when you were young. I remember him telling your mother you'd be the one who made a difference."

"Did he?" Chev said and sounded surprised.

"Oh yes. I remember it because he turned to me right afterward and said -- hell, he said I should stay close to you when you needed me. A long time ago, in the pueblo. Your mother didn't think much of it. Grandfather hadn't exactly given her any good advice in the past, but he'd always told her the truth."

"Where does that leave us?" Chev asked.

"Still bridging the gap between two worlds; still looking for answers."

They rode in silence for a mile or so. Lee sat back, breathing in the scent of the desert mixed with pinion pine. He could hear birds in the trees as they passed, and deer darted away from the side of the path -- he could no longer call the two indentations a road, especially since the furrows were as often grown over with grass and weeds.

"How the hell did you ever find this place?" Lee asked

"Hiking," Chev said. "I had brought Sandra to Taos after our marriage, and I needed to get away for a day. So I drove up to the ranch, grabbed a horse and came up here.

Actually, I had gone to visit my mother to see if I could get her to come down to Taos and meet my wife, but she wasn't interested, and there was no way I could get Sandra to come to the pueblo."

"Sounds unpleasant," Lee said.

"Different worlds," he said. "I sometimes have a hard time remembering growing up there."

"And you grew up there too, Patrice?"

"Yes," she said. She gave an uncharacteristic little shrug. "I actually made my escape before Chev left, but then I am older. I went off to college, got enough education to be a bookkeeper/secretary at a few places and went to work at different museums. I suppose I was learning skills to be ready when Chev needed someone to help him out."

"Does your wife --" he started, and stopped, shaking his head.

"Does my wife know about the past Patrice and I shared? Yes, she learned. Someone sent her an email, right after I turned down the first offer for my land. I never saw it. I wished I had. She deleted it in a fit of rage. Grandfather told me there had been some men out at the pueblo asking about me. So he told them all about Patrice and me."

"Your grandfather did. He doesn't like your wife?"

"I don't think he considers Sandra my true wife," Chev said.

"Not your spiritual mate, certainly," Patrice said -- and did not say that she was that person. She hit the gas as they started up another steep hill.

"It caused problems?"

"Oh yes. Its one of the main reasons we went back to Europe and I left Patrice with most of the work of setting up the museum." Chev said. From the quick look the words won from Patrice, she must not have realized it. "We signed a pre-nuptial agreement, though, and Sandra couldn't divorce me for anything from my past and expect a cent -- nor could I turn her out for the same reason. It had been her idea, so I kind of suspect she has a few things hidden in the closet." He shook his head as though trying to make sense of any of it was beyond him. "I really don't have the time or the energy to deal with her right now. I want to get all of this settled -- if I can. I'm hoping I can at least embarrass the bastards from Red Sun into backing off. And then there's the other problem with the olla and all the questions it has raised."

"One problem at a time. Almost there," Patrice said. She glanced at Chev and away again, apparently willing to let Chev handle all of this in his own way and his own time. It seemed odd since Lee knew that Patrice's life was tied up in Chev's decision. He wondered what choices she would make if the decision were hers.

"There we are!" Chev said and leaned forward again.

They topped a hill and came down the far side. Someone with a rifle stepped out from a stand of trees and watched, worried until Patrice reached out of the window and waved. They had reached the camp. Lee wondered what wonders he would find here.

CHAPTER TWENTY-THREE

Cheveyo mentally braced himself as the truck came to a stop at the bottom of the hill. He could already see movement by the tent, which had been covered over with brush and sand to hide it from sight if the plane flew overhead. Marty waved, put down the rifle, and started their way.

Marty's hair had grown longer, and he had a beard as well. They lived rough out here, and Chev would have felt bad about it, except they insisted that they were having a great time. He had stopped wondering if they lied to him to make him feel better. Chev admitted, given the same choice, he would have been out here as well.

"Hey!" Marty shouted. "Company at last!"

Others came from behind the tent. They had probably heard the truck coming for the last couple miles, and he hated to interrupt them, though only because he wanted to do the work so badly himself.

"Patrice!" Chico yelled and waved as he came into view. He picked up speed for a moment and then slowed when Lee slid out of the truck, showing his mistrust strangers. Chev slid over to the side of the door and peeked out -- and won a shout of surprise. Chico came running again, shocking Chev with the pleasure he saw in the man's face. The others were coming as well, and he hardly had time to feel embarrassed as Lee and Patrice helped him into the wheelchair.

Marty drove the truck into a makeshift covering by the jeeps while Patrice pushed him up the rough trail to the tent. He hoped they could make it the rest of the way to the ruins. Chev really wanted to see those lovely, half-fallen walls again. He had started dreaming about them, and fearing his dreams were no longer at all connected to reality.

"Your timing is good as usual," Chico said, slapping Chev on the shoulder. "This morning we found a new passage. We got some of the debris cleared out today, and we should finish it off tomorrow."

"What kind of debris?" Chev asked, looking up at him.

Chico grinned brightly before he spoke, and the look on the usually somber Leanne's face mirrored it. "The kind of debris that would make most archeologists think they'd hit the mother lode if we handed it over to them. Broken pots, cloth scraps, beads. But it was just shoved in to fill a space, Chev. We know there's something beyond it. I suspect it's going to make the debris look like what it is -- trash thrown in to fill the hole."

"God," Lee said. The others looked at him with a little worry still, but it wouldn't take long for them to get used to Lee being around.

"How far in?" Chev asked, shifting in the chair, anxious to be out of it.

"Right at the back of the wall behind Storage House ruin," Alicia said as she put a hand on Chico's shoulder, leaning there and catching her breath. She looked tan, thin and healthy. "We can get you there, don't worry. I don't know about through the opening, though."

"I want to see," Chev said and hoped he didn't sound too anxious. He wanted to still be professional. He wanted to go back to the work he loved.

They went to the tent first, and there they showed him what they'd brought down from the ruins already. It was like unexpectedly waking up and finding out that not only was it Christmas, but Santa was real.

"Oh," Patrice said from behind him. She had stopped pushing forward, as stunned by the sight as he felt. Tables, chairs, and even the floor were stacked with pieces of pottery, baskets, and what might be hides and cloth.

Marty put a hand on Chev's shoulder, drawing his startled look. "This is mostly the debris Dr. Rey. And at least now you can tell why none of us have been in a hurry to get back. Even before we found the opening, there was work enough to keep us busy for years."

"Do you have an age range?" Chev asked, forcing the chair forward over a bump.

"Oh yes." Kitt, who had said nothing until now. He picked up a few things from one of the tables. "Late Pueblo. We found a couple Spanish Colonial crosses."

"Excellent." The link they needed? He let his hand brush over a couple pieces of pottery sitting side by side, trying to see if they matched up. He looked up at Lee who was keeping close by him. "So, was it worth the trip?"

Lee reached out and let one finger touch a piece of broken pottery. "Damn impressive. All of it. What is this? A Chacoan bowl, maybe?"

Marty, who had stopped on the other side of the table to watch, nodded approval. "That's a good guess, and without even seeing the entire piece. What do you make of this?"

He picked up a small carving from the table to his right and held it out to Lee, who took it in the palm of his hand as though he held a very small baby. Cheveyo felt a surge of annoyance that it was too high for him to see, especially when Lee kept shaking his head.

"This doesn't belong here," Lee finally said. He did lower it for Chev to see; a tiny green stone bird, about two inches tall and expertly carved. It glittered in the faint light beneath the tent.

"What makes you say so, Lee?" Marty asked.

"Aside from the fact that there are no emerald mines in this area?" Lee asked, letting his finger trace the edge of the carving again. "I would guess it's Aztec from some of the engraving, and probably a representation of a quetzal, since they're mostly green anyway."

"Well, damn," Leanne said with a laugh.

"Lee's good at this," Patrice offered, as though they needed to be told at this point.

"I can tell. Can we keep him?"

Lee laughed, handing the statuette to Chev, who stared at it with a more than a little wonder. South American artifacts were not unheard of in the Southwest, but emerald ones the size he was holding -- this was a damn fortune, just in the stone. This site had produced too many surprises. He couldn't guess what might be next.

Although anxious to get to the ruins, he didn't push the others who would have come down to the tent for a noon meal and some rest through the hottest part of the day anyway. He wasn't going to order them all back out just because 'the boss' had shown up.

Besides, they all had prizes to show off, and though none of the others showed anything as startling as the emerald bird, they still had some excellent finds. Most were from inside the main ruins, but Kitt had also found a secondary site up behind the hot springs which seemed to be a storehouse for statues.

"I think it might have been a temple of some sort," Kitt offered as though he expected to be corrected. Cheveyo nodded agreement. The items showed signs of being ritual objects, including a lovely set of bowls with kill holes poked in the bottom. "I know there's never been a temple associated with this sort of find --"

"But there's been so many things found here that have no antecedents that you can't rule out anything, just because it's not been found before," Patrice said. She handed Lee a burlap-covered canteen. "Drink some of this. It's water from the spring."

Lee sipped while he examined an ancient sandal. Then he frowned and looked at the canteen. "This is good. You could make a fortune on this stuff. Much better than some of the bottled spring water people sell in the east."

"Well, if Dr. Rey ever goes broke, maybe we can fund the site from this," Marty said with a laugh.

They had a light lunch; pasta salad with garden vegetables and caramelized apples for dessert. They weren't suffering under poor rations.

"This stuff is easy to make," Alicia explained. "We put the pasta in a pot with holes in the bottom and set it in the hot springs. Water rushes over it, and it cooks very well. We have powdered mix for the sauce and some spices. We grow the vegetables in plots about a mile away -- they look wild from the sky. The apples come with the supplies once a month, and when they start getting old, we cook them like this overnight in the campfire."

"Very nice," Patrice said, running her finger along the inside of the plastic bowl.

"You people are okay out here, though, right?" Chev asked. The others seemed surprised by the question. "I never meant to strand any of you here. If any of you want to go back with us tomorrow --"

"You'd have to tie us up and drag us out of here, Dr. Rey," Kitt said with surprising force. "Do we look like we want to leave?"

His words brought a hardy round of agreement from the other four, which didn't surprise Chev. This was the find of a lifetime, and he'd been very careful about the group he put together for this site. Although relatively young, all of them had already spent years at digs throughout the Southwest.

"I had to offer, you understand," Chev said. "I know I wouldn't want to leave. I don't want to leave."

"You should stay here." Marty looked serious suddenly. "We could keep you safe."

Those words surprised him. He thought he should be embarrassed, but he felt touched instead.

"We've had planes go overhead, but I don't believe we've been spotted," Kitt said as he collected dishes from everyone. "Grandfather comes by every now and then and lets us know we're still safe."

"Good. I don't know what's going on with the people after me, or with Red Sun. And you heard about Lee's trouble, right?"

"That was you!" Alicia said. "The one the bastards took out to the desert? We heard some of it from Tim."

Lee nodded, looking embarrassed.

"I'm amazed," Chico added with a grin. "I thought you would have packed up and escaped by now."

"No," Marty said. "You saw him with the potsherds. He knows the stuff too well to abandon the work. I suppose you are anxious to get up to the ruins."

"Will there be a problem?" Chev asked, tapping the chair.

"We'll get you up there, don't worry. You have to see this, Dr. Rey," Alicia said. "We've been waiting months for you to get here. You aren't getting away this time."

Going up the hill felt damned hot, and he wasn't pushing the chair. The day was desert bright, and the air so dry that sweat hardly had time to form on his skin before it sublimated into the air. The others panted as they climbed, taking turns pushing him, and with frequent rests in this short half-mile. They knew how to handle themselves in this terrain.

Then he heard a sound that stopped them all for a moment. A plane, apparently back among the hills still, but they were in the worst position, out in the open along a ridge trail.

"Shit!" Marty waved his arms as he shouted. "The rest of you get up the trail to cover! We'll get Chev to cover!"

The others scattered. Chev raised a hand and shielded his eyes from the sun while he tried to find either the plane or a shadow of it. He could hear the growing roar of the engine as it echoed through the valleys and ravines.

Patrice hadn't followed the others up to the ruins. Marty and Lee shoved his chair, trying to force it up over the hill, through sand and rock. It was not a quick ascent, and he was ready to get up and crawl the rest of the way. It might have been faster.

"Go, Patrice," he said, waving her ahead. "The fewer of us here, the better."

"We're not going to make it," Marty warned, and began to look frantically around for any kind of cover.

"Tree down there," Lee said, pointing down the slope

where a stately old pinion had spread protective branches. Then he shook his head. "If we go down, we'll have a hell of a time getting him back up here."

"I'll get back up. You can hoist me up with a rope if need be. Let's go!"

"That's awfully steep," Patrice protested. Then she nodded at his look. "Hold on tight!"

That proved to be a useful warning. They went over the side of the hill at such an angle he would have slid right out and down the cliff on his face. Patrice, wisely, darted in front and caught hold of the chair's arms, backing down. Dangerous for her. She slipped twice and must have wrenched her ankle because she limped. But they got down in good time with her holding him steady from the front and Lee and Marty at the back and side.

They had nearly reached the tree, and Chev could hear the plane very close. He craned his neck around to see a flash of light off to the north, and knew it would fly over them at any moment.

They brought him to rest up against an ancient pinion pine probably with roots down to the heart of the world. They jammed the wheel up against the trunk at the last moment, but they were under the branches now, and the others crouched down as close as they could.

"Damn!" Cheveyo suddenly hissed. "Give me something to cover the metal on this chair! It's reflecting!"

Lee and Marti began stripping off their shirts. Chev looked up at Patrice and grinned.

"Not on your life, Kimo Sabe," Patrice said and batted at his head. He laughed, helping the others cover the glaring spots. He could see the plane as it flew over, a few hundred feet above the ground. It went on, dipping down over the hills, but not in the direction of the camp. He had the feeling they were still safe there, at least.

"Give them a minute," Patrice said. She kicked at a scorpion, sending it flying off into the debris. "I think they're making circles, and they'll be back in this general direction soon."

"Good point," Chev said. He leaned back in the chair and lifted one leg, trying to shake the sand from his pants before it worked down into the boot. "That was damned close. Sorry."

"Not your fault," Marty said. He looked up the hillside, as though trying to gauge how to get back out of this mess. "I don't think we can go up the way we came down. Maybe we better scout down the ravine a bit."

"Hold on. The plane's coming back," Lee said.

They held their places again, but the plane didn't go directly overhead. It was, however, clearly in view for a brief moment, and Chev saw the emblem on the body: Red Sun.

"They must know there's something in the hills," Patrice said, kneeling beside him this time, and frowning up at the sky. "They could be a problem."

"We always knew they'd find out sooner or later," Chev said. "I'm open to suggestions on what to do, though."

"We haven't been found yet," Marti said. "Let's not do anything that draws their attention."

"Maybe..." Lee started and then shook his head.

"What? Spit it out." Patrice jabbed at him as she stood again.

"Maybe you need to make it look as though you are somewhere else entirely. It might keep them away for a little bit longer."

"Oh, nice plan," Chev agreed. "Yeah, we can set up a

second camp somewhere. Not make it too obvious, but let something show. Yeah, I'll send out tents and stuff as soon as I get back. But how do we get me out of here?"

"This way, I think," Marty said. He started to turn down the ravine and then stopped in mid move. "Lee?"

Chev looked over his shoulder. Lee had moved in the opposite direction, as though totally unaware of anyone else. He saw a nasty scar on Lee's back from his shoulder and down his right side. The skin still looked reddish as well, as though the sunburn hadn't completely gone away. Chev wanted to grab Lee's shirt and throw it to him, but he stopped himself.

"Lee?" Patrice said, and started to cross after him.

He looked back, his smile so bright it startled Chev.

"Look at this." Lee knelt by the hillside and pulled away some of the brush.

Petroglyphs carved into the rock face -- and at the base of the petroglyphs, he could see the sherds of bowls laid out on a flat surface. As Patrice and Marty worked him and the damned chair closer, he saw animals bones first, some of them gnawed. The petroglyphs formed a tall, semi-circle around --

Around an opening sealed with flat stones in a Chacoan Type III style wall with narrow bands of layered sandstone alternating with larger blocks.

"Damn, look at that," Marty said. "Good work, Lee! You get an extra brownie tonight."

They all laughed. Chev reached out and brushed a hand over the closest petroglyph, dusting it lightly. The symbol shown clearly under the dust, as though it had been made that afternoon instead of the gods knew how long ago.

"Hopi Migration symbol," Chev said, pointing to the

mark of spiral arms. "Ah, and Kokopelli there at the top -- lying on his back."

"Famine, so they left the area," Patrice said, brushing against the same petroglyph. "I see Fire Clan, Gray Flute Clan... maybe others."

"A number of Kachinas, too," Marty added. "Oh, I can't wait to find out what's behind this door."

Chev knew they had stumbled across another incredible find. He could understand Lee's grin.

"Hey!" Kitt yelled from above them. "You guys all right?"

"Get down here!" Marty shouted and waved his hands. "You guys aren't going to believe what Lee found!"

People started sliding down, kicking up dirt and rock, but in a moment they had all gathered around the wall, standing in stunned silence. He saw fingers tracking the petroglyphs. Leanne knelt and picked up a couple small shards, turning them over in her hand. She shook her head, and Chev couldn't tell if that came from shock, disbelief, or that something was really wrong.

She finally looked up at him and shrugged. "Chev, we're going to need more people."

They all laughed. Lee and Kitt pulled debris away along the edge of the cliff side, and it looked like a rock fall had covered something more. There was, Chev suddenly realized, years of work in this one small location, and he was going to need a damn army to guard it all. Good thing he had the money to buy one.

"I can't tell if it's more of the same complex or not," Marty said. He pulled down his canteen and passed it around. "I can't wait to see what they put behind the wall, though. Damn good work, Lee. I bet whatever site you left to come here is in a world of hurt. You've got a real feel for it."

"This is my first time in the field," he replied, letting his fingers brush petroglyphs. "I was training to be an architect." He could have as soon told them he had arrived from Mars. Everyone stopped and stared at him. "Yes?"

"You've never worked at an archaeology site before?" Kitt asked. "You're sure?"

"Yeah, I'm fairly positive," Lee answered, and won laughter again. "What do we do now?"

"I think we should move the camp up here," Marty said. He looked around and nodded, waving toward the area off to the left. "It'll be a hike back to the water, but not too bad. This looks flat enough. We can rig a ladder up to the side to get up to the main trail. I think it's better than trying to climb down here every day."

"What about drainage?" Patrice said. "This doesn't look like a good place in a rain storm."

"Could be a problem. We might have to rig some drainage from the cliff side, but then we do that at the camp now," Kitt said, waving a hand in that general direction. He looked toward the end of the little ravine, hardly more than two hundred yards away. "Looks like there's a crevice up toward the top leading down behind us and it must funnel pretty well. The water can't be bad here since that pottery never would have stayed there through it."

"Excellent point," Chev said. "I leave the camp stuff up to you guys. Just one question: How the hell are you going to get me out of here?"

CHAPTER TWENTY-FOUR

They weren't in any hurry to get Cheveyo back up out of the ravine, and he seemed quite happy to explore the new site anyway while the others went back to camp for some ropes. They had started to call it Lee's Find, and Lee suspected the name would stick until they came up with something official. They did not try to get inside that sealed door. First, they had to come back and document the find, photograph everything, and act like serious archaeologists again.

Lee felt a little shiver every time he thought about spotting the petroglyphs. He had turned and somehow saw the markings, even covered in dust, sand, and tumbleweeds. He felt as though he'd been drawn to them.

And he never wanted to leave.

He needed to go back to Taos with Chev and Patrice because staying would feel too much like running away. And need, at the moment, outweighed want -- especially since he knew that he would be welcomed back to this site at any time.

Despite the time they'd taken at Lee's Site, once they got Chev back up to the trail they went on to the ruins. The group acted like kids turned loose in a toyshop, and they all wanted to take their friends to their favorite area. Lee followed along behind Chev and Patrice, pulling at the collar of his shirt where it kept sticking to his still sunburned skin. He had protective creams covering any part of his body that might see sunlight, but they didn't help against the heat and dust. The day felt so hot and dry that he felt like he drew dust down into his lungs rather than air.

The trail they took from the ridge down back into the hills would have given the site away if the others weren't so careful about moving brush out over it and breaking up the image of a path straight to the hillside. It was hard to get Chev around the obstacles, and through a narrow defile which looked as though it might have been hand-carved out of the stone -- like the entrance to Shangri-La, Lee thought as he went through.

When Lee saw their destination, he forgot everything else again.

The red tinted sandstone ruins sat well back in a natural overhang -- one of the reasons no one had spotted them from the air. The cavern appeared to be at least forty feet high in the large center stretch, and manmade walls rose up to the ceiling in a couple places, dotted with small dark windows opening to a world of the past.

The valley dropped away from them, pinion pine descending into the V-shaped opening and spread up the other side. Lee could not see the bottom from here, and watched two hawks flying upward from the trees below.

Then he looked back at the ruins which sat about 500 feet away across a wide, stone path. Some of the buildings had fallen, but a large section of the structures appeared to be intact, making it an extraordinary find. He saw a large circle of a Kiva at the front of the cavern, most of it still covered in dirt and brush, and unexcavated. Behind it stood a long, low wall of one story rooms with a balcony for the roof -- it looked, for a moment, like parts of the Taos Pueblo. He almost expected to see people walk out.

"Lee?" Alicia said from behind him.

"It's breathtaking."

"Come on inside. There's more."

They had pushed Cheveyo up to an opening at the corner of the wall where a larger building had fallen over and had been cleared away to give access to the rest of the site. Lee wondered if they had purposely made the area easy for Chev to get in and out, and smiled as he followed. They seemed like a good group.

They wandered through a series of rooms, heading toward the cavern's back wall. Leanne pointed out a room with pieces of pottery all over the floor, and another looked as though the storage bins must have had corn until something broke into them.

"The place was abandoned, wasn't it?" Lee finally asked. "And quickly."

"It looks like it," Leanne agreed with a glance around. "We've found no sign of an attack or fire marks on the walls and the fallen areas seem to have occurred later and from natural causes."

"I'd have expected them to take pottery, food --"

"Unless there weren't enough of them left to take it all," Kitt said. "We have had some sign there may have been an outbreak of disease, and it wiped out much of the group. And you'll see some pictographs back here on the wall, which also seem to point to disaster."

"We found that damned interesting olla on a shelf in a room back there," Chico said, waving toward a narrow opening into a small room with more doors. The area appeared almost entirely intact.

But they didn't turn in that direction. Marty led the group straight through to the cavern's wall. The ruins stretched all the way to the back of the cavern, but he found the builders had left a vast area clear -- a room of some sort, though not a Kiva as he might have expected. In the darkness, he saw the outlines of designs on the wall, and gave a startled little leap with Chico turned a floodlight on them.

"Sorry," Chico said. "I didn't consider what that would be like."

"It's all right," he said, stepping closer to the wall. "These are lovely."

Kokopelli stood high on the wall, enormous and brightly colored -- he didn't think he'd seen one like that before. Below the figure stood rows of other symbols -- corn, life, birth, war: a dizzying array of history.

And there, crowded into the far right corner, near the ground... a line of body symbols, and a hastily pecked-out migration symbol -- and a Christian Cross.

"Those last might have been added later," Lee said, pointing out the cross, but afterward shook his head. "Though that's not likely, is it? If Europeans had been this way after the site was abandoned, we would have known about it."

"Exactly," Kitt said. "But they had some contact, as shown in the cross. From the location of the mark, though, I suspect a native made the symbol. Spaniards tended to put the cross more prominently in the scenes, even if it meant destroying other symbols. This person had respect for what had come before."

Chev had no trouble traversing the remarkably flat cavern floor. Lee couldn't begin to guess how many years had gone into making this place and all hand-carved symbols and carefully painted emblems. Generations? And how long ago? Pre-Columbian, for a good amount of the work, although the cross symbols brought the final phases into a recognizable timeframe.

This wall represented history in every sense of the word; generation upon generation of history, and he wished he could know the reason they had put so much care into the work only to abandon the location later.

He couldn't say how long he had been there before he noticed the others were sitting by the wall, watching Cheveyo and him.

"Sorry." He waved an arm toward the wall. "This is overwhelming."

"It is," Marty answered. "You don't need to apologize. We wanted to make certain you and Chev had plenty of time here."

"This is not my first trip, but it still takes my breath away when I see the work. Chev leaned close to the wall so he could study the runes. "I had forgotten how damned impressive this place is. I wish we could show it to the world, but not yet."

"We've had some thoughts about that possibility," Kitt said. He stood up, brushing his hands against his shorts. "As much as we'd love to have this all to ourselves for the rest of our lives, it may be time we think about opening it up."

"Opening it up?" Chev asked with a frown.

"We started talking about it after what happened to you," Alice added. "We got worried about what would happen to this place."

She stopped and shook her head, unwilling to say more.

"Yeah, I know," Chev said. "I thought about it too.

You're in the will. The lands will go to all of you, Patrice and Lee."

"Me?" Lee said, startled. "I'm not --"

"You're my friend, and you love this as much as I do," Chev said with a wave of his hand. "Those were the only requirements. But let's assume I'm not going to get myself killed. What do you think we should do, Kitt?"

"Something like the Salmon Ruins," he replied. "They were private for years. They've got a great library, right there on the site, and a few things for tourists. I figure we can set up building down by the spring and make them walk up here to the ruins."

"That's a long hike," Patrice said.

"Exactly," Marty agreed, nodding emphatically. "It'll keep the number of tourists down. We'll put barriers up around everything and have a guard on duty, day and night. We'd need to make some sort of facilities, too. And now that we've got Lee's Find, we might have a secondary set of ruins to open. Chev, with a hefty entrance fee and maybe a small campground like at Chaco --"

"You really want to deal with tourists?" Chev said, looking startled.

"We aren't going to get people driving through looking for a quick thrill. No matter what, this place is never going to be easy to reach. We might even give Chaco a run for the money as the least accessible public ruins site in the Southwest. We'll draw enthusiasts. It was our desperate attempt to come up with a plan that might continue funding to this place if we could somehow keep all of this in our hands."

Chev nodded. He leaned back in his chair, shifting a little in discomfort, but Chev had started considering their suggestion.

"I'll keep this in mind. I created the museum because I wanted to share. We might do day long expeditions from there. Now, what about the new find?"

Marty grinned and walked to the far left side of the wall. Patrice pushed Chev closer, and Lee followed. He still felt odd to have such acceptance, but here was the life he had always wanted. Yes, he missed his wife -- ex-wife -- and son, but he didn't need to deny himself the joy of this place because of what had happened in the past.

Kitt lifted the light to the dark corner of the cavern wall and showed a slight indentation. He pointed to a pile of stone slabs stacked up on the side.

"The outer layer turned out to be a series of flat plates, covered in petroglyphs like the rest of the walls. I was studying them when I noticed a scorpion slipping in and out of the cracks. It took us a while, but we finally figured out the people here had covered an opening. We carefully pried those five slabs off. Heavy bastards."

"Then we found more debris shoved into the opening. Some of it looks like offerings," Alicia said. She turned on another battery powered lamp so they could see the outline of an archway, very carefully carved out of the mountain wall and lined with a lintel of wood. There were a few carvings around the opening, some of them familiar and few not. Lee, Chev and Patrice all headed straight for them, which won a little laughter from the others.

"That looked like a remake of our first sight of them," Alice explained. "We nearly tripped over each other trying to get to the archway."

They all laughed again. Lee felt giddy. He looked into the opening wishing they had gotten the debris completely cleared. He wanted to know what they would find on the other side.

"Do you think this was a burial site?" Patrice asked.

"If so, it was one they didn't use very often," Chico said. He ran a hand over the lintel, like petting a cat. "This material is packed tight. You can see we've already cleared out about two feet of the debris, and there's no telling how much farther it goes. It's slow work. There are wonders -- like that little bird -- in here."

"We tried pushing a wire through to see if it went all the way and we could measure the distance," Kitt said. "But the material is packed in too tightly, and a wire couldn't get through. We decided against using something stronger for fear of damaging anything along the path."

"Damn," Chev said. "I wish I knew how much farther you have to go. I'd love to be here for this one."

"Well -- maybe we can work for a little while," Kitt suggested. He'd already gone to the makeshift wall and started pulling out a few little bits of rock.

The group had gotten used doing this work and soon had Lee, Patrice and even Chev pulling out small pieces of debris and sorting it into the appropriate boxes along the wall. Every couple inches they stopped for new pictures and notes. Lee found a nearly intact plate, black on white and early Anasazi with a little of the edge chipped off. Patrice leaned over his shoulder, amazed -- and he realized something important.

"I can hear dirt falling inside."

Every head turned in his direction. Kitt and Marty came close enough to put their ears up to the spot where he had worked the plate free.

"Damn!" Marty said, stepping back while Kitt kept examining the little area. "You are our good luck piece, Lee. We may not let you go back with Chev after all. What have we got, Kitt? Can we get through tonight, or should we come back tomorrow --"

"Tonight," everyone chorused.

They laughed, waiting impatiently while Kitt did a little exploring. He carefully pushed a bit more of the debris out of the way, and they could all clearly hear some of it falling on the far side. Kitt stuffed his hand in and grinned.

"I wonder why it hasn't fallen down already," he said. "Maybe five inches at this point, probably more down toward the bottom. Shall we try to work the stuff out from the top?"

He didn't have to ask twice. As anxious as everyone had been to get through, they still worked very carefully, taking pictures every few minutes, and making sure all the debris went into containers to be carefully sifted later.

They found more treasures -- first a pottery jar filled with seeds, and beneath it a slab that looked like some sort of table. They worked carefully across it and found two more jars. One held pieces of turquoise, and another held bits of rock crystal.

"Offerings of some sort," Chev said, holding both jars in his hands and looking inside before he handed them to Alice. Lee watched as she carefully packed them in a box filled with sand for protection when they took them down to camp. Chico had taken dozens of photos and switched to another memory card for the camera. "Neither the turquoise nor the rock crystal had been made into beads. That's unusual. I'm used to finding these things strung together."

"Petroglyphs on the surface of the slab," Alice said, shining the light on it. They could see a little beyond as well, and what looked like a tunnel. Chico took more pictures. Were they going to find another pile of rubble at the far end? Lee couldn't tell from here and really didn't care at this point.

He glanced at his watch, shocked to find it was a little past midnight. No one else appeared to have noticed how fast the day had passed, and he refrained from mentioning it for fear they would want to stop. He wanted to see what these people had hidden on the other side.

Marty and Kitt knelt down on the ground, looking at the underside of the slab.

"Yeah, looks like nothing but a few large rocks under here," Marty said, pulling free a stone and brushing away more sand. "All the way to the other side. I think we can pull the slab down on an incline of sand, and slide it off to the side, and then see if we can pull out the rocks. It shouldn't take long. We can push it off to the side and sift through later. Does that sound good to the rest of you?"

Lee got down on his knees and helped. Kitt and Patrice worked at balancing the slab while they cleared enough to pull it down and out of the way. Lee wanted a closer look at the carvings on it, but the others had already begun clearing the last of the obstacles to the tunnel.

And he could see, as they worked, that it turned a few feet ahead, enticing them to hurry ahead and look. If Chev hadn't been there, they might have climbed over and gone on -- but none of them considered going on without him.

"Just about," Patrice said, she sat back on her heels and brushed dirt from her hands, laughing. "I didn't think I was going to have this much fun coming up here. It isn't every day that a museum curator gets to play in the dirt while her boss watches."

"If I had a choice, I'd be right down there with you," Chev reminded her.

"A couple more inches on the side," Lee said, and began to pull the dirt back. Kitt took it from there, and then on to Patrice who, with Alice's help, packed it up against the wall. Team work.

They had the way cleared. Kitt picked up one of the lamps and stepped in first, but he didn't go far, waiting as Patrice pushed Chev in. Lee started to step back, but Marty signaled him in next with a grin of delight.

"There's a curve here," Kitt said. His voice echoed oddly in the little opening, and Lee looked up to see the cavern's ceiling rose much higher here. No sign of bats anywhere, which meant there likely was no other opening.

Kitt had waited for the others before he went any farther. Patrice had some trouble turning Chev at the corner.

"Screw this," Chev said. "We'll all go crazy trying to get me through here."

He stood and with a hand on the wall, went the few steps while Patrice folded up the chair and followed. Lee had never seen Chev on his feet. It startled, frightened, and pleased him, but he was glad when Chev sat down again.

They were past the curve and cavern opened up, all dark and shadowy. The others followed, and Kitt lifted the light.

"Good God," Chev said.

Lee stepped forward. The light filled a large area and shown on ... things. Even with a coating of dust, many of them glittered brightly from niches in the walls.

"Gold?" Patrice said, her voice barely a whisper.

Lee started to shake his head in denial, not of what they saw, but that it could be here at all. Everything here came in shapes he had only seen in pictures. Niches cut into the walls held statues and carvings of ...

"What the hell have we found?" Chev whispered.

"Aztec," Lee said. "Think of the olla. We knew they'd

traded a little in this area, but this... this isn't trade. This is -- hiding? Storage?"

"Keeping it out of the hands of the conquistadors?" Chev ventured.

"No way of telling --"

"Oh, I think there is," Kitt said. He lowered the light.

The body looked like a thin covering of dried skin on bones, preserved in the dry desert heat even in this cavern. A conquistador's helmet, a crude cross, and a sword sat beside him. So did a flask, and a book with a quill lying upon it, all of it surrounded by several flat plates. Lee suspected some had held candles, burnt down and finally sublimated in the dry air.

"Oh hell," Lee said. "I think we're going to have answers. I'm betting that's a journal."

"Get the cameras in here," Chev suddenly ordered. "We don't dare take another step until we get this documented. "This is so outstanding that we ought to call the government in before we do anything."

"We'll contact them when we get back, Chev," Patrice said. Her hand was on his shoulder. "And it's not like these people aren't qualified to handle it."

"But Aztec," Marty said, protesting. "We need an Aztec expert!"

"It's a damn good thing Chev is here then, isn't it?" Patrice said, patting his shoulder.

"Oh hell, yes!" Alice said, laughing. They all looked drunk.

"And Lee, apparently," Kitt added.

"Just a passing interest," Lee said.

"Really?" Chev looked back at Led. "How many people do you think could tell Aztec from Incan at a glance? Tell me what that statue straight across the room represents."

Kitt lifted the light again, and it showed on a large, shadowy figure that nearly took Lee's breath away. "He's an eagle warrior. They were the elite nobles."

"Right," Chev said and finally stopped to look at him. "How do you do that? Photographic memory?"

"Close," he said with a shrug. "I remember things if they interest me. It didn't help when I needed it, though."

"When you needed it?" Patrice asked, stepping aside for Alice, Chico, and the cameras. "In school? I can't believe you wouldn't do well in school."

"I wasn't interested in most aspects of architecture," he explained. "And it became apparent to anyone who knew me."

"So you changed majors?" Kitt said.

"No." Lee realized he had put more emotion in the word than he had intended, since the others turned to him, and Chev put a hand on his arm. "Sorry."

"There is nothing you need to apologize for," Chev said, and then very obviously changed the subject. "Kitt, is the printer still working? I'm going to want some prints to show certain people when we go back."

"Working well enough," Kitt said.

Everyone went to work. No questions -- but in some ways, that felt worse.

"I might as well tell them," Lee said, feeling his face color. He felt, inexplicably, as though he had been lying to these people.

"Lee was arrested and convicted of a crime that later proved to be done by someone else," Patrice said before he could. "He sent five years in prison for it, and we're damned lucky he got out at all."

"We're lucky?" Lee said. Odd words.

"Damn right," Chev said.   "Lee, you've helped me more at the museum than you probably realize. And we need people who can help with this type of material. How well versed are you?"

Lee started to deny he knew anything at all, but he didn't need to do that here, he realized. In school, he had annoyed people trying to teach him things he really hadn't given a shit about. And in prison, the worst thing he could do was to admit to knowing anything.

Time for that to change as well.

"I read everything I could," he finally admitted. "We had an excellent library at college, and I spent a lot of time in prison, reading anything I could out of the library. They weren't too keen on letting me have access to stuff on the Aztecs, though."

"Why not?" Kitt asked.   Then he lifted his hand. "Never mind. It's not important."

"They thought I was a serial killer," Lee said. People shook their heads in disbelief -- odd to see them have such faith in him.   "And to them, the Aztecs were just people who cut out the hearts of their victims. Not the sort of thing they like to give to people like me."

"Hell," Kitt said.   He looked straight into Lee's face. "And you weren't popular in prison, were you?"

"No, I wasn't," he said.   He looked around at the others. They'd all gone mad, standing there staring at him, listening to his story.   "Will you start taking the damn pictures! I want to get in there!"

Alice laughed, and Chico began to take the shots. Light flashed here and there, reveling crevices where faces of stone, gold and silver brightened for a moment, and then went back into the dark.   He held his breath and waited. He didn't bother to look at his watch this time.   No one was going to sleep for a long, long time.□

CHAPTER TWENTY-FIVE

C hev tried to lean back and curb his anxiousness as Lee and Kitt slid the wheelchair down four hand carved steps into this sanctum. He couldn't imagine how they had gotten some of this material up here. The stone statue of the Eagle Warrior, for instance, had to weigh half a ton or more. Had they brought the statue, and the others, all the way from the Aztec world to here? Why?

Chev hoped they would find answers in the journal. He wanted his hands on that book and was getting impatient as Alice put in more batteries, and did a half dozen more shots of their nameless conquistador and everything around him. They had filled the memory sticks for the other camera as well. Back at the camp, they had several laptops and extra hard drives. He'd be taking a dozen of them back with him.

Lee knelt down beside the book and looked at it without touching. Chev wanted to be right down there with him.

"Here," Kitt said, handing Lee a pair of cloth gloves and a bag. "Put the quill in there and we'll seal it right up. I hope the spines don't break on it."

Chev watched as Lee very carefully opened the plastic

bag and slid the quill in. A couple of the feathery spines fluttered off but most remained intact. Kitt had brought one of their storage boxes in, and they cautiously nestled the quill between flat slats of cardboard and sand, protecting it as best they could.

And that left the book. Kitt handed Chev gloves as well and then nodded to Lee. "Give it to him."

The book lay open on the last page, and Lee picked it up without closing it. The dry binding flaked at the little movement. Patrice had brought a flat board to place across the wheel chair's arms, and Lee carefully put the book on it. Chey blew a little of the dust away. The ink had faded slightly with age, but he could read the words.

"It's a diary," Chev said. He brushed his gloved finger over the writing. "Signed by Alejandro De Seville, our friend from the olla, and dated May 19, 1540."

The writing looked elegant and cramped. Having wanted to know everything about his own ancestors, Chev had taken the time to learn to read the language of his Spanish great-great grandfathers so he could read their papers. He wanted to turn to the first page of the journal and to start there. It felt wrong to skip ahead, like reading the end of a mystery first.

He contented himself with, carefully flipping through a few pages. Chev stopped to stare at a small drawing for a long moment before he realized what he was looking at.

He tapped the little drawing, so well done. "Kin Kletso at Chaco. Look -- you can see Pueblo Bonita in the distance. It was still nearly intact then."

He let the others look before he went on. He found another drawing, this time of some Native Americans, and then a drawing from one of the Pueblos showing laughing women on the walls, and men carrying in a deer. The date was 1535. He must have been the first European to ever come this way. Chev dared to stop and read a few lines this time --

"Oh hell. We have a vindication for the good Fray Niza," he said, looking up. Everyone had stopped in their movement around the room. He didn't know how long he'd been looking at the book, lost in the words. He would have to start sharing more. "It says Alejandro's group had been hiding at Zuni Pueblo -- Cibola -- when the Friar came. They didn't want to be seen by a Spaniard, mistrusting him, so they hid during his visit. But one of the children showed Fray Marcos a room filed with their treasures, brought from Tenochtitlán."

"And he went back and told the officials about the gold, and that sent Coronado into this area," Chico said, shaking his head. "Everyone has assumed the Friar never really got this far -- but he did!"

Cheveyo nodded, looking down at the words again. "He says they were so worried they packed everything up and were heading for an abandoned pueblo nearby, to hide out. And here they are."

"History come alive," Patrice said. "It's going to be quite a tale to find out how he brought it all to this area, to begin with."

"Yes, it will," Chev said, already drawn back into the man's journal, turning again to the last pages. Alejandro had had much to say, and little space, so he cramped his writing into every usable corner of paper down to the final signature -- and a date, slightly smudged, but readable: May 20, 1540,twenty years after the death of Montezuma, nineteen years after the fall of the Aztec Empire. Alejandro had traveled a long ways with all these Aztec treasures.

"Here," Chev said. The light was poor, and he

squinted. "These are the last words he wrote:

It is done. We have come here, to this land of desert, a place of such strange beauty that I cannot feel at home -- and yet I feel at peace again at last. And that is well. My heart pounds at any little movement now, and I know that the fever that plagued me for years has taken its toll. I climbed to the cavern this afternoon and watched them lay Mazatlcalli to rest in his chamber. I brought my journal, the last candles, and had the bearers bring my breastplate, sword and helmet. I think they suspected what I already knew, that I would not leave again. Some wept, and I was touched at their devotion, for they never wept when they put their graven gods to rest here. Some kissed my hand in parting, as they had seen me kiss Mazatlcalli's hand in his last hour, and wish him well on the journey to his heaven. They begged to let them carry me back down again, and promised to take me to a green place that is not far away. But I said no. My work is done, and I am too weary to travel on.

"*Ah, I have seen such wonders! I have walked in places no one from Spain has ever seen, and I have lived with a simple people who are closer to God than those who pray each day in their Cathedrals. God has granted me a full life, and I know I die in His Grace. There is peace at last.*

Though I miss the roses of home. I miss them still-- and the fine wines, and soft music. I wonder if there is a Spain in heaven, the Spain of my dreams where I still ride in the hills.

When someone of Spain finds me here and reads this journal, pray find a priest to bless my bones and assure my final passage to paradise. I know my people will come. I have no doubt they will spread far and wide, always searching for gold -- the curse of my cousin, Cortes -- when they should have searched for grace instead. God grant them the peace I have gained, and God grant them the love of this place that I have found.

And you, friend, who read this journal, pray keep these treasures protected. I put them in your trust now. God keep you safe and go in

His Grace.

And remember me.

*Alejandro De Seville, the 20th of May, in the Year of Our Lord, 1540.**

Chev ran his finger over the name, wishing he had a face to go with these words. He was not going to forget Alejandro. Neither would anyone in this room.

Chev looked back at the body once more, which was no more than the tatters of cloth, the sandals that had obviously been native made, and the metalwork brought from Spain. This man had come to conquer a new world, but instead, he had become a part of it in ways few people of his time ever did.

"What are we going to do now?" Lee asked.

Chev carefully closed the journal. "We're going to find him a priest."

CHAPTER TWENTY-SIX

They'd made it back to camp barely before dawn, rested until mid-afternoon -- although no one, as far as Lee could tell, actually slept. For the next few hours they helped the others prepare to move the camp up to the site of Lee's Find and made lists of what he, Patrice and Chev needed to bring back from town. High on the list were a priest and Professor Belinato from Santa Fe and having a few small items authenticated -- quietly. It might take a few days to track her down, but everyone agreed she would be important to bring in at this stage. She had the connections to officials they were going to need to bring in soon.

"We're not going to do anything with your site, Lee until you can come back and work here," Marty said as Lee climbed into the truck.

"You can't --" he began to protest.

"We already voted. Besides, it's not like there won't be enough else to keep us occupied for the next ten lifetimes."

Chev nodded agreement and before Lee could argue anymore, Patrice had kicked the truck into gear, and they backed out. He frowned in her direction, and she grinned. Lee finally gave up and leaned back in the seat, relaxing for the first time in days.

Surprisingly, he slept through most of the trip back to Taos. He sat up finally, his neck sore and his body lethargic, to find them parked in front of the museum, and long past sunset. Patrice had already climbed out from behind the steering wheel and stood outside his door.

"Oh," he said. "Sorry."

"It's okay," she said and eased the truck door open. The night had turned wonderfully cool, but he felt wobbly as he slipped out. "We're going to spend some time here collecting material. I hope you don't mind sleeping on the sofa in Chev's office."

"I can help," he said. "At least I've had some sleep. Maybe the two of you ought to get some rest."

Dr. Rey gave a little nod of agreement as he slid to the edge of the seat. Lee helped Patrice get the chair out of the back and brush the sand and dust off of it, though he suspected it would hardly matter since Chev had far more on his own clothing. He slid down into the chair and looked relieved to be in it for the first time since Lee had met him. The trip had been rough.

"I'll park the truck in the lot," Patrice said after she pushed Chev inside. "No use making a target out of it."

"I can replace the truck," he said, looking up at her.

She almost argued, but Lee put a hand on her arm. "He's right."

A car drove past slowly, and Patrice looked toward it with a start and then looked relieved to see a police car. Lowell stopped, giving them a friendly wave. The relief almost made Lee giddy again with another surge of adrenaline.

"I'll put the truck in the lot," Lee said, easily extricating the keys from Patrice.

"If Lowell will stay and watch," Patrice said.

Chev had almost argued, but he looked outside and nodded instead. "Yeah, take it in back. Maybe no one will notice we've returned. A few hours of peace won't hurt. Tell him we were out at the ranch, checking on damage to the ruins there. We need to keep this quiet for a few more days."

Lee nodded and opened the door. "Lock up behind me. No use being careless here, either. I'll see you at the back door."

Patrice came to the door and locked it, and he watched a moment until the two moved out of the direct range of the glass window.

"At least you people are careful," Lowell said. "Good to know you've picked up some tips from Tomas."

"Yeah. I need to get the truck off the street and into the lot. They'd only let me do it if you kept watch."

"Wiser and wiser," Lowell said.

"Has there been trouble?"

"Nothing serious," the cop said. "Get the truck off the street and we'll go inside and talk about it."

Lee nodded and hurried into the cab of the truck, noting that it was almost out of gas. The engine kicked over, and he barely had to give it any gas to coast to the end of the block and around the corner heading toward the turn to the alley.

Another car came at him, and going a bit faster than he should have been doing on a town street. The driver obviously didn't know there was a cop car behind Lee's truck and about to turn the corner. It would probably scare the shit out of them --

A gunshot. The windshield cracked in a spider web design that blinded Lee for a moment. He braked out of panic, and slid down --

"Yes, he's all right!" Lowell yelled as he came up the truck door. "Come on! We have to get after them, and I can't leave you here!"

He could already hear other sirens.

"Call Chev and Patrice. Tell them I'm fine and not to come out!" Lee threw himself out of the truck, not bothering to shut the door as he ran to the police car. "Get someone here to watch them!"

"Tomas is on the way," Lowell said. "Get in!"

He barely pulled the door closed and grabbed the seat belt before Lowell hit the gas and spun them around in the street, heading after the other car. Taos wasn't large, and this late at night the winding streets were nearly empty. Even so, they had reached the north edge of town before Lee saw the car they were following.

Lowell had been talking to others via the radio. "State patrol is going to try and cut them off. We're going to keep them in sight until then. The others are back watching over the museum." Driving at this speed apparently didn't have much effect on him, although it had certainly woken Lee up. "These people are idiots to try something like that in town."

"Lucky you were there," Lee said.

"It wasn't luck. We've been keeping watch over the museum, with a drive by nearly every hour."

"Well, I sure appreciate it," Lee said and tried to relax. His shoulders felt like they were set in cement. The bullet could have killed him.

"If they're smart, they'll cut off across country, cut their lights, and lose us," Lowell said.

"I didn't see the type of car."

"Black pickup with good tires," he said. "The kind of

vehicle you get for off-road in this area. But it was shiny and new, so it may just be for show. I can still see the taillights, so they haven't gone off-road yet."

Lowell grabbed at the radio when it squawked and spent some time talking with others in a combination of English and codes again. Once they were on Highway 64, the dark countryside swept past them, too fast and shadowed to see anything except for an occasional distant light. The pickup -- he hoped it was still the right vehicle -- passed a slower moving car. They did as well. Two semis headed the other direction, toward Taos. A quiet night, at least, and Lee had no trouble keeping the truck in sight as they slid up over hills and around curves, heading northward.

"Some fog up on the Rio Grande Gorge," Lowell noted. Lee could see the line of white cloud, hugging the earth along the deep trench of the river, and drifting across the bridge where the road cut across it. He'd been out here once during the day, amazed by the view. At night, with the moon high and the fog rising up above the crevice, it looked like a line of smoke on the horizon.

"Getting closer," Lowell said, pushing down on the gas pedal. "The fog could hide them long enough so they could disappear before the state patrol can get there."

"How far away is the patrol?" Lee asked.

"They had an accident up north, but they won't be more than five miles away by now."

Lowell started to gain on the truck. They were close enough, in fact, that when they reached the bridge, he could barely make out the shape as it went into the fog.

And then lights danced before them, a glow of bright red in an unexpected arc, and then white --

"Damnation!" Lowell shouted, already starting to

break. "Bridge is slick. I think they spun out trying to slow down --"

And they, unfortunately, were doing the same thing. The police car started to slide to the right, bumped the curb on the wide sidewalk where people stood during the bright day to look down at the gorge.

"Where the hell are they--"

Black truck in fog on a dark night: They slammed into the side of it, but Lowell had already slowed, and though they bounced and he heard glass break, the airbags didn't inflate. He was damned glad, having a moment of panic at the thought of being trapped, while people with guns came after them.

Lowell cursed as the car stopped, and shoved open his door, but the truck's tires squealed, and he jerked it closed again as the truck rushed past so close they broke off the mirror, before heading back out of the fog, and toward Taos.

"You all right?" Lowell asked.

"Fine, as long as you don't count being angrier than I've ever been in my life."

"I'm getting right up there with you," he said. The engine caught, but the car wouldn't turn. "Damn. We aren't going anywhere. I'm afraid we're going to lose them. I better get some flares out. It would be wise if you went and stood on the bridge, instead of in a car hidden in the fog -- but for God's sake, try to stay hidden. Someone did shoot at you!"

Lee nodded and got out, flexing his shoulders and trying to ease new kinks out as he hurried toward the bridge. The fog at least partially hid him. He didn't go too far. It had already been a damn long few days. He decided, all in all, to take advantage of a few minutes of quiet.

Lowell put out flares and leaned against the car door while he talked to others, reporting what had happened and directing them after the truck.

Lee saw the flashing lights bouncing through the fog. Another car pulled up behind theirs, the one they had passed following the truck. The driver had seen the truck, still heading toward Taos, about four miles back.

Three state patrol cars arrived, and two of them headed on toward Taos. Lowell called to Taos and put in a warning, and added another to contact Dr. Rey and his people to tell them what happened and Lee was safe, but trouble had headed back their way.

Lee finally walked along the sidewalk, looking down into the dark abyss. He couldn't see the bottom, and it seemed an analogy of how things were going right now. He knew Chev had people trying to find out who was causing this trouble, but it seemed like blankness sat the bottom of everything.

"Lee!"

He came back to where Lowell stood talking with a state patrol officer, a large man with a face like set stone; square-jawed, crew cut, and the epitome of something out of a comic book.

"This is Officer Peltin," Lowell said. Lee nodded, remembering the name from somewhere -- hadn't he been part of the group who had picked him up in the desert? "I'm going to wait here for the wrecker, and you can ride back with him."

"You shouldn't wander off," Peltin said. "We don't have time to go hunting you down. You people really shouldn't waste our time with this pottery crap, you know. We have real work. Are you ready to go?"

This was not the night to push Lee. He'd had enough,

and this attitude didn't help.

"You know, at this point, I'd rather walk back than ride with you," Lee said. "Mainly because if you don't take someone shooting at me very seriously, why the hell should I trust you?"

Lowell looked skyward for a moment. Peltin glared and shifted his feet like a cartoon bull about to charge. There was no way in hell Lee was getting into a car with him. He'd had enough of this already today. He turned, intending to head back toward the sidewalk and watch the fog for a while.

Peltin grabbed him. Lee started to swing, and Lowell stopped him in time. It had been a stupid reaction.

"You might as well go back to patrol, Peltin," Lowell said. He sounded amiable enough. "I guess Lee won't be riding with you after all."

"I know all about you," Peltin said. He still had hold of Lee's arm, and if he didn't let go soon, Lee feared he might end up hitting the man after all, which was stupid and reactionary, and the worst thing he could do. But it might just happen. "I know about the time you did --"

"And the fact the real killer was caught, of course," Lowell said. He had lost his own tone of friendliness now. "I think you better release Mr. Constantinos, or else give me a damn good reason why you shouldn't."

Peltin unexpectedly shoved Lee aside, and he ended up on his ass on the sidewalk, looking up at the man with more confusion than anything else.

"I don't give a damn what you and your boss have up there in the canyons," Peltin said. "You aren't going to run this county and Rey isn't as all powerful as he thinks. You remember that."

Peltin spun, stalked back to his car and slammed the

door as eh got in. Then he drove away with his tire's squealing.

"What the hell was that about?" Lowell asked.

Lee stood, and brushed his hands against his pants. "Lowell, do you know Peltin very well?"

"No."

"Then you're going to have to trust me," he said. "We need to get away from here before he comes back."

"What the fuck are you talking about?"

"He just did something incredibly stupid," Lee explained, inching back toward the edge of the bridge. "He said *up there in the canyons.* Only the people who have been looking for Dr. Rey's site would know that they're hunting in the canyons, not the flatlands."

Lowell pursed his lips for a moment, started to shake his head, and then stopped. "I've read all I could find on Rey's work," he said. "Part of the job, and part interest. I saw pictures of ruins, and they were on some plateau."

"Those are some of the sites, but I've been into the canyons," Lee said. He wanted at least some of the fog between him and the road. Lee could still hear the sound of Peltin's car. He could hear it slowing, somewhere not nearly far away. "Lowell --"

"Damnation!"

He didn't dart for cover. He went to the car. Codes passed again, and then words Peltin no doubt heard as well. "We have a situation here, and I'd like to have some backup as soon as possible. Please note we suspect Officer Peltin may constitute a danger. I will be out of radio contact until the tow truck gets here. Please have it escorted."

The two jogged along the walkway, past the scenic turn off, and off into the scrub.

"We can't go too far from the fog," Lowell said. "The

moon's too bright, and he'd pick us out."

"Coming back," Lee said, gasping a little at the exertion.

"Yeah, he is. Take cover and stay still."

"Sirens," Lee said.

"Good."

Lee could hear the sound of the sirens, too far off, but they were coming quickly. Unfortunately, he could hear the sound of Peltin's car much closer. Lee figured they were safe, though. Peltin wouldn't have time to search, and Lee suspected the man wasn't going to want to stick around. He'd made a mistake, and he knew it.

The state patrol car braked to a stop and he could hear a door open. Somewhere nearby a truck downshifted for a curve, and a coyote howled from down in the gorge, a haunting sound that rose up into the foggy night.

Footsteps.

"God damn! You're going to pay for this one, Constantinos!"

Running. Lee could see red lights refracted in the fog, growing brighter as the wail of sirens nearly drowned out all the other sounds. In the next moment, Peltin's car door slammed, and the car drove away, tires squealing as he spun around. Lowell and Lee stayed where they were, silent for the next few heartbeats.

"This is getting too damn weird for me," Lowell said. "I don't like to think we were in real danger, but he sure as hell acted strange."

"I know." Lee sat up, carefully brushing dirt from his hands.

"I don't get why there's this much trouble over some damn, desert land."

"Money, pride, stubbornness," Lee said. "Corporate

Mentality. All in all, nothing to be proud of."

"Those kinds of things are pretty rare in this area, you know," Lowell said. He stood and offered a hand back to Lee. He wasn't so certain he wanted to get up, but he did. "You get that stuff down in Santa Fe sometimes, but out here -- hell, there's land enough for everyone. It's stupid."

"Yes, it is. But people are stupid all over the world."

"True enough."

The police cars had arrived, and the two jogged back through the fog, startling a couple cops who apparently thought something awful had happened.

"What the hell is going on?"

"Any of you know Peltin?" Lowell asked, looking from face to face.

"Nah. He's only been on the force for a couple months," one said.

"Does he pilot a plane?" Lee asked.

"Yeah. Peltin has a prop plane. Flies quite a bit on almost all his days off. You aren't going to tell me he's flying drugs, are you?"

"No," Lee said and forced himself to give a little laugh. Standing in the midst of all these cops made him nervous. Lowell must have noticed, since he slipped up beside him, instead of forming more of the circle. "I don't know if he's involved in anything."

"But he did act damned weird," Lowell said. "You don't have to be nervous about it, Lee. I know these guys. Jose is my cousin, and Jimmy and me went to school together."

"Good. Sorry. I'm an outsider here, and I have to admit that working with cops makes me uneasy."

"Can't imagine why," Lowell said. "Ah, here's the wrecker. I don't suppose anyone caught up with a new black pickup with a big dent in it?"

"No."

"Of course not," he said. "Bastards. I don't know what the hell is going on, but I didn't appreciate this game."

Lee gave a little smile and then looked startled as another car pulled up behind the police cars. A van -- and Patrice stepped out, looking worn and worried.

"You didn't have to come out here, Patrice!" Lee said. "In fact, I wish you hadn't!"

"It was on the way," she said and looked grim. "We've closed down the museum, and the three of us are going to drive up to Denver, out of range of this madness for a few days. Don't argue Lee. We all need a break and some time to think things through."

"I had a run-in with a state patrol officer," Lee said and explained the situation.

"Great," she mumbled. "And Petlin went north?"

"Yeah."

"I'll escort you up to the border," one of the officers said. "It's my patrol area, mostly, anyway. We'll get someone from Colorado to take you on from there."

"A bit anxious to get rid of us, aren't you?" Lee asked.

"Yeah, we are, at least for a while. Let us try to sort this out for a few days."

Patrice agreed with a weary nod. She put a hand on Lee's shoulder. "Come on. It's a damn long drive to Denver. And since you had some sleep, you get to do the first stint."

"Fine." He followed her back to the van. Chev sat in the back seat this time and had some paperwork and his computer. He didn't look happy either.

"Lee has more great news," Patrice said as she slid into the passenger's side of the car. "But it may be a break, too.

At any rate, we're on our way."

They drove out of the fog, following the state patrol car. Lee told Chev about Peltin and tried very hard not to panic because the man had gone off in this direction and could be anywhere ahead of them. No paranoia, he told himself.

But he still felt damned tense when they finally caught up with the Colorado state patrol car at the border. He waved to Jimmy and silently thanked him as the New Mexico State Patrol turned away at the Combres Pass. They'd made it safely this far, at least, but the world looked dark and dangerous out there, and they had a long ways yet to go.□

CHAPTER TWENTY-SEVEN

By the time they reached Denver, they had a plan. It was, Chev thought, born of too much caffeine, no sleep, annoyance, and fear. In fact, he distrusted it so much he decided they should have a couple days rest before they acted.

Two days at a fancy hotel gave them time to send material out to be processed in labs -- they still needed authentication for the site. It also eased aching muscles, settled nerves -- but did nothing to improve or change the plan.

Chev stared out at the view of the mountains and wondered if he'd lost all sense of proportion and shouldn't get to the proper government officials and university departments and hand all the finds over to them --

Then he thought about the people they'd left back at the camp. They'd worked damned hard on that site. And, from experience, Chev knew he couldn't blindly trust any agency to do the right thing. His people would be replaced, his lands would be confiscated, and probably half would be given to Red Sun anyway if they were willing to hand over a little cash. No, he was going to hold out as long as he could, in hopes he'd still be able to settle everything well.

On the second night, they went to dinner, ate a nice meal, and still hadn't quite made a decision on what they were going to do the next morning.

"We have to make a decision," Patrice said as she played with the last few bites of desert. "And I only see two real options now."

"And they are?" Chev asked.

"Back off and give in, or go all the way and make sure that they have no choice but to back off."

Neither choice sounded like the sort of decision Chev would have expected from Patrice, but he wasn't surprised by the passion. They'd all been pushed too far in the last year, even Lee, who had come late to the show. Chev would have liked to dissuade the two from leaping into his plan, but he knew they would be in danger no matter what they did now. This might be their best chance to get clear of the trouble.

"First step is to get a priest and Belinato," Chev decided, and in those words committed them to Patrice's second choice. He pushed his plate aside. "But we're going to have to be discreet. It's time I was rid of the wheelchair."

Lee looked surprised, but Patrice nodded, which pleased him.

"You're not going to be up and running anywhere," she said, "but Dr. Holm told me that you'd be ready soon. Just don't do anything stupid, Cheveyo."

Chev nodded, thinking about how clumsy he had felt with the canes when he practiced but figuring he'd have to go to them sooner or later. He'd been practicing, alone in the house with Morton to come and help out if he fell. Chev hadn't fallen yet. Now he suspected Patrice had always known what he did.

"So what do we do next?" Lee asked.

Chev smiled, though not for the reasons Lee Constantinos might think. In the last few days, Lee had finally put himself entirely in their camp, rather than considering himself an outsider. Good. So far Lee had proven to be more of an asset than he probably realized. He didn't have trouble adapting to new problems, and contrary to what people might think when they first met him, his quiet demeanor was not a sign of fear.

"We're going to fly to Albuquerque tomorrow," Chev said and won startled looks from both of them. "We'll rent a car there and drive up to Santa Fe. There we'll collect Belinato and a priest."

"How? Kidnap them?" Patrice asked.

"We can lure Belinato without much trouble," Chev said. He reached into his pocket and pulled out the envelope with pictures they'd printed off at the site. He also still had the lovely emerald bird. "The priest might be more of a problem. Finding one we can trust, for instance."

"Let's talk to Perez while we're in Santa Fe," Patrice suggested. "Even if he isn't Catholic, he still might know someone."

"Good plan." Chev felt strangely at ease, though they would soon be heading back into trouble. He did look forward to getting the news about the site out in the open, before something unfortunate happened and they lost this strange bit of history forever. He didn't trust Red Sun to care about a find as incredible as the conquistador. While they probably wouldn't destroy something like the find, Rey had started to have nightmares about a Conquistador Theme Park.

After everything he had been through, he wasn't in the

mood to let anyone have anything of his, least of all the credit in something this spectacular.

Patrice made the plane reservations for the next day and called Tomas to add a little bit more misdirection. He would head up toward Denver in one of the company cars and maybe draw some of the people with him. Chev had to trust the man would be careful. Everything had been quiet in Taos, but he suspected it would change soon.

Before they checked out the next morning, Chev called on his law firms in England and in Santa Fe. Then he phoned his portfolio manager who gave him some interesting news.

"I talked to Mina this morning," he told Lee and Patrice over a hurried cup of coffee before the cab arrived. "She had something interesting to say."

"Mina?" Lee asked.

"My investment broker," Chev said with a little frown. "Sometimes it sounds so damn elitist I hate to say those words aloud. I asked her to do some research on Red Sun for me. Guess who's poised to unveil their secret project this afternoon, and hits the stock market for public trading tomorrow?"

"Red Sun? Really?" Patrice said. She sat down her cup, already suspicious. "And what do you suppose they plan to show?"

"We know they plan a closed community site. Maybe Red Sun has found other land," Chev said.

"But you don't think so," Lee replied.

"No, I don't. Mina said this presentation has been on the boards for half a year, and to pull out now would pretty much ruin their first days on the market and they might not recover. I think they're going to try and bluff their way through."

"Not much choice," Patrice said.

"Yeah."

"Once they make that presentation, they're going to be desperate to make it come true," Lee added.

"Yes, I know," Chev answered. He pushed away his cup. "Like I don't have enough desperate people after me. We've no choice on this one, though, except to sell the land and walk away."

Patrice finished her coffee and shook her head at that idea. "Let's see what happens next. I'm not in the mood to make this easy for these people."

Lee smiled. Chev had already guessed they were both crazy.

"Cab's here," Patrice said. She threw some bills down on the table. "Let's get moving."

"She's always like this when she's outside of New Mexico," he told Lee, rolling out toward the Lobby. "Hell, she used to be this way whenever she was off the reservation."

"Like you were any better," she said.

"True enough," he conceded. "Time to get rid of this."

It took an act of will for him to pull the two canes from the back of the wheelchair and stand. Not because he couldn't do it physically, but he couldn't be as certain about his mental readiness. The feeling surprised Chev -- there had never been a challenge he hadn't been ready to face before this.

He stood. It wasn't particularly uncomfortable, although the weakness bothered him. He would have been more mobile in the chair, but people would be watching for him in it. He looked over at the concierge's desk and gave the man a nod. "Be sure the chair is donated to some worthy charity, will you?"

"Certainly, Dr. Rey," the man said, coming over to take charge of it. "Thank you."

Chev smiled and nodded to his two friends. The driver and doorman had already started loading the limo. In a moment the three settled into the back, encased in luxury. For a moment he felt the temptation to hire the limo for the drive all the way back to Taos -- but it would be a little ostentatious, not to mention showy. Since the trick was to not draw attention, he reluctantly decided on going no farther than the airport in this excellent car.

Amazing how easily everyone accepted 'skiing accident' when they got to the Denver airport, despite it being this late in the season. He and Patrice took a ride in one of the carts while Lee followed on foot, making it harder for people who might be looking for the three of them. Chev and Patrice also conversed in Spanish. People asking about two Native Americans were not likely to remember two Hispanics.

They made it through security without a problem, and on to the plane ahead of everyone else. Lee insisted he not ride in first class, although Chev thought he had deserved a couple hours of comfort before they went back into battle.

Flying out of Denver was, as always, spectacular. The Rockies stretched out beneath them, rolling brown and white, still with much of the snowcap in place. Every time Chev flew over the mountains, he stared at the winding roads and the vast expanses of wilderness wondering what lay hidden down there. Like the vast desert and the empty sea, the forests could conceal any number of secrets from the past. Chev loved mysteries. He wanted to see what hid beneath each pine, and behind every rock. He wanted the answers to everything.

He would not find them up here in the plane, and he

finally leaned back to ease a crick in his neck from staring out the window for so long. When the crew brought food and drink, he leaned back and enjoyed a quiet morning meal with Patrice.

Why the hell had he ever married Sandra? Was it the Indian Boy from the Reservation still looking for acceptance in the outside world? Look at my pretty blonde wife? I have to be doing well if she'll marry me, right?

"Chev?" Patrice said.

"I've screwed up a lot of things in my life," he said with a shake of his head. "I'm not going to mess this up as well."

She gave him an odd look, but then they went back to their food and enjoyed each other's company for a little while longer. The flight to Albuquerque would go far too quickly, and once they were down, they wouldn't have much time to relax for a while.

Again.

CHAPTER TWENTY-EIGHT

L ee felt incredibly uncomfortable walking into the Santa Fe Police Department building alone. Asking for Perez nearly brought on a bout of stuttering, which he hadn't done in so long he couldn't remember the last time. People gave him odd looks when he asked someone to tell the detective that Lee was here.

Perez came out a moment later, frowning at first and then looking surprised. Lee really hadn't spent much time with the man, and it amused him to see the man look suspicious and worried.

Lee smiled. It didn't seem to help.

"What's gone wrong?" Perez asked softly as he came out into the lobby.

"Nothing really wrong, but we could use your help. Chev and Patrice are out in the car."

"I heard you people were in Denver after that last fiasco."

"We were, but we had to come back," he said and almost laughed at the look Perez gave him. "Can we meet you somewhere?"

Perez sighed. "Lunch at the café where we ate?"

"Sure thing," Lee said and started to step away. He

was surprised when Perez caught hold of his arm.

"Peltin got kicked off the State Patrol force, and he's disappeared," Perez said his voice soft. "I don't know all the details, but we've been warned to keep an eye open for him. Apparently, they found some really questionable things when they started looking into his background, and no one is quite sure how he made it as far as he did. We think someone higher up the ladder maybe took some bribes. Do I have to tell you to be careful?"

"No, you don't," Lee said. He tried not to sound depressed or worried. Perez still gave him a long look. "There's some great stuff going on, and I wish these people would crawl back into their holes for at least a few weeks. When do you get off?"

"I'll see you at noon. Three hours. That all right?"

"Yeah. We need to go watch a CNN Money report anyway."

"I'll see you at the café, then. Now go and stay out of trouble."

Lee hated lines like that, as though they were little omens looking for a place to start trouble. He left the building and scurried from air conditioned halls to the air-conditioned car.

"Okay, we'll meet him at the café where we ate at noon," Lee said as he slid into the driver's seat as Patrice slid back over. He looked into the back seat where Chev sat. "Where now?"

"I think a nice, plush business-orientated hotel," Chev said. "Patrice can rent a room, and we'll slip up there and watch the show."

Chev handed her the cell phone with a smile, and she went to work while they sat in the police parking lot. Lee wondered if he was supposed to feel safer here.

Half an hour later, they found a very expensive hotel in the middle of the Santa Fe's answer to Silicon Valley. Patrice checked them in as Mr. And Mrs. Barnowl, and Lee played 'driver' to the pair, though he didn't really think he looked the part.

"You're going to have to buy me a uniform," Lee said as he put the suitcases inside the door to the suite. No use taking them farther. After all, they weren't going to be staying long.

Which was a shame, since this looked like a nice set of rooms: a massive outer room, two bedrooms off the sides, a bar and a small balcony. Lee walked around and finally looked back, shaking his head.

"I grew up in an apartment smaller than this," Lee said. "This is crazy."

"Yeah," Chev agreed. He sat down in a chair Patrice pulled over, looking exhausted. Lee flopped down on the very plush sofa, and Lee wondered if they could stay for a day or two. He really didn't give a damn about Red Sun and their show.

They didn't have long to wait after the coffee and rolls arrived. Chev and Patrice leaned forward as the presentation started, and Lee found himself interested if for no other reason than they were.

Edward James Stillman, CEO of Red Sun Enterprises looked like a crew-cut right wing wanna-be. Lee wasn't certain why the sight of the man hit him quite that way until he saw all the other people around the table with him were white, well-dressed, crew cut men. No women. No minorities. He wondered if anyone else noticed.

"Don't they look like a wonderful group of thugs," Patrice said. "I'm calling for some more coffee. Let me know if they say anything I want to know about."

Lee looked at her, a little surprised, and then realized her anger with these people made watching them on television difficult. Lee, on the other hand, watched in fascination, wondering more about Chev's other type of business. He listened to a discussion of stocks, marketing, and finally -- just as Patrice handed him a cup of coffee -- they began unveiling something from under cloth on the table before them. Patrice stopped to watch.

The layout looked perfect. The Red Sun people had modeled the mountains, plateaus, and the dry creek running through Chev's land. And there, growing like some gigantic spider on the landscape stood a city of stark black and white buildings, about as out of place as a panhandler would have been in the lobby of this hotel.

"Good God that's ugly," Chev said. "There is no way in hell they're going to build that on my land!"

"Well, they seem to think they're going to. Oh, look -- they plan to build a reservoir about where the Conquistador Ruin is." Patrice tapped the screen over the area.

"Like hell, they will!" Chey growled. "Turn the damned thing up."

"We have a site in mind," Edward James Stillman said. "The land is perfect for our needs and useless to anyone else. There has been no land improvement done on it in more than fifty years."

"But word is the owner is reluctant to sell," a reporter said.

"We believe the state government will, in fact, confiscate the land and pay the owner a fair price. This is too good of an opportunity for the people of New Mexico, and especially for this depressed area of the state to lose because of the stubbornness of one man. He's holding out for more money, and frankly, if he had been more cooperative, he would have gotten it."

"Lying bastards!" Chev said. He had started to stand. Patrice pushed him back down.

"Don't worry," she said. "We still have a few aces to play."

"Yeah." He sounded sullen. "But he's had the first word, and that's what people will think is true, no matter what we do later."

"They aren't all that shallow," Lee said.

Chev nodded, but he still didn't look pleased. There had been more questions from reporters, and they came back to the man again, smiling through perfect teeth.

"I have assurances from government officials this will not be a problem. We'll have the land long before we plan to start building," he said.

"Ha," Patrice said. "You know what he's really saying?"

"That they don't have shit yet." Chev gave a little laugh. "He's bluffing his way through this because they didn't dare stop the presentation or their first day on the stock market would be a disaster. Good. Why do I know this man? He's familiar."

"I don't know," Patrice said. "I don't know him."

Chev shook his head again, watched for a moment more -- but they were going off to a reporter now who stood outside the building and commented on the Red Sun presentation --

"Oh shit," Lee said. He got up and went to the window, looking down. "Yep."

"We're in the same hotel where they gave the presentation?" Patrice said, coffee cup halfway to her lips.

"Sure are," Lee said. He slipped back from the window and pulled the drape partially closed. "And now we're supposed to leave to go meet Perez."

"Might be fun," Chev said. "I'm tempted to go down and crash their little party. CNN is still here. I'm sure they'd like to have some juicy tidbits to go along with that presentation."

Patrice turned off the TV and sat down. "No. We'd look petty. We'd look like we had planned to be here for this and ruin it for them."

"Yeah, I suppose so." Chev leaned back, looking as though he'd had the last bit of fun taken out of his life. "I would have so enjoyed it, though."

"You'll get your chance," Lee said. "We better call Perez and say we might be late, though."

Patrice nodded and called. Perez had already left his office, so they called the restaurant instead. Then they watched until three huge limos pulled up, gathered their precious human cargo, and sailed off again, disturbing traffic patterns where they passed.

"I'll get the car. Watch for me. Don't come down until I come around," Lee said. "Shall I take the luggage?"

"No," Chev said. "We should come back here for the night. It's going to take a bit to find a priest, and we still haven't talked to Belinato. We'll head up to Taos tomorrow. I think it might be a good idea to lay low tonight. After that little show, Red Sun is going to be really anxious to make things right. I don't want to be somewhere they can find me."

"Good point!" Patrice put a hand on his shoulder, and he put his hand on hers.

Lee left them. They didn't get much time alone together. He went down to the second floor and then took the stairs to the first. Elevators were so damned noticeable. The lobby looked empty, and he crossed quickly and out again in the hot desert air.

This was still spring. Lee began to think he wasn't going to do well around here come summer. Suddenly the snows of the East didn't seem quite so bad. Maybe he'd go up to Denver and the Rockies if he needed a break.

The valet got the car, accepted a tip, and went back to stand in the shade. Lee pulled the car around to where he knew his friends could see him, although he couldn't looking up, he couldn't be certain of the room.

The car had been a steam bath when he got in, but the AC unit had made it pleasant by the time his two companions arrived. Cheveyo fairly skipped to the car in his haste to get out of sight, and slipped into the seat by Lee with a nod. Patrice pushed his door closed and then got in behind. In a moment they headed back on the road.

"You'll have to direct me," Lee said. "I wasn't exactly cognizant the last time we went here."

"You know, thinking about everything that's happened, I have to wonder why you're sticking it out, Lee," Patrice said.

"If I told you it was for the adventure, would you have me committed?"

"I'd think real hard about it."

"Then we better go on to the next question."

They both laughed. They tried to direct him to the little restaurant, but they got lost twice along the way and by the time they arrived Perez looked nervous. He stood and smiled, waving them over to the table.

"Damn glad to see you on your feet, Chev!" he said, pulling out a chair. "Looks like a chance for another celebration."

"Yeah. Lots of celebrations," Chev said as he settled into the chair. Patrice sat next to him, and Lee by Perez.

They ordered quickly and over chips, and salsa got straight down to business. Chev leaned over the table and looked at Perez. "We need a priest."

Silence for a moment. "Priest?"

"Catholic Priest. It was a last request from someone."

"Someone's dead?" he said. He looked startled. "If someone is dead you're going to need more than a priest --"

Patrice pulled a piece of paper from her purse and handed it across to him. Lee glanced at the digital picture printout as Perez picked it up. It showed the chamber, and although the color wasn't great, he could still see the hint of gold where the flash had caught it. He could also clearly make out Alejandro de Seville and everything around him.

"Dead," Perez said. He looked as though that might be the only word he knew right then.

"About 500 years dead," Chev replied as he grinned.

"God," Perez said. "You found him? He's what I think he is, isn't --"

He stopped and put the paper down when the woman brought them more drinks. Lee smiled, grateful to know that Perez could be discreet, which was probably a big part of his job.

"Food will be here in a few minutes. Do you need more chips and salsa?"

"Yes, that would be very nice, thank you," Patrice said.

The woman went away. Perez looked at the picture again as if he had expected the scene to change in those few seconds. Then he looked back at Chev.

"Conquistador is the word you're looking for," Chev supplied, still grinning. "See the book beside him? That's his journal. It's going to give us a lot of answers."

"Holy Mary," Perez said. His voice rose before he took a deep breath and calmed again. "You're certain?"

"As certain as we can be," Chev answered. "There will be tests done, but I don't see how this could have been faked. I was there when we broke through the wall, and I know my people didn't set this up."

"Damn!" Perez looked at the picture again and then handed it back to Patrice. "Why the priest?"

"He asked that when someone found the journal that they get him one," Chev answered. "I want to have it done before we move on to other things."

"Yes. Good. All right. You know, I don't know much about archaeology, but even I know this is a pretty spectacular find."

"And he's not alone," Chev said. He leaned forward, and Perez's eyes widened in anticipation. "We have another unopened chamber. We have every reason to believe there will be an Aztec prince buried there."

"Oh." He looked around the room as though afraid someone might have heard.

"We need a priest before we go back. One who will be willing to go there, and keep quiet," Chev said. "Do you know one?"

"Yeah, no problem. We'll grab my brother, Father Antonio. He has a traveling mission, and heads off into the wilds often enough he won't be missed. I think he's in town right now. We'll go find him after lunch. And I'll take the next few days off -- I have them coming anyway -- and go along with you if that's all right."

"That's a great idea," Chev said and with evident relief. "Glad to have you along, if for no other reason than you can be an official witness."

Perez nodded, looking excited. Lee realized the man's reaction would be just a taste of what they were going to see later.

The food arrived, and they settled down to a calm, long meal.

"We're going to take an archeology professor back with us as well," Chev said. "I'll talk to her first thing tomorrow. Then we'll head straight to the site. We will not go near Taos if we can help it."

"You want to tell us about Peltin now?" Lee said.

Perez made a face but nodded. "I suppose so. He could still be a problem. His superiors decided to look into things after Lowell's comments about what happened out there by the gorge. The first thing they came across was that his wife works for Red Sun. This was quite a surprise since he has no wife."

"His own second income?" Patrice said.

"Yes. Electronic banking between Red Sun and Peltin right into a 'joint' account, which he has full access to. We have a lookout for him, but nothing formal. His department is still sorting through his application and acceptance to find out where he slipped in because he didn't come in through any normal channels. He suddenly turned up on the roster."

"And they want to know who put him there," Chev added.

"Yeah."

"I hope it's not too high," Patrice said. "Especially after what the Red Sun CEO said about state backing for the project."

"I think you have an ace in the hole that's going to win this over to your side. Eat up. Let's go find out what my brother has to say."

They finished a pleasant meal. Lee had never been this involved in life before. He hadn't allowed himself to feel it until now, and to realize he had his hand in something historical. Damn. The realization stunned him -- and the moment wiped away an entire layer of darkness that he'd been holding on to.

Perez called into the office, said he was taking his sick leave for the rest of the day and the rest of the week as vacation time. It took him a bit to finagle it and get any work redistributed, but no one seemed to argue much. He drove this time, with Chev and Patrice in the backseat, and Lee beside the cop. He had stopped being uncomfortable, and might stop feeling uneasy around other police soon. He hoped the Red Sun people stayed clear of them for a few more days. After that, Chev would have the information out in the open, and Lee suspected Red Sun would have to back away.

Red Sun, having made a national announcement, would now be caught in their own timeframe which was dangerous, in some ways, since they would be desperate. But they continued to underestimate Dr. Rey and his people.

Perez drove to the outskirts of town and a small church half hidden behind a line of lilac bushes, though it was too early for flowers.

Perez hurried into the church, and came out, waved, and walked next door to a little adobe building that must be the rectory. In a moment he came out with a man who looked like a younger version of himself.

Perez slipped behind the wheel, and his brother slid in on the other side of Lee. The priest looked around and shook his head. "I'm not used to clandestine stuff, you know," he said. He had a little laugh in his voice. "That's Pablo's work. What is the problem?"

Patrice pulled out the picture and handed it to him. Chev told the story of the journal. He had to repeat it again when the priest finally got over his initial shock and could actually make sense out of words.

"Can you come with us in the morning?" Perez asked.

"Yes," he said. He smiled. "This is a unique circumstance, but I don't see any problems. What time can you pick me up?"

"We'll be here about seven in the morning," Chev said. He sounded relieved since they weren't going to have to go search for another priest. "Then we'll pick up someone else on the way out of town, at least if we can find her. She's not as essential as you are, but we can get her to do some verification for the site."

"We better get a different vehicle tomorrow," Patrice added. "Especially if we want to head to the site without anyone else taking notice. Taking a caddy off into the wilds might be a little too noticeable."

"I'll handle it," Perez said. "I'll borrow dad's SUV and tell him some friends, and I are heading to the mountains."

"Thank you. The less Patrice, Lee and I are seen, the better. Then we're set." Chev settled back and looked relaxed again. "We'll head to our hotel and suck up the luxury for the night. You want to come and get us about six, Perez? That way we can be out before most everyone else in the place wakes up."

"Want? Six in the morning? Want is not the word I would use. But I'll be there."

Father Perez went back into the rectory, and they returned Perez to his car at the restaurant. Afterward, the three headed to the hotel again. Lee wondered if he would sleep tonight. It looked like they were in for some real excitement over the next few days.

CHAPTER TWENTY-NINE

P erez showed up at the hotel the next morning with 2001 blue Suzuki SUV; a bit battered and scuffed but large enough to hold all six of them, and with a rooftop carrier so they had no trouble storing suitcases. Perez quickly packed everything but the canteens away, and they were out of the hotel parking lot within ten minutes.

Patrice had also arranged to pick up a lightweight wheelchair. Chev had almost argued, but she had rightly pointed out there might be a time when he didn't want to slow them down. He bit back his surge of macho pride and agreed.

Patrice took the place behind the wheel, and Perez sat shotgun. They picked up the wheelchair, folding it up and storing it in the back, and then went to gather Father Perez, who with one small knapsack, stood outside the church, already waiting. He looked more awake than any of the rest of them and smiled greetings as his brother stored his case.

It was too early to go the college, so the group settled for breakfast at a quiet little diner. Cheveyo watched with amusement at how much attention the priest drew.

After breakfast, Patrice drove to the college. She had checked her laptop the previous night and tracked down

Professor Belinato's schedule. The woman should be in today, but there were never any guarantees.

Sitting in the parking lot of the college felt like being in a carnival road show, Chev thought. Kids walked by, looked inside the SUV, stared at the freaks, and went on. Lee started to squirm. Even Father Antonio looked uneasy.

"There she is, heading into the building!" Patrice said. "Damn. I had hoped we would catch her before class started!"

"I'll see if I can get her attention." Lee got out of the car, and Perez hurried to go with him.

"I'm not letting any of you wander around without a keeper, not here in Santa Fe," Perez said. He poked his head back in and grinned. "Lock up. We'll be back soon."

Patrice nodded and hit the lock key. She kept the engine running, at least, and the AC kept them all from baking in the few minutes it took Lee and Perez to deal with the professor.

More kids walked by, stared, walked on. Chev moved uncomfortably. At least today they'd be in the car most of the time. And they would be heading in the right direction, too -- back to where he really wanted to go.

"Here she comes," Patrice said. "She's not happy."

"Unlock the doors and get the pictures out. Quickly," Chev urged, leaning forward. When Father Antonio gave him a curious look, he shrugged. "I was her student. I know that look, and I'd like to circumvent the worst of the lecture."

She came to the car in a few more quick strides, pulling open the door by Chev and glaring. "I don't appreciate being called out of class," she said. "These kids paid for their education and --"

Patrice held one of the pictures up by the edges. Belinato leaned closer. She took the other three printouts from Patrice's hands and shuffled through them. Then looked at the first picture again.

"Where?"

"Up in the mountains on my land. We're going now if you'd like to come along."

She started to climb inside and then stopped herself with a startled look back at the building. "Can you wait half an hour? I'll get the students going, and set up someone to take the class, and get my suitcase from the car. Damned good thing I planned to be in Santa Fe for a few days. How long will I be gone?"

"Better clear the rest of the week if you can," Chev said.

"I will. I'll be right back."

She forgot to close the door, and Lee and Perez had to hurry to keep up with her. They were not going to let her wander around alone now that she was part of the group as well. Father Antonio leaned over Chev and got the door shut, and Patrice locked up again, grinning at Chev.

"There was a moment there where I thought we were in for some real trouble," Patrice said.

"It's all in the ability to divert attention," Chev said. "And having something incredible to wave in her face."

A little later Lee and Perez walked back out of the building with Professor Belinato and started across campus, heading toward her office. Patrice drove them over to that area and looked anxious to be on the road.

"Did your brother tell you about all the trouble, Father?" Patrice asked as they parked outside, waiting.

"Call me Tony. Yes, Pablo told me about both the trouble in London and with Red Sun. I imagine they aren't going to be happy about this find."

"They want to make a giant reservoir where our ruins are located. I suspect they are not going to want the news of the site made public," Chev said. "So we have to move before they find out."

"Why don't they go somewhere else? It's not like there is a paucity of open land in the state -- or the rest of the Southwest, for that matter."

"I really don't know anymore," Chev admitted. "Hell, I'd offer them money to help buy other lands if I thought it might give me a little peace."

"Chev, I've been thinking about something," Patrice said. She had all their attention as she turned to look in the back seat. "I thought about what more it would take to build a city on your land besides equipment and supplies. I remember Mina calling me about some stocks you had in local utilities. She said your wife wanted them in her name. They weren't much --"

"Yeah. I let her have them. She wanted to make a gift of them to her former brother-in-law who had put together some sort of local..." He stopped and blinked several times. "I assumed he was trying to corner the energy market. Hell, that's where I know that bastard CEO from! He's the half-brother of my wife's first husband. I saw him for a moment a couple days after our wedding!"

They all fell silent, and Chev felt a fire of rage starting to grow that he was having a hard time holding back.

"Be sure and tell Pablo about this when he gets back," Tony said. "Can I ask about your wife?"

"Don't bother," Chev said. He felt another wave of anger he hadn't expected. "I have to ask a lot of questions myself first. Like how far back her involvement in this really stretches. I am beginning to think I was married for my land."

"And your money," Patrice said. She didn't mince words.

"I was a fool."

"No, actually," Patrice said. She started to reach back and pat his hand, but refrained, though she did smile brightly, which almost annoyed him. "Chev, in the end, they were the ones who were the fools. They should have done a hell of a lot more checking on you before they rushed into this scheme."

Father Tony nodded agreement as well. By then the other three were heading to the vehicle and Chev fought his annoyance back so he didn't snap at them. Belinato leapt into the SUV and found a seat in the back.

"Let's go," she said. "And let me see the pictures again. Anything else you can tell me?"

Patrice immediately headed toward the highway. Chev thought Lee looked tense -- and then he remembered this was where Lee had been grabbed and taken off to the desert. While he told Perez about the connection between his wife and the CEO, he found himself watching the road behind them. Lee, at least, began to relax.

They didn't find any trouble until they nearly reached the turn off for the Rey ranch. Patrice started to slow down as they came up to the road --

"Keep going," Lee said. "Plane."

Lucky that Lee had spotted the plane before they had slowed down enough to draw attention. It wouldn't have been noticeable so far, and she swept past pinion pines and the chain. "What now?"

"Go on up to the Nambe turnoff," Perez said. "It's only a few more miles, and we can pretend we're heading for the Pueblo, like good little tourists. I want to make a call."

He popped his phone out. Chev started to protest, but it seemed unlikely anyone had actually put Perez with them. He had to trust that the cop would be careful.

"Think you can get us a couple F-16's to chase it off?" Tony asked.

"No, but I can find out a few things about the plane," he said, holding the phone. "Like how long it's been up, and when and where it's going to go pick up fuel."

"Can we get it grounded somehow?" Chev asked.

"Well, if Peltin flying, they're going to short a pilot when they put down."

"That's a good start," Lee said. He smiled brightly.

They turned down the Nambe road, passing along the Sangre de Cristos foothills. Nambe's museum, dark reddish adobe in the bright light, already had several cars parked in front of it.

Perez still talked to the police while the rest got out of the car. The problem, Chev realized, was that they were a noticeable bunch, no matter what they did. It didn't help that a state patrolman pulled up, and they all looked uncomfortable at the sight.

"Hey, it's all right," Lee said and waved. "Popovi!"

"And Tomas with him!" Chev said, feeling better again.

Tomas climbed out of the patrol car, pulled off his sunglasses, shook his head, and came over. "Yeah, we've got problems," he said as he leaned against the car door. "As if any of you are surprised."

"What now?" Chev asked, shifting to get his footing better with the canes.

"The plane you spotted apparently belongs to Red Sun. They've dropped tear gas at the campsite, but I got an email saying it was all right, they had mostly packed up from there and already moved."

"We've stopped people three times from going in onto your land," Popovi added. "And they stopped another group trying to go through the reservation. Grandfather spoke to them personally."

Lee, Patrice, and Chev all winced.

"We have some time to kill," Perez said, getting off the phone as he slid out.

"Do we?" Chev asked.

"Oh yes. About an hour. And then we're heading for a private airfield at Chimayo and see what lands there. Chances are Peltin will be present since he's the only small plane pilot we can find associated with Red Sun. We'd like to get the plane grounded at least long enough for us to get to their site. If Peltin is there, we have a good chance."

"But we're going to have to go carefully on this one," Popovi said, shaking his head. "Some people on the force who got close with Peltin says he has all kinds of fancy communications equipment. We don't dare call in help. We've been discreet on the car radios. We're sure this plane is part of that trouble?"

"If the plane belongs to Red Sun," Perez said, staring up at the sky as though he could see the craft, "it might be the same one that found the campsite. I don't know if we can actually get them on anything, but we might as well give it a try. And we'll see when they're down."

So they wandered through the Nambe art galleries and drew a few more stares. Chev finally shrugged it off -- they were a strange looking group, considering how diversified they were. Belinato and Lee talked about the art, while Popovi and Patrice discussed old times at the reservation. The conversations revolved around everything but where they were headed. When Perez looked at his watch and nodded, Chev knew it was time for the next step.

"Look, it would be better if the rest of you say here --" Perez warned.

"No," Lee answered, surprising everyone. "We need to see who comes off that plane. Don't worry. We aren't stupid. We'll stay back. But I want to see the people we're up against."

Popovi and Perez both nodded. Tomas looked worried, but then it was his job to keep Chev from danger. Chev met his look, stopping Tomas from arguing before he began.

They went back out into the hot, bright day and quickly to the cars. Popovi and Tomas still road together, and headed out first, half a mile ahead so that it didn't look as though they traveled together. They headed north toward Chimayo, skirting along the edges of the hills, then up and down again into the Chimayo Valley. They passed through the town -- adobe houses, the Chimayo Museum, and Chev could see the Santuario's famous twin bell towers. He wondered if he should stop there, at that place of miracles, where the lame came to see the Franciscan Brothers who maintained the sanctuary.

Not now. The patrol car stopped by a small café, the car mostly hidden in the shadows. Popovi and Tomas got out and signaled them over.

"We're going to walk down to the airfield. A patrol car sitting down there would be too much of a giveaway," Tomas said. He pointed to a dusty little alley between rows of adobe buildings. "Drive down to the edge of town. You'll see a metal shed about a quarter mile further. That's the place they store fuel. Stay back and don't put yourselves in danger."

"I'm coming with you," Perez said.

"So am I," Lee added. He raised a hand when Chev started to argue. "I'm not going any closer than the cover of the shed, but I want to get a look at them."

Chev wanted to argue. He didn't.

As the four walked away, Father Antonio whispered a little prayer and swept his hand in a sign of the cross.

"You never know what might help," he said with a quick smile.

"I'm going to head back to the Chimayo Museum," Belinato said, getting out the car as well. "You know where to pick me up."

By the time she had slipped away, the others were halfway down the alley and heading toward the shed. Chev wanted to call them back. He couldn't. He could only hope the righteous won, and he wasn't certain if he had that much faith anymore.

CHAPTER THIRTY

L ee didn't really feel the heat this time while he worried about making the wrong noise or even that he might panic. He feared he would sneeze at the dust the plane kicked up as it landed or that his shadow would show. Everything seemed ready to rush to disaster.

Perez stayed with him at the edge of the shack, a hand on Lee's arm, stilling him as well. In a moment the engine died, and Lee could hear voices, and they seemed far too close. He glanced back and could see the van at the edge of town, almost inconspicuous, and a quarter of a mile too far away for his tastes.

"Well, if you don't have any warrant, I don't see why you are here bothering us at all, officer," someone said rather loudly.

"I'm here to see your pilot," Popovi replied. "When he comes out, we'll see if I have reason to stay here. Your pilot is Peltin, isn't he?"

"I wouldn't know."

"Really? How odd, since you are listed as a student, aren't you Mr. Stillman? And you don't know the pilot's name?"

Oh hell. Lee hadn't expected to find the CEO of Red

Sun himself on that plane. That could be trouble.

"I won't put up with this harassment. I have important friends."

"Many of us do," Popovi answered, and his voice remained calm. "If one of you would ask the pilot to hurry? And if all of you would please keep your hands in sight, it might save us all kinds of unpleasantness."

Lee slipped forward to see how many his friends faced. He could see around the corner and --

Shit.

He pulled back as quickly, and Perez gave him a very curious look. He bent close to the man's ear and whispered, "The two guys standing behind Stillman are the ones who took me out into the desert."

"Bingo. We have them. Peltin is superfluous at this point."

"Maybe so, but they probably murdered Mary Powers," he reminded the man. "And if that's true, this is way past harassment over some land. We need to be careful."

"This is where, we hope, training pays off. Get back to the car, and when I give the signal, turn it on, race the engine, and hit the horn -- but don't come any closer until I signal you again. I'll take that moment of confusion to move in and help Officer Da and Tomas. Hurry, before this goes any farther."

Lee nodded and carefully jogged back to the car, doing his best to be quiet and keep out of the line of sight of the group standing by the shed. By the time he reached his friends, he felt the air suffocating him with the heat -- although panic likely added to the condition.

He climbed into the car, accepting a canteen of water from Father Antonio and quickly sipped before he spoke.

"You ready for some good news? You don't have to

pay the people in London to hunt down whoever is still after you. They work for Red Sun," Lee said. "The two who took me are standing behind Stillman down there."

"Well, hell," Chev said, shaking his head. "That simplifies my problems. I can stop worrying about crazed drug lords, right? What are we doing?"

"Waiting for a sign from Perez. When he waves, Patrice, turn the car on, rev the engine and hit the horn, but don't drive toward them until Perez gives another signal."

"They work for Red Sun," Chev said again. He shifted in his seat. "And my loving wife is the former sister-in-law to the CEO of Red Sun. I suspect I've been looking in the wrong place for who shoved me out in front of the lorry."

"God, Chev," Patrice said. She sounded as shaken as Lee had ever heard her. "I didn't like her much, but I never considered that she might have tried to kill you."

"Neither did I," Chev admitted. "This is looking more and more like a set up from the start. It's lucky, really, that she's in Europe right now."

"There's the signal," Lee said, though he hadn't needed to. Despite being upset, Patrice had kept her eyes on the scene below. The van made enough noise to draw everyone's attention.

Perez darted away from his spot to help Tomas and Da. Perez had his gun in hand already, and that deterred English and Texas from drawing their own, though they did reach.

They had, Lee could tell, taken the group by utter surprise, and it gave him hope until he realized that the plane had started up and began to turn.

Perez fired at the tires, but it didn't stop the craft. In a few heartbeats it had taken off, but it left three rather disgruntled looking men behind.

After Da, Perez and Tomas had searched the three, removing guns from the two kidnappers, and put them all in handcuffs, Perez finally gave the signal. Patrice coasted down the dirt road, hitting the gas a little at the bottom. They pulled up by Tomas and Perez, and Da took that moment to go back to the car, no doubt to call in more help.

Lee saw Mr. Stillman's attention turn from the plane that lifting off into the clear blue skies, and rivet on Chev as he rolled down the window and looked out.

"This is harassment," Stillman said. "I'll sue you."

"Well, we'll see," Chev answered cheerfully. "Seems like you may have your hands full explaining about those two men with you. You know, the ones who kidnapped my employee, and likely murdered a young woman. And then there's all that trouble with Peltin -- they will track that plane, you know. Oh, and the fact that you are the former brother-in-law of my soon to be ex-wife might bring up a few questions as well."

Stillman had reddened right up until the last statement -- and then he went pale and silent. The other two remained devoid of emotion. Professionals, Lee thought, and he was damned glad that Perez and Tomas had guns on them right now.

"I have back up about five miles away," Popovi said as he came back to the others. He smiled a little, hand still on his gun. "Then we'll go somewhere and talk for a while."

Lee frowned. He didn't really want to go talk with police about this. Lee wanted to get out of here and back on the road to the site. He wanted to go back and see everything again, to know it was real.

Instead, a few minutes later they drove up to the small Chimayo Police station and city hall.

"Just as well," Chev finally said as he opened the door. "We don't know where the plane is yet, though I suspect it hasn't gone far, not if it was coming in to refuel. And driving across the desert in midday was never my idea of fun."

"Yeah," Patrice agreed. She didn't sound very sincere, but the others nodded as well. And really, they had no choice.

Hours passed. Lee had to sign so many papers and make so many statements that he started, finally, to get the shakes. It had begun to feel too much like his arrest, and he had the suspicion the local police -- all three of them -- knew it.

The tiny room had only a small fan for air circulation, and it ruffled the papers every time it turned their way. People came and went, whispering to each other, looking glum and angry. Lee began to fear those emotions were turned on him, and he couldn't dismiss the illogical feeling and the panic growing with it.

He must have looked as bad as he felt when Perez came into the room. The cop cursed quietly, signaled the local sheriff over to him, and had a very short, quiet conversation with the man, who then left the room.

"Lee?" Perez said, taking the chair across from him.

"Shit. I'm sorry."

"Are you all right?"

"I can't do any more of this. I need a break. I need out of here." He knew he looked frantic as he glanced around the little room. This was not like the police station where they took him in Boston. Not at all, he told himself, but it didn't help.

"Come on," Perez said. He caught hold of Lee's arm. "Come on."

"What the hell is wrong?" a local cop asked. "Some kind of fit? Drugs? We didn't do anything --"

"I'm taking him out to the SUV. Then I'll be back to answer any more questions you might have."

"Yeah, sure. Whatever."

Lee tried to stand. He couldn't. He looked at Perez with total, unexpected and inexplicable terror.

"Relax. We're going. You want to go?"

"Y-yes."

"Then you better get your ass out of that chair and come with me."

Lee stood with a hand on the table. Perez had headed out the door, and if he didn't follow, he would be trapped here. He rushed to the door, made it out, and his legs gave way in the hall. Perez barely caught him and pushed him against the wall.

"Damn!" Perez cursed. "Tony!"

The priest arrived, caught hold of him under the arm, and helped get him out of the building. The bright light and heat felt like another blow. For a moment he couldn't stand or get his breath.

"Hell, this isn't good," Perez said. "Stupid bastards in there."

"All right," Lee said, his voice barely a whisper. "Stupid, me."

"No, not you." Perez sounded as though he meant it. Lee took one breath and another. He thought he could stand on his own, but when he tried to pull free, neither of them let go. "No. You look like you're going to pass out still. Tony, go back in and get the car keys from Patrice -- try not to alarm Chev. He'll be holy hell on wheels if he sees Lee like this. We'll get him in the car with the AC on, and I think he'll be fine. I'm going to go in and finish up the paperwork here, gather the rest of the gang, and get the hell out of here. We have other places to go."

"What about the plane?" Lee asked.

"Didn't they even tell you that much?" Perez growled while Tony darted away. "It made a forced landing in a field near Taos. Out of gas. Peltin was picked up and is in jail there."

"Ah. Good."

"Yeah. I've heard the police found a crate that had held tear gas canisters, but it was empty. Another black mark," Perez said. He looked toward the mountains and shook his head. "I hope we can get this settled soon."

By the time Tony returned with the keys, Lee could almost stand on his own. The car felt like an oven when they opened the doors, but the AC kicked on, and he settled in the back seat by the priest, forcing calm again.

When he could finally speak without stuttering, he hoped, he looked across at Tony -- Father Antonio -- with a little smile. He sipped from the canteen of tepid water again. "Thanks. I was doing fine, but ... do you know anything about my past?"

"Yeah. Pablo told me about you back after you got dragged out to the desert. You don't live a dull life, do you?"

He had been drinking and now coughed it out in a surprising laugh. "Sorry, sorry," he said, dabbing at his chin. "No, not a dull life, though it really wasn't my choice in any of it."

"If it was your choice, what would you do for excitement?"

"What I've already chosen: I'd work with Dr. Rey. I love archeology here in the Southwest. So much so, I've stuck it out, despite unexpected walking tours of the desert and far too much time with police."

Tony laughed and looked pleased. Lee couldn't decide why. He'd made all kinds of a fool of himself in there. The thought of it nearly set him shaking again.

Tony said nothing, but Lee looked at him and sighed. "I want out of this nightmare," he said. "The best way to do that is to keep walking away from it and going on to do the things I want to do."

"Wise decision. But is there nothing from before you would go back to? Parents? Family?"

"They went away. They never came back." He realized those words sounded very childish, and he frowned and shook his head. "Sometimes it's better to go on, Tony. If I can't have it back, I don't want to keep trying to reach for it. I want a new life. Yes, I miss a lot of my old one. I wish I could see my son again --"

"Son?" he said, eyes gone wide.

"I was married. She's remarried and changed his name. I talked to her after I got out, but she asked me to go away. I said I would. I always keep my word."

Tony nodded and said no more. As a priest, he probably had some strong views on marriage and family, but he didn't say them now. Lee was grateful.

"Did you hear anything else about the plane? Peltin?" Lee asked. "I don't know why they didn't tell me."

"Because they are looking for excitement in their own lives," Tony said. He leaned back, sighing. "This is a really small town, Lee. You have to forgive them. Holding Mr. Stillman was trouble for them. Once his lawyer called, there was no way they were going to risk the wrath and a possible lawsuit --"

"Let him go already?"

"Yes, on bond -- but with the understanding that he

would be in Santa Fe. He left without Trader and Barnes -- those are the two you identified. And he had a hard time getting back to Santa Fe. Peltin would have flown them there after refueling. Stillman had to hire someone locally, and it sure wasn't in the luxury he was accustomed to. So, if it's any consolation, he was at least put out by all of this. He's not out of the woods yet, although he is out of the jail."

"I really didn't think they'd hold any of them for long," Lee said. He shrugged. "There's money on their side. Money always buys a little more freedom."

He nodded. "And you accept such an answer?"

"Right now I want to get this over with so we can get up to the site. It's so incredible, Tony. It's a wonder to be part of this. That's what I'm going to hold on to."

"Good. Leave the police stuff to Pablo. I've seen him when he's mad. It's just as well we got you out of there."

"Mad?"

"Mostly with himself, I think. He'd lost track of you while he dealt with Rey and Stillman. Now there was a meeting. I didn't know Pablo knew such words, and in several languages, too. When Rey asked where you were, the local cops mumbled something about questioning your story on Trader and Barnes."

Lee looked at him, silent for a long moment. Then he nodded. "Thanks."

Tony smiled. "Drink a little more water."

A few minutes later the others began to filter out of the building. Patrice jogged down to the museum and brought Professor Belinato out, filling her in on what had happened as they came back. Tomas opened the door and stood by the car, his eyes watching the area around them while he spoke.

"They'll be holding Trader and Barnes here until we can get proper authority to drag their sorry asses down to Santa Fe or Taos -- it's a toss up right now on which one," Tomas said. "Peltin is already locked up in Santa Fe. Rey is raising Holy Hell over Stillman's release. Your pardon, Padre."

Tony waved it off. "I can imagine."

"They'll all be done in a few minutes," Tomas said. "Popovi is going back on patrol, and I'm going with him to Taos to keep my eye on things. You people have three days up at your site, and then Rey and Lee have to show up in Taos for any more questions. I'll be there with you."

"Thanks, Tomas," Lee said. He offered his hand, and Tomas shook it, smiling brightly. "We'll see you soon."

He nodded and headed toward the state patrol car a few steps behind Officer Da. Lee half wished he could be in on that conversation, but then he saw Chev, who was in the wheelchair, and came to the car ready for a fight. Lee looked at him with shock, wondering what the hell had gone wrong now.

"There you are. Perez told us about that little game they played over there. You all right?"

"Fine," he said. He smiled, which finally calmed Chev and Patrice. "And at least with Stillman grounded, we finally are safe to head up to the site."

Rey nodded and climbed into the car. It didn't take them long before they were heading back past Nambe Pueblo and toward the turn off again. Nothing stopped them this time.

CHAPTER THIRTY-ONE

They reached the camp by late afternoon and found a scene of destruction -- tear gas canisters littered the ground, and it looked as though part of the tent had caught fire. Chev had bought the most expensive, fire-resistant tents and tarps he could find, besides supplying extinguishers, and it was a damned good thing, or most of northern New Mexico would likely be on fire by now.

His initial panic eased when he realized the camp appeared to be abandoned, and he saw no sign anyone had been injured. Stillman was going to have a hell of a lot to answer for when this all came to light.

By the time they got out of the car, he could see Alicia rushing down the trail. She waved happily, and immediately eased Chev's worries.

"You are all okay?" Lee asked.

"Fine," she said, slapping him on the shoulder. "We'd already transferred almost everything up to the new camp. We better move fast. There's no telling when --"

"They won't be back anytime soon. Their pilot is arrested, and their plane grounded for the moment," Chev explained as the other climbed out. "You made the new camp up at Lee's Site?"

"Yeah," she said. "Are you going to try to walk it, Dr. Rey?"

"No. Chair is in the back. We'll take it most of the way," he said. "I've had about as much walking as I care to do for the next few days."

"Wisdom at last," Patrice said. She went to the back and pulled the chair out. "Lee, can you hand down the cases from the top? Then I'll park the SUV under the tarp. No reason to be obvious."

"Alicia, this is Father Antonio, and his brother, Officer Pablo Perez. You know Professor Belinato, right?"

"Yeah. The Professor threatened to fail me in a couple classes," Alicia said with a bright smile.

"She did the same with me," Rey said. He eased himself down into the chair and let Lee get the canes into the holder on the back.

"Yeah, well, if you've messed this site up, I'll do more than fail you this time," she said.

"Oh, don't worry. We've been professional," Alicia replied, still grinning.

"Let's go." Chev looked up the trail. Life looked good right now.

When they reached the new camp, Rey looked down into the narrow ravine. The tent covered tables and bedding, and they had spread sand and debris over the roof, so from the air, it would have been hard to tell the difference. Chico, who joined them on the trail, pointed out the hidden, and ingenious set of ropes and pulleys they had rigged to get their own supplies in and out of the ravine, and which would work very nicely with the wheelchair when they came back to the camp. They lowered the suitcases down to the camp, although both Patrice and Father Tony held on to their bags.

Belinato looked intrigued by the doorways they pointed out below the ridge, and she got down on her knees to look over the edge.

"We'll get back to this," Chico said with a laugh. "You don't want to waste time here."

"Waste time? Those doorways are like nothing I've seen before --"

"Yes, I know," Chico said, offering a hand as she got back to her feet. "But *you don't want to waste time* here."

Belinato took a deep breath and looked up the trail again. Alicia, Lee, and Patrice started out, the others following. They fought the wheelchair over the more difficult areas. Chev knew it wouldn't be long before he walked these paths on his own.

The others met them at the ruins. Belinato had pushed ahead and had already begun examining the walls and staring into the shadowed rooms. She nodded at things Marty said and looked impatient as Patrice introduced Perez and the priest.

"Some of these walls are McElmo style," Belinato said, waving a hand toward the rooms. "That's pretty damned late in construction for a cliff dwelling." Then she laughed. "Yes, yes -- you people already know."

"We have reason to believe this may have been built -- or at least resettled -- very late. People came here after the Spanish had landed in Mexico," Kitt said. They were heading back toward the cavern wall again, and Chev felt his heartbeat picking up. Belinato gave the petroglyphs a few moments, but soon they were into the stone-walled hall and around the corner to the opening. Kitt reached down and flipped a switch to a row of small lights they'd put at the corner of the room.

"Oh," Father Tony whispered.

For a moment everyone stayed quiet. And then Professor Belinato walked into the room and looked around, shaking her head in wonder. "I really didn't think this could be real. Good God! We need to get this documented and bring in some specialists."

"We haven't moved or touched anything since Dr. Rey left," Leanne said. "We've been busy enough relocating the camp, and taking pictures and notes on everything. And besides, we needed Dr. Rey back to translate the journal. I want to know what is in there."

"We all do," Rey said. "But first, Father Tony, if you would?"

Father Antonio stepped forward and knelt by the bones of the fallen Conquistador. Everyone else stood still and waited.

"I'm going to say the prayer twice," Father Tony said. "First in Latin, since this good man would have recognized such a prayer, and then in English."

He opened the bag and laid a cloth on the ground, put a few small items on it. Then he opened a book and placed it in front of him.

*"*Fidélium, Deus, ómnium cónditor et redémptor, animábus famulórumfamulárumque tuárum remissionem cunctórum tribue peccatórum: ut indulgéntiam, quam semperoptavérunt, piis supplicatiónibus consequántur: Qui vivis et regnas insæcula sæculórum. Amen. Réquiem ætérnam dona eis, Dómine. Et lux perpétua lúceat eis. Requiéscant in pace. Amen."* He bowed his head for a moment, sprinkled holy water across the body. "O God, the Creator and Redeemer of all the faithful, grant to the souls of Thy servants departed full remission of all their sins, that, through our devout prayers, they may obtain the pardon which they have always desired. Who livest and reignest, world without end. Amen. Eternal rest

grant unto them, O Lord. And let perpetual light shine upon them. May they rest in peace. Amen."

Amen whispered and echoed around the room. Patrice stepped closer and pulled something from her bag, carefully unwrapping it -- a rather travel-worn, but still fragrant, rose.

"It's not from Spain, but it's still nice," she said and laid it across the Conquistador's chest.

The three days passed far too quickly, and even Father Antonio reluctantly hiked back down to the SUV with his brother, Lee, and Chev. Belinato absolutely refused to leave. She stayed, along with Patrice who had taken over the much-needed computer file updating for the group, although she did walk with them to the car.

"I'll call Tomas as soon as we reach the road," Chev promised again. He reached out and took her hand, and then let go. "Get the work done. I'm going to start making contacts."

They drove back down past the ranch, and Chev called ahead to Tomas, who started out from Taos and met them by the road. When they got there, Popovi was already standing outside his car and waiting.

"What now?" Chev asked as he walked over to the window.

"Things are calm, but we thought we'd be safe," Popovi said, nodding at Lee. "You didn't come back with as many people as you took with you."

"Patrice and the professor are staying for a few more days," Chev said, leaning back in the chair and relaxing again. "We're waiting for Tomas, so we'll ride back to Taos with him, and these two can take the SUV back to their father."

"I'll hang out with you for a few minutes, then," he

said. "Stillman worries us, and there are still things about Peltin that has the force uneasy -- like if he had someone else working with him. So I'll stick around as long as I can. Tomas shouldn't take too long. Things went well on your end?"

"Yeah. Arrange a day off, and I'll take you up there," Chev said. "Before the madness hits."

"Madness?"

Chev grinned, but Tomas arrived before he could say more, and they parted company with the priest and the police officer. People in cars slowed and watched and Chev had to remind himself it was likely the state patrol car and the priest that drew the attention.

Once they were in the van with Tomas, Lee kept watch behind, but he didn't seem to notice anyone following them.

"Any news we should know right away?" Chev asked.

"I heard from your lawyers, and they're being buried in paperwork from Red Sun's people. They've hired someone part time to sort through it. I talked to Smithers in London, and he's redirected the detectives to looking into your wife's background."

"Good plan," Chev said, and barely kept from growling the words.

"Bad news is she's disappeared."

"I want her found, at least long enough to sign the divorce papers."

"I suspected as much. Smithers and his people are on it. We're going to go straight to the Taos police, and they'll fill you in on anything else. How long do you intend to stay in town?"

"Only as long as we have to. I do need to start making arrangements to bring this find out into the open, though.

A private showing first, and then we go public."

"If Red Sun gets word of the find, it's going to be hell. We need more guards. I've arranged to hire a group out of Denver. They should be sufficiently removed from the area so they won't be involved with the local stuff, and I can't find any link between them and Red Sun."

"Good. Excellent!" Chev smiled all the way back to Taos, the three of them coordinating some of the work. He didn't want to stay long in town, and the more they got this worked out, the better.

Chev and Lee went into the police HQ while Tomas stayed guard at the car. They found Lowell inside the building, his hat in hand. He smiled and waved. "Heard you two were heading back in town from Officer De. I was going out to hunt you down."

"Sounds like a line out of a bad b-grade western," Chev protested. He settled on a chair, a bit more tired than he expected. "Anything you want to tell us about what's happened in the last three days?"

"Stillman has everything here put on hold, which means your trip into town was wasted. Sorry. We don't know when you're going to be needed, but it won't be for another week at least."

"That's fine," Chev said. "I don't really care. We had to come back to settle some other matters anyway. Anything else?"

"Well, your wife's lawyers have called several times a day demanding to know where you are," Lowell replied with a bit of a snarl. He leaned back against the wall. "Off at the dig didn't cut it with them either. They wanted an exact location. Since they called from Europe, we thought it wasn't really necessary they know, even if we did. They're threatening lawsuits."

"Are they?" Chev said. He leaned forward. He had feared dealing with his wife would make him maudlin, but suddenly he felt angry. "Did they happen to leave a number?"

"Yeah," Lowell said. "Are you going to call?"

"Oh no. I pay someone big money to do that for me," Chev said. He pulled out his billfold and handed over a card to the Santa Fe law firm. "Have someone here call and relate all the conversations to them. I'll send word that I want it handled."

Lowell took the card and grinned. "Looks like we're no longer on the run, huh?"

"Right. Time to turn the dogs loose," Chev said. "Or the sharks. Anything else?"

"Stillman got Trader and Barnes out. Damn high bail, though."

"On a kidnapping charge?"

"There was some irregularity with the paperwork from Chimayo, and we suspect some money might have bought the problems with the reports. Those two are down in Santa Fe and not supposed to leave the city, although Stillman and his lawyers have arranged for them to come here to Taos for various reasons related to the case. Be careful. We're still trying to find the links to tie those two to the Powers murder, and we think we're getting closer, thanks to help from some detectives of yours in London."

"Glad they could help," Chev said and didn't glance at Lee this time.

"Beyond that, things were quiet at the museum."

"Won't be for long," Chev said. "I'm calling in a few other archaeologists and maybe some reporters. We have work to do. I'll have everyone here on Friday. It's probably going to be a circus, so I thought I ought to warn you. Once I go public with the find, there's going to be more traffic through here than in peak tourism season."

"Oh." He didn't look as happy.

"I'm going to look at building down in the area, later." Chev stood. He wanted back to the site as soon as he could get everything settled. "We're going to the museum, and then we'll do some shopping -- and then we're heading for the backcountry again."

"Already?" Lowell looked surprised.

"There's a damned lot of field work to be done before Friday," Chev said. "And, to be honest, I really don't want to stick around here any longer than I have to. It seems safer up there."

"Well, it's certainly quieter down here when you people are gone," Lowell said, and still smiled. "But I'll be glad when you have this matter settled. One last thing you need to know: Stillman has made it clear he intends to start working on his dream city within the month. I assume that means he doesn't think the fact you own the land is any problem."

"Damn. Okay, I better check into it." Chev glanced at Lee and frowned. "Let's go. Looks like we have a hell of a lot more to do than I thought."

"We? It's your land," Lee pointed out as he went to the door and pushed it open. "Hell, I haven't been here long enough to get a license yet."

"Do take care of that, Lee," Lowell called out as they left.

Chev laughed. They headed back around the corner from the station, discussing what they needed to do next. And then Lee stopped, a hand to Chev's arm as a limo came to a stop between them and the van. Tomas had already gotten out of the van as three men climbed from the limo and came toward Chev and Lee. Another headed for Tomas.

"Lee go back --"

"No. They have Tomas cut off. I'm not leaving you. But they'd be fools to try anything in the police parking lot -- and damned desperate."

The three men cut them off so quickly Chev would have fallen if Lee hadn't caught hold of his shoulder and steadied him.

"Dr. Rey, we'd like to have a few words with you."

"Write me a letter," he said.

"Mr. Stillman has an offer to make. If you would come this way? He's in the car."

"No," Rey said. One of the men reached for him, and Lee slapped the hand away.

The other two grabbed Lee. They must have thought it wouldn't take more than one to take on Chev, but he proved them wrong. It was amazing how fast the man danced back out of the way after being hit across the shins with one of the canes.

Lee, Chev noted, had no trouble snaking out of the holds of the other two. Shame about getting those nice, fancy suits all messed up. And Stillman stepped out of the limo. He brushed at his immaculate gray pinstriped suit as though letting it out into the air was a bother. He walked over to Chev with the gliding step of a man owned the world.

"Mr. Rey -- so sorry about --"

"Dr. Rey," he corrected.

"Dr. Rey," Stillman repeated. He met Chev's look without flinching. "I'm sorry if my people were out of line. They were meant to direct you toward the car. I would like to have a few words. If you don't mind?"

"I do mind. You have nothing at all to say that I give a flying fuck about."

Stillman's cheeks colored. Good.

"I am offering you four million dollars for your land. That's far more than it would ever be worth to anyone else."

"You can't buy it. The land is not for sale. You could offer me four billion and immortality, and I wouldn't take it, you stupid bastard. This has nothing to do with money. Oh, and be sure to tell my wife to stop calling, will you? I'm sure you talk to her far more often than I do."

His face colored and then went ash white, which was a strange reaction he kept having whenever Chev mentioned his wife. However, he backed away now, as though for the first time he took Rey seriously -- and that bothered Chev as well. The man had been trouble enough before this; he didn't like to think things were about to get worse.

On the other hand, Chev knew he was about to cause trouble for Stillman. So far, Red Sun didn't seem to think that they were dealing with anything more important than some crumbling walls and a few broken bits of pottery. Once Dr. Cheveyo Rey made his announcement, the perception would drastically change. He smiled at the thought.

"Trouble here?" Lowell said walking up behind them and startling Chev.

"No trouble," Stillman said, and signaled his men back to the car. They began to head that way.

"Unless we press charges for attacking us," Lee said. Chev looked back at him, surprised. "I'm damned tired of finding you people everywhere I go."

"You want them arrested?" Lowell asked, reaching for his radio.

"Yes, I think --"

Stillman's group had climbed into the limo and left so quickly Lowell barely had his radio in hand. Lee gave him a subtle sign to hold up. Odd game. Chev couldn't quite figure out what he wanted.

"They're going to think we want them arrested," Lee said once the car had gone. "I don't want to spend the rest of the day doing reports and answering questions, just to have Stillman bail everyone out again. However, as long as they think they're in trouble, they're likely to stay clear of us, Chev."

"Oh. Good point!" Chev said, grinning again.

Lowell looked more inclined to arrest the group, but they had already disappeared down the road. "We'll keep an eye on you two while you're here. No use doing anything stupid now."

Chev agreed. He had a hell of a lot of people to talk to in the next few hours, and then he wanted to leave Taos as quickly as they could. Once Stillman heard Chev had a big announcement to make, he feared they would get aggressive again. Chev wanted himself and Lee out of their reach.

Once they finally reached the museum, he put Lee to work gathering equipment to take back with them, while he made call after call to people who owed him. It was interesting to see which ones happily jumped into the morass with him, even when he explained the dangers -- but would not tell them the reward as well. He was not going to let any hint of what they'd found get out.

He also called the places where he had sent a few items for study. Preliminary reports would reach him via email no latter than Friday morning. Everything seemed to be falling into place at last.

Four hours later he had arranged for flights and transportation from Albuquerque to Taos for everyone who agreed to come. On Friday morning the people he wanted to see would be at the museum. In some ways, he regretted they would no longer have this wonderful site all their own.

When he came into Patrice's office, he found Lee on the phone as well, which seemed odd. Lee grinned and gave a thumb's up. There was a new bruise on his cheek. If Chev had realized the bastards had actually hit Lee --

He could see Tomas out in the hall, watching people down in the museum. Well, with luck he'd be done babysitting them soon. Maybe. What if they annoyed Stillman so much he swore a vendetta and never left them alone again? What if --

"That's it," Lee said, putting down the phone. "I called the grocery store and told them exactly what we need. They'll have it boxed up and ready when we get there. That's going to save a lot of time, though it will cost a few dollars more."

"Damn smart move," Chev said. He looked around at the packs Lee had lined up by the wall. "You're good at this."

"I'm anxious to get back."

Chev understood. He and Lee were about as much alike as two people could be without being born of the same blood. Actually, his own family had never been much like him.

Lee and Thomas took out the packages from the museum, and then the three drove out and picked up the supplies, Lowell in the car behind them. Tomas helped Lee check the boxes and load the van, but then he headed back to the museum again to field any trouble and get ready for

Friday -- and to have someone who could keep watch for trouble from Stillman and his group.

Lowell honked at the edge of town. Chey waved, and Lee honked in return. They were on their own again. He tried not to feel nervous about it, but he did see Lee was also looking in the mirror, expecting trouble.

CHAPTER THIRTY-TWO

Lee glanced in the mirror again. "I don't see anyone, but you know, I just don't trust it."

"Yeah." He saw Chev shift a little in the seat. "I hate being paranoid."

"Me, too." Lee looked up at the sky and frowned. "Nothing. In some ways, I'd prefer to see them so I knew where they were. Since they found the old camp, they think they don't have to follow us anymore."

"This is either going to be over very soon -- or get a lot worse," Chev admitted. "I'm betting on it being over. I'm betting everything on it, in fact. After Friday, we won't have any secrets anymore, Lee."

Lee felt a little surge of emotion at the statement, and couldn't quite decide if it was excitement or fear. "Yeah, but we'll have a hell of a lot more people interested in what's going on. Red Sun isn't going to want to look bad in front of the whole world."

"That's what I hope." He shifted in the seat and Lee gave him a curious and worried look. "I'm okay, but I'll be glad to get where I can rest without everything bouncing all over hell again."

"Should have gone to see your doctor while we were

still in town. We really didn't have to race back --" He had
started to slow down, clearly with the intention of turning
back.

"We go back there now, and Lowell will shoot us."

"Chev--"

"No. Keep going. I'm fine. A bit sore and ready for a
break -- but I'll take it at the camp where I'll enjoy myself."

"Out there with the snakes, the scorpions, sand, dust,
and a damn lot of heat. I'm from the East Coast,
remember."

"I forgot. You've taken to this place like a native,"
Chev said. Lee grinned back at him. He knew Chev hadn't
lied, and it felt good to belong somewhere again. "I take it
you intend to stick around for awhile, right?"

"Yeah. I like the work."

"And people think I'm crazy."

Lee laughed. Then he glanced up at the sky again, still
looking worried. "I know Peltin is grounded, but he's not
the only pilot in the state. And our friends are desperate
since they made their announcement."

"I did call my stockbroker, and she suggested I grab as
much of the Red Sun stock as I can. It's soaring. I told her
I wouldn't give money to that company if they were the last
company on the market and I could make a million a
share."

"You know, you're the first rich person I've ever
known," Lee said. He saw Chev squirm a little. "At least
known well. What makes you so different from Stillman?"

"The land," he said. "The way I was raised, the fact I
chose to hold on to my roots and believe in the old ways --
at least to some degree. And you want to know something?
Right now those old ways are telling me we're still going to
face trouble."

"Damn." Lee looked in the mirror again, but he could find nothing out of place. Two semis's followed behind them, loaded with construction equipment, and they had slowed the other traffic. Lee kind of liked having them there, like a solid wall between their car and the others.

"Lee -- would you consider going back to college for a degree in archeology? I'd like to formally put you in charge of some of the stuff here, and I don't want any questions later about whether you are qualified. You're too damn talented, and you love the work to well, not to be given the full chance you would have with a formal education. All right? If you go back to college, you won't be tied to this single dig forever -- or as long as it's in my care. I'm going to pay your way through. And don't argue with me."

"I will certainly argue with you about it --"

"Don't," Chev said softly, and the tone stopped Lee. "Don't argue. Let me do this. I love this work, and I know you do, too. I know you could put yourself through college -- eventually. But this way you can get on with it, still work for me, and neither of us loses time. You want a real truthful answer about why I want this, Lee?"

"Yes." He looked into the mirror again, and then glanced at Chev.

"I trust the people out at the camp. I trust Patrice. I don't trust a hell of a lot of others. Once we open this up, we're going to need people who are qualified to handle this site, and who are above question. I called the college and had them send info to the museum. We'll go over it after this madness and see how we can spread the classes out."

"And I don't have any say?"

"Sure. But if you stick around, we're going to be arguing about it at every turn. Better to give in now and get it over with."

"I can be very stubborn."

"You don't think I've figured that out? So, you want to specialize in Pre-Pubolean or something more esoteric?"

Lee looked at him, looked at the road, looked at the mirror. Then he sighed and felt a little surge of excitement and fear. Maybe it was how people were supposed to feel when they took chances on life again.

"Tell me my options," he said.

They spent the rest of the drive going over various disciplines and sub-categories. Lee couldn't help but get excited about the possibilities. By the time they reached the turnoff to the ranch, Chev had decided he was going to take a few more courses as well. He said he was old enough to appreciate them now.

They reached the turnoff, and Lee pulled the car up into the drive and started to step out --

"Son of a bitch! Look at the trucks!" Chev shouted and pulled himself out of the car.

The semis which had been following them had Red Sun logos on the side. The first truck driver honked twice as he went past, already slowing. At the curve ahead they could see a makeshift road from the highway and a parking lot filled with crates, bulldozers, and a couple campers. They could not have been there more than an hour, Lee thought. They were still unpacking things.

"That's my land, the bastards!" Chev shouted. He pulled out his phone and snarled. "I'm in a damned node, but my service isn't working. I suspect I would have heard about this from the ranch by now if it was."

"Is it not working or is it disconnected?" Lee asked.

"Damn good question. Maybe someone didn't want me to know they were setting up camp here."

"There's a state patrol car," Lee said, shielding his eyes

as he looked. "Not Popovi's."

"Let's go have a few words with them," Chev said, getting back into the car. Lee had half expected him to walk there.

Lee turned the car around and headed back onto the freeway and into the new lot. The state patrolman was standing at the front of a semi and apparently arguing with someone. It looked good. Lee got out of the car, and Chev followed almost as quickly.

"I want you people off my land," Chev warned. "And I want you off in the next half hour, or you're all going to be spending more time in jail than you really want to think about."

Lee grinned. People had begun backing away. Chev looked dangerous when he was mad.

Something made Lee stop and glance back at the road. They'd come down a little dip, and he couldn't see the highway clearly from here. And no one up there could see them --

"Chev --"

The state patrol officer moved toward Chev. Peltin -- his hat pulled down enough so Lee hadn't recognized him. Lee leapt forward, panicked --

Peltin slugged Chev right before Lee bowled the officer over, but he hadn't a chance to do more than knock him down. Someone else came along and pulled him off.

And Stillman stood there in his gray suit, immaculate even in the dusty camp they had made. He grinned.

"I knew something this blatant would pull you like a magnet," he said. He gave a signal. Trader and Barnes came out from behind a truck. "Get them in their car, and get rid of them -- somewhere far enough out in the wilderness that they aren't a problem for me every again.

No more games."

Lee started to stand, but a blow to the back of his head put him down in the sand.

CHAPTER THIRTY-THREE

Chev had no idea where they were or how long they'd been on the road, bouncing around in the back of an SUV. At some point, he had found the knot on the rope around Lee's wrists, and began working at getting it untied. He thought Lee might be conscious enough to know what he was doing. Chev sure as hell hoped so because Trader and Barnes had already said they were far enough out in the desert.

They were not going to have many chances to survive this mess. Damn, Chev knew he had been stupid to fall into such an obvious trap. Why had he felt so damn safe --

His fingers slipped on the ropes as they hit another bump.

"The bloody road has gone to hell. This is far enough."

The car began to slow.

God, God -- he caught the rope again and worked at the knot, trembling. Trader got out of the car and Barnes followed, slamming the door. There was no doubt what they'd do. They'd killed Mary Powers, after all.

"Lee --"

"You nearly have the rope undone."

The steady sound of his voice calmed Chev. And he heard Barnes say he had to answer the call of nature. Praise God. A moment longer.

The rope loosened.

"I don't have time to untie you," Lee said, his voice soft as he moved slightly. "I'm going to try and take them when they open the door. Chev --"

He had no chance to say anything more. Barnes came back and yanked the door open. Lee stayed still with his hand behind his back.

"End of the ride, boyos," Trader said with a laugh. "Damn glad to finally do this job right."

They grabbed Chev first, yanking him out with a hand under his arm. He hit his legs and went limp, hoping it at least slowed them --

He didn't see Lee make the first move. He heard Barnes' muffled grunt before the man tumbled into Chev and Trader. They all went down.

Chev used his elbows and his knees to try to keep Trader down. He saw Lee kick Barnes hard in the groin, and the man doubled over before Lee grappled for the gun. Chev's own ploy worked until Trader got hold of the ropes around Chev's arms and nearly yanked his shoulders out of the sockets --

Gun shot.

Trader let go of Chev, stumbled and fell to his knees, blood running from his shoulder. He looked stunned. His hand moved --

"You go for that gun, and I'll shoot you again," Lee said, his cold, calm voice stilling Trader's move. "Barnes, untie Chev."

"Why the hell should I --"

"Because if you don't, I'm going to shoot you and go

do it myself. Now, which would you prefer?"

Chev rolled over on his side, watching Trader while Barnes untied him. His back hurt like hell, and he didn't think he could walk, but since he hadn't thought they would live this long --

Trader's hand suddenly snaked into his jacket -- and Lee fired. The man tumbled backward, moaning, but still alive.

Barnes rushed at Trader, and would have a gun in hand. Lee fired as Chev threw himself under the car, shimmying his way to the other side. Lee had darted around the side of the car as well.

"I think I hit Barnes too," he said, quickly untying Chev. "But he kept going. He has a gun. Let's get away from the car. I looked -- they took the damned keys. We can't take it, so we better get away."

"I don't know if I can walk."

Lee leaned down and Chev threw his arm over his friend's shoulder. He made it to his feet, and his legs held, though he didn't have the coordination to stay there. Chev could hear the other two -- Trader saying he had to get to a hospital. He thought Barnes might be agreeing.

Lee tried to get he and Chev away from the car, but they almost immediately bogged down in the sand and brush, so he moved back to the hard-packed dirt of the road, where they might make some distance.

The van's engine started and revved.

"Good. Let them go," Chev said. "We need to get away --"

"Damn!"

Lee yanked him off to the side, and Chev looked to see the backup lights as it racing toward them.

Lee shoved him aside, tried to follow -- but he heard

the dull thud of flesh and metal -- a sound that had haunted him since the accident in London.

Lee landed in the dirt beside him, but he rolled and came up with the gun and fired it at the driver spun the car, hit the gas, and headed back past them, dust filling the air the sound of the engine like a jet. Barnes drove -- tried to swerve to get them, but nearly got bogged down in the sand.

Then they drove away. Chev watched for more than a minute, holding his breath while the car lights swept up to a mesa top, across, and down.

Gone. Lightning danced across the horizon, and thunder shook the air. He could smell rain close by. He hoped they were all right at the camp.

Wished he was there.

"I think we need to get away from here. They'll c-come back," Lee said. He sat up, his left arm tight to his chest. "Yes, the arm is broken. Damn. We're in trouble, Chev. Once they get back to Stillman --"

"I know. I need to find something I can use for a cane or crutch. We can use a belt as a sling for your arm." He sat there for a moment, letting his eyes adjust to the dark. He could still hear the distant drone of the car. "I have no fucking idea where we are."

"Ah, well." Lee moved carefully, shifting a little. "I do know we're not in our graves, so I really don't care where else we might be. I walked out of a place like this once before, and without a clue what I was doing. We can do it again. It will be better with the company."

"Oh yeah." Chev finally began to crawl forward. "We're in an arroyo. There might be some deadwood washed up I can use."

"You can still lean on me."

"Let's try for a cane, first. I'll probably need you as well. Here." He pulled his belt off and as carefully as he could, got it around Lee's neck and arm. He could see the swelling below the left elbow which was a bad spot since the belt would rub against it. He ended up taking off his shirt and using it to help brace the arm as well. Maybe they could do better -- after they got at least a little distance from here.

They both got to their feet. It looked harder for Lee than for Chev. Maybe it was because Chev had righteous indignation on his side.

"Do we follow the road where they went?" Lee asked.

"We don't dare. They could turn around. Hell, for all we know, Stillman might have followed them and is waiting a couple miles away. We need to go. Down the arroyo for a distance and then up."

"It's storming," Lee said, and thunder shook the world again.

"I know, and I'll be pissed as hell if we suddenly get caught in a flash flood and drown, but this is the fastest way we can make distance and stay out of sight. You up to it?"

Lee nodded. Chev put his arm across Lee's shoulders, and they began to walk. It wasn't difficult with the adrenaline still surging through his body.

"I'm sorry I dragged you into the ambush, Lee. That was damned stupid to head straight to them."

"We were both damned stupid. Let's hope we survive this and give Patrice a chance to lecture us about it."

"Yeah. Damn. She's in danger, too. They all are, as soon as Stillman finds them."

"I hope Perez and Father Tony stay safe. All of them."

Chev's misstep nearly took them both down, but they stayed on their feet. They kept going.

And it wasn't so bad, as long as they could talk to each other through the long night.

They walked, rested, walked -- Chev found a branch shaped by water and sand that worked well as a cane, but he still had to keep his arm on Lee's shoulder. He regretted it at first but then began to believe it helped keep Lee moving.

Walk and walk. They spoke about classes, about the site, about the museum.

Dawn came, at last, after the longest night of Cheveyo's life, but he had walked his way through it with a friend. The storm had washed over them, in the metaphysical and literal ways. They'd climbed out of the arroyo then rather than tempt fate.

As the light of dawn came up over the land, Chev looked up to see a hawk heading in the direction they had been walking, and he knew it was a sign, and he took pleasure in it.

They rested, though neither of them dared to sit. Chev studied the area around them.

"Lee, I know this place. This is Sanista Canyon. This is the land where I grew up. I can get us to the pueblo long before the desert can kill us -- if we're careful."

Lee grinned and straightened. They started walking again, which proved easier in the light of day.

"You been out to Chaco?" Chev asked.

"Haven't had a chance," Lee answered. His voice sounded scratchy, reminding Chev how much he wanted a glass of cool water, and how long and hot they were going to get before they got near one.

"We'll go after we get this mess settled. I haven't been to Chaco or Mesa Verde in a few years. Time I went back. Those were the places I visited that finally woke up the love of this history in me."

"You were born and raised in a pueblo, though, right? And you didn't feel it there?"

"That's where I was born and grew up, but for me, it was just home. I feel differently about it now, but back then it was the place where anyone with ambition wanted to leave. What kind of place did you grow up in?"

Lee took several steps in silence, and Chev wondered if he would answer about his own childhood. If he had stopped and thought about it, he never would have asked. It couldn't be pleasant, remembering a life with a family that had since abandoned him.

"Lee --"

"My parents didn't speak much English," he said. Chev couldn't see his expression, though his voice remained calm. "For a long time, we lived in an area of New York where you heard little English at all. And the food ... I really hadn't thought much about the food until now. Souvlaki, baklava, real gyros. When I was ten, we went back to Greece to visit family, and it shocked me, the differences. My brother -- he was sixteen -- didn't like it at all. He had lived in America too long and liked the comforts. The week we spent on one of the islands -- I got to climb all over some ruins and help herd goats. If my parents had said they were staying, it wouldn't have bothered me at all. But we came back to America. They had ambitions for my brother and me. My brother went into contracting -- the hands-on side of building. I was supposed to be the one who went to college and learned how to design buildings to make my father proud."

"Did they really believe you had killed someone?"

A coyote sang to the rising sun and danced away ahead of them. They paused, watching him disappear into the brush. Then Lee started to walk again.

"I like to think they didn't believe, but I don't know," he finally admitted. "My father believed in law and justice and the American way. He couldn't believe American Justice, for which he had dreamed and slaved his whole life, could do wrong -- so he had to believe I was guilty. But you know -- as much as he embraced America and loved it, he still left after the trial and went back to Greece. So I think, maybe, he had some real doubts he could never say aloud, or admit to himself. And my mother -- well, she loved him very much. I saw her in court the day they found me guilty. She looked twenty years older. I don't like to think about what this did to her."

"And your brother?"

"My father and brother were very close. I think, in the end, he probably had to abandon me or lose my parents. Under the circumstances --"

"Under the circumstances, you were the one who needed him more."

"No. Under the circumstances, I was already dead to them. I was never coming back out of hell. I don't blame any of them for anything. It's not worth blaming people and being bitter. I don't want to drag what happened into my new life. I've done everything I can to forgive them, Chev -- and to forgive my former wife. I want to get past the nightmare, and the one of prison. When they killed Mary -- that brought it all back to the surface again."

"Lee --"

"Let me talk it out," he whispered. "Let me say it and get it out because I can't stand to have this shadow sitting there any longer. Though this may not be the time --"

"There's never going to be a good time to talk about something like this," Chev said. "You're right. Talk it out now. No one else is around."

"I'm sorry. It's not fair to you --"

"That's not what you're worried about. You're afraid I'm going to judge you because of what happened," Chev said. "It's not going to happen. It's not like I didn't know you were troubled."

"I thought I was doing well," he said, his voice showing a hint of worry and upset.

"You've done damn well. But you lived at my house for a while. You have hellacious nightmares, Lee. Sometimes you shout in them."

"Oh. Yeah. I wake up in cold sweats nearly every night. I didn't realize it was more. Shit. At the camp, too?"

"Yeah."

"So everyone knows."

"Yes, they do. Did it make a bit of difference in how anyone treated you?"

Silence for a long moment. "No. Not at all."

"Then get it out. And if this doesn't help, we'll find some way that does."

"You are not responsible for my well being."

"Yes I am," Chev replied and drew a startled, worried look. "I made myself responsible the moment you picked up the first potsherd in the museum because I could see you come alive with it in your hand, and I hadn't seen it in anyone else before -- except for me. My people believe in ties that have nothing to do with blood. Leander Constantinos -- I had three older brothers. One died drunk falling off a cliff near the pueblo. Another died in a shootout with the police over a damn stolen car. When I was twelve, I asked the last one why they kept dying. He told me they died because they couldn't see anything else in their futures. They were going to live and die just what they were, and they couldn't see any reason to drag it out. And I remember he looked down at me and said I had all their dreams and all their ambition. They gave them to me because I was always to be something more. And then he went out and shot himself in the head the next day."

"Oh hell, Chev. I never -- I thought, somehow, you'd -- you don't need to listen to me --"

"What I need is to know someone else has dreams like mine, and I didn't steal them from my brothers. I need to know that if I couldn't help them, I can still help someone else. Tell me the story. And then we can talk about the future and college and the site. It's time both of us stop holding on to the past, and do things for ourselves, instead of trying to appease the ghosts or bury the darkness."

"I don't want to relive the years in prison. They're starting to fade, you know since I went to work for you." Lee looked at him, a quick movement of his head. "They put me in a prison with people who were never going to see the light of day again. Not people doing hard time -- people doing *life.* I was there for five years, and my choices were to be alone in solitaire and deal with the guard on the days when he felt mean or go back in with the rest of the community. I was young, small, and I knew what I was going to face if they put me back with the others. Solitaire gave me hours of dignity. They let me have some books. I tried not to think about the years passing -- fifty or sixty of them, with nothing but the books, the silence, and a sadistic guard now and then. Then one day the prison warden walked into my cell and said I was free to go. I couldn't trust them. I thought it was another of their damned games. So when I stepped out, I ran. I wanted away as far as I could get. I wanted to go home to my wife and child and heal. I didn't get to, but I finally got here. I think, oddly, this is where I was always meant to be."

Silence, except for the crunch of sand beneath their feet.

"You know the one good thing about this, Lee?"

"Aside from the fact, I'm becoming an expert at desert survival?"

Chev laughed. His throat felt so dry it almost hurt. "We're going to have the satisfaction of seeing Stillman get exactly what he deserves, Lee. You know, I'm looking forward to it almost as much as I look forward to working at the site in peace."

"That's assuming we're going to survive this," Lee said.

"Oh, we'll survive. We're too damned stubborn not to. And besides, if we don't, Stillman wins. I'm not going to let it happen."

"How far do we have to go?"

"At the rate, we're moving -- probably another ten or twelve hours walk to the pueblo."

Lee nodded. They kept walking.□

CHAPTER THIRTY-FOUR

The sun stood high above them. Lee had noted it moving all day without looking at it as he watched his shadow change. He hoped Chev guided them. He had lost the strength to look up. They had nothing more to talk about.

"What the hell?" Chev whispered.

Lee lifted his head. His neck hurt. He saw movement ahead of them, something too fast, inhuman, and strange. Dust and heat waves rose around them. And thunder --

"Hell. Horses," Chev said. His fingers tightened on Lee's shoulders. "Riders."

"Trouble?"

"You know -- I don't think so," he answered. His voice sounded scratchy, and his hand shook as he lifted it. "I think they're my people, *Kimo Sabe.*"

Lee tried to laugh, but the movement hurt. The riders came quickly, and he could hear shouts now. They brought dust with them, but two men slid off the horses before they were fully stopped.

"Cheveyo! I thought Grandfather was crazy when he sent us out here to find you and your friend. Damn those people! Give me the canteen! Broken arm?"

"Yeah, he broke his arm," Chev said. He looked stunned, and he would have fallen as he took his arm off of Lee's shoulder, but one of the others caught him. Someone took hold of Lee, too. "Careful. He's not had the best few weeks since he came to work for me."

"Now you know why you can't hire any of us," another said. The others laughed.

"Grandfather sent you?" Chev said as he took a canteen and sipped. Someone held another one to Lee's mouth, and he drank, grateful for the tepid water.

"Yeah. Grandfather would have come himself, but he had to go to the State House."

"Pardon?"

"He said to make sure the two of you got down there as soon as we found you. Ready to ride?"

Lee realized, suddenly, they were rescued. They weren't going to have to walk the rest of the way to civilization, although the idea of riding a horse did not exactly appeal to him. He sipped the water again, caring more about it than anything else.

Another pulled out a phone and talked to someone on the other end. Lee wanted to sit down. They wouldn't let him.

"You're going to ride with David," Chev told him, a hand on his arm to get his attention. "I'll ride with Mark. We're going to head for the highway, where state troopers are going to meet us. Stillman is already in Santa Fe for a meeting some government people, and Grandfather wants us there --"

"Let's go," Lee said, piecing some of the situation together, realizing they needed to stop the bastard.

"We can drop you at the hospital --"

"No. Let's go. I want to see this. You owe me that

much, Chev."

"You're crazy, but I understand. Let's get you up on a horse. Careful."

The rescue proved to be a rather unpleasant introduction to horseback riding. Lee hoped it didn't put him off it forever because he had always thought it might be fun to ride out in the countryside. Right now he concentrated on not jarring his arm any worse while they moved over the land of rolling desert hills, across a small dry stream, up the far side and on again. Lee closed his eyes. He hadn't intended to lay his head back on David, but the man didn't complain.

The others talked around him. He heard snippets of conversation but didn't try to follow what they said, lost in the haze of pain and wondering if they would ever stop.

He heard cars and lifted his head as they topped a little rise and came out on the edge of the highway, startling someone in a pickup who swerved, honked and gave them the finger as he kept going.

"Idiots think they own the world," Chev said.

"They do own it," David said. He patted Lee's shoulder. "You still with us?"

"Almost."

"Damn hard ride for someone with a broken arm. How are you doing, Chev?"

"Better for me than walking."

"I don't know why you've put up with this shit from these people. I'd have been counting coupe by now."

"Oh, the thought crossed my mind. But I decided on the high road a long time ago, for all the good it's done me."

"We're about a mile from the Gorge where we'll meet your friends," David said. "Easier riding here along the road, at least."

A couple other cars went by, and people stared. Lee wondered if they thought him another of the tribe. He was dark enough at least, and it felt odd -- it made him feel as though he belonged to something again.

By the time they reached the bridge, Popovi had come at a run, followed closely by Tomas and Perez. It looked like a reunion.

"You two are going to give me a damn heart attack!" Popovi said. "You're a full-time job just by yourselves! The minute I found out your cell phone was disconnected, I knew there was trouble."

Lee watched as Chev slid down from the horse beside him. People gathered, taking pictures again. They must have looked like quite a sight.

"Okay, swing your leg over and let me take your weight," Tomas said. "Lee? Are you listening?"

"Oh. Sorry."

"Shit. We need to get Lee to a hospital."

"Santa Fe," Lee replied. "I'm going to Santa Fe with Chev. I want to see these bastards when we show up."

"Are you masochistic?" Tomas asked.

"Maybe." He finally swung his leg over and slipped down. It really wasn't so bad after all he'd gone through already. "You have any aspirin? Maybe some ice?"

"I've already radioed Holy Cross Hospital in Taos," Popovi said. "They're going to be ready for you, but I said they had to make sure the arm was stabilized, and we were taking you on to Santa Fe. We have time. We don't know exactly where Stillman is right now, but we know where he will be in three hours -- trying to talk some government people into signing away Chev's land."

"And that's where we nail the bastards once and for

all," Chev said. Tomas kept Chev to his feet as they walked to the cars -- but it looked likely he could have stood there on his own right now.

Lee turned around and held up his hand to David, who looked startled and reached down, fingers locking around his. "Thanks."

"I'd say anytime, but I don't think you really want to do this again, right?"

"Right. Though I would like to learn to ride a horse. This was my first time."

"Get Chev to bring you out to my ranch. Later, when you're ready for it."

"I'll bring him. Thanks, David."

"No problem. Hey, take this." He slipped off his shirt and tossed it to Chev. "You can't go the capital looking like a savage."

Chev laughed. "Thanks. One last problem everyone -- we need to make certain Stillman didn't get to the people at the site. It's back in the hills. Do you have a car, Perez? You're the only one who has been there."

"Nothing that will make it back into the canyons," he said. "I'll pick something up in Taos and go out--"

"Or you could ride with us," David offered. "Horses can get there fast."

"I'll owe you, David. Patrice is out there. She's going to want to come back --"

"She rides well. We'll get her back."

Lee had the feeling David fully understood Chev's worries. David pulled Perez up behind him, and then gave a lift of his chin in a little salute as the group turned and rode away. It was a good show, but Lee was as glad to turn around and head for the Popovi's car. In a moment he and Chev settled in the back. Air conditioning, soft seats --

heaven. Tomas brought an ice pack and some aspirin and water that he'd gotten from tourists.

"You want to tell me what happened?" Popovi said.

"Yeah -- but I want you to drive while I tell you," Chev said.

"I'll ride and take notes," Tomas offered.

"Wake me up when we get there," Lee said. He settled his head against the corner of the seat and the window and fell asleep before they got turned around on the bridge.□

CHAPTER THIRTY-FIVE

C hev told them everything he could about the encounter with Stillman, including how stupid he had been to walk right into it. Popovi called in other information about Trader and Barnes, the SUV, and gunshot wounds. Chev wondered if they would ever catch the two.

"Okay, so here is what has happened on our side," Tomas said, looking into the back seat. "First, your wife is in Santa Fe, preparing to sign away all your lands."

"It will never stand up," Chev said with a snarl.

"Well, it probably would have stood up long enough if you never showed up to disputed it," Popovi replied. "I've checked into it -- hell, they've had so many people check into it in the last two days that the law firm started getting snippy."

"But it was still going on," Chev said.

"She's your legal wife."

"I have my London firm working on the divorce. I already had them cut her off from my bank accounts. I forgot to say the same thing to the lawyers in Santa Fe. I never expected her to come near New Mexico again. Stupid mistake."

"We can get this stopped without you two being there," Tomas said glancing from one to the other. "Now that we have this story, there is no way anything they do will be legal, you know."

"I know," Chev said. He looked at Lee -- but Lee lifted his head and shook it. "Hell, Tomas -- we need to see this to the end. Both of us."

Tomas shook his head and looked at his watch. "We should get there in time for the big show."

"I don't get it," Popovi said. "They can't possibly think this would stand up, even if you never turned up. You've talked to too many people, and I don't know what the hell you've found in your mountains --"

"The burial of a conquistador who escaped from the bloodshed at Montezuma's death and Cortez's escape, and made his way all the way here with Aztec treasures he was keeping out of Cortez's hands. And it looks likely there is an Aztec prince buried in the next room from him, but we haven't opened it up. We want experts on hand when we do."

Popovi slowed the car and pulled over to the side. He turned around, pulling off his sunglasses as though to look more clearly at Cheveyo.

"You're serious. And you haven't let word of this out yet?"

"We just found it a few days ago. And I wasn't going to let it out when I had Red Sun breathing down my neck. I want the site safe, and these people have no respect for life, so how can I expect them to have respect for history? I've already arranged to make everything public on Friday. Can you get the day off? You can come up with the archeologists. We're going to have a real party."

"I'll try to be there. I hope you and Lee are up to it,"

Popovi said. He turned around and pulled back out into traffic. They had had nearly reached Taos.

"Nowhere else I intend to be," Lee said. Chev saw him wince as they hit a pothole, but his voice stayed steady. "This is the most important thing I've been part of in my life. I've survived to make it this far. I look forward to seeing Stillman dragged off to jail, too."

"Hospital is a couple blocks away," Tomas said. He looked at his watch. "We have time. None of us are going to miss this show."

The stop at the hospital didn't take long, despite the flurry of work they did on his arm. Popovi stayed close, and Lee wondered how many people passing through thought the State Patrol Officer stood there guarding a prisoner.

For some reason, the idea amused him. It wouldn't have a few weeks ago, and that told him how much life had changed.

Chev had commandeered a computer with an Internet Connection and a printer. Tomas helped him, and they both looked pleased when Lee came back out.

"Amazing what you can find when you know what you're looking for," he said, grabbing up the papers and putting them into a file folder. He turned to the people in the office. "Thank you."

Despite a broken arm -- or maybe because of the drugs they gave him -- Lee felt better than he had in years and ready to face the bad guys one more time as they headed out of the beige abode building into the covered walkway. Popovi brought the car while Tomas stood with them, still playing guard. Cheveyo had latched onto a cane and looked steadier for it.

They'd wrapped Lee's arm in a brace, though he could still feel the dull ache under the painkiller. He felt awkward with his arm immobilized, but all in all, the two of them had come out of this with doing well.

Lee looked at Chev and smiled, obviously startling the man. "Someone is in for a real surprise."

Even Tomas laughed this time.

CHAPTER THIRTY-SIX

C hev had borrowed a phone from Tomas and started making calls as soon as they hit the road. Along with the information he had gathered from the Internet, he came up with a rather damning scenario for Red Sun and its pretentious CEO.

Theirs was the first police car to arrive at the state capital building, but others weren't far behind. Tomas climbed out of the car, cautious again as they prepared to face the enemy down.

"Almost high noon," Popovi said as he offered a hand to Lee. "Do you think that's symbolic or something?"

"I think it means it's been a damn long couple days," Chev said as he got out and leaned on the cane, surveying the walk to the building. "I'm looking forward to having this over with and getting back to the important things in life."

Popovi led the way into the building, past security, and into the vast rotunda, with the state's seal embedded in the cream colored tiles. While his cousin tracked down the meeting, Chev stopped to look down at the American eagle with wings spread protectively over the smaller Mexican eagle. He wondered what his Conquistador would have thought of the melding of the cultures that made New Mexico unique.

They couldn't have timed their arrival better. They found the meeting in a large room with a round table and another gorgeous seal of New Mexico on the wall, this time in burnished wood. Stillman and Sandra stood side-by-side, papers in their hands. Lawyers stood in array beside them, and Grandfather stood the other side with two of Chev's Santa Fe lawyers. Grandfather looked like something wild brought into the building. Between grandfather and the others sat two men and a woman, none of whom looked pleased.

Sandra had dressed well for the show. Conservative, her makeup not quite perfect, her hair a little bedraggled. She held the papers in her right hand, the left on her chest as she spoke.

For a moment no one saw Chev, Lee, Tomas, and Popovi. Chev paused and watched the show and forcing himself to calm before he rushed in. He wanted to do this right, and getting into a shouting match, or beating Stillman about the head with his cane, was not going to look good, no matter how rewarding it might feel.

"No, I haven't heard from my husband in months," Sandra said, shaking her head with a mock look of worry. "I've been working hard to find him ever since he disappeared from London. There's been ... well, concern about his mental health since he purposely stepped out in front of an on-coming vehicle. He has run his business into the ground and turned down half a billion dollars from a reputable firm in the Orient. The man is not well. This ... this is unfortunate that we have to do business this way, but I do not see any reason why Mr. Stillman, who had assurances the land was his, should be forced to suffer through my husband's mental problems."

"He turned down a more than adequate offer for the land," Stillman began.

"Because he doesn't want to sell it," Grandfather said with a snort of disdain. "The money has never been the point."

"I think, sir, you have delayed these proceedings long enough," one of the lawyers said. "I understand you are Rey's grandfather, and we've reason to believe you may be acting in your own best interest here since we have paperwork showing you intend to file suit to obtain rights to the land yourself, and take it out of Mrs. Rey's hands. We're willing to make a settlement with you for the area as well --"

"It is not my land to settle with, nor does it belong to this woman. It belongs to Cheveyo, and he has made the decision not to sell."

"We have three psychiatrists flying in from London," Stillman said. "They'll testify to Mr. Rey's unfortunate state of mind --"

"It's *Doctor* Rey, you stupid bastard," Chev said as he stepped forward. He had the joy of seeing both Stillman and his wife take a step back in shock. "The land is not up for sale. Nor do I think these people want to give it over to someone who is about to be arrested for attempted murder."

"Oh Chev," Sandra said, shaking her head with mock sorrow. She was better at the act than Sillman. "I'm so glad you arrived. We've arranged take you some place where you will be cared for now."

"I've already filed for divorce, Sandra, so you can stop the act. I know you heard from Smithers in London. I did make the mistake of not telling my Santa Fe firm to cut you off from my funds. I know you've spent the last two days draining as much money out of the banks as you can."

"You aren't thinking clearly," she said, her face paling.

"Oh, I think I am." He turned to the other three who looked a little more interested now. Grandfather grinned. "I'm Dr. Cheveyo Rey. This is Officer Popovi Da from the State Patrol. He's here to assist in the arrest of Mr. Stillman and my soon to be former wife on charges of fraud and attempted murder."

"Chev, please," she said, a hand going to her lips.

"Damn good act," he said and grinned and held out the file to the government people. "You'll want to look at these."

"I believe if you are making accusations, my lawyers should be the first to see them," Stillman said, nodding to his people.

"No," Chev said. He walked around the table to where Grandfather stood, and laid the folder on the table.

"I can see there is enough dispute here already that no decision would be made today," the woman said as she opened the file folder.

The pictures were pretty damning, really. Mr. and Mrs. Stillman -- Sandra, in fact, though the name said Mia -- on a cruise in the Bahamas five years ago. A second picture showed the two at a Red Sun affair when the company first launched. Various other notes and mentions of the two involved in business practices that might not have been legitimate.

"I rather suspect she married me to get my money and my land," he said and gave a little shrug. "I looked like the perfect patsy -- Indian Boy made good."

More police had shown up at the doorway. Lee stepped out of the way, letting them through.

"We've located your missing vehicle, Dr. Rey," one of them said. "It was dumped in an arroyo south of town, with two bodies, bullets through the head."

"Damn," Lee said and leaned against the wall.

"That would be Trader and Barnes, two men who worked for Mr. Stillman, and who had attempted to kill Lee Constantinos and me. We didn't kill them."

"We have a witness, John Peltin, who is turning evidence on the murder," the policeman said. "Mr. Stillman, Mrs. Rey, if you would come this way?"

They gathered the two in a circle of police and headed for the door before anyone could protest. Stillman and Sandra looked shocked, as though someone had changed the script and not told them. Chev heard someone reading the Miranda rights, and the lawyers trailed after them while the three government people watched on, looking stunned.

"There is going to be an announcement tomorrow you'll want to watch," Chev said as he gathered the papers back up and handed them to the nearest policeman. "And the land is not going to be sold."

"I rather gathered as much, Dr. Rey," the woman said. "They were too desperate. I had my doubts already. I don't know why they took this chance."

"I talked to my lawyers and detectives in London and my stockbroker on the way from Taos to Santa Fe. It looks as though I was not the first businessman Sandra -- or whatever her name is -- married and swindled out of funds. There's some question about at least one having gone missing as well. It looks as though the two had an ongoing scheme of marrying into money -- one or the other -- and walking away with as much as they could to build their little empire. Unfortunately, they were bad in business, and their own funds had dropped so low it looks like they were about to lose Red Sun entirely."

"Ah. So the two wanted your land and your fortune."

"I think the land was a subterfuge," he said, leaning against the cane. "I suspect they did it to keep everyone focused on saving the land, while they worked on draining funds from every account they could reach. I had already cut Sandra off from my European funds, so she raced back here before I thought to do the same locally."

"But the equipment they took to your land," Lee protested. "They planned something."

"All rented, and they didn't have the money for supplies to get started. I think they would have needed my money to bolster their European investments, which had a far better chance of netting them returns. Amusing, really -- it looks like the one thing I really worried about was pretty much safe all along, and that was the land. They didn't have the resources to build."

The other three, still looking stunned and a little confused finally ended the meeting. In a short time Chev, Lee, and Grandfather were back out in the rotunda. People had gathered in groups, gossiping about what had happened.

"Can we give you a ride, Grandfather?"

"No, no. I'm going home. You get your friend to the hospital before he falls over. Go. You still have a lot of work to do."

Grandfather walked away, pausing to pat Lee on the shoulder. Tomas grinned and waved as the older man stepped out into the sunlight. By the time Chev made it to the door, Grandfather had disappeared.

The police were still sorting out things when Chev, Lee, and Tomas stepped out into the bright hot New Mexico day. Stillman stood handcuffed, and they were herding Sandra, weeping loudly, toward another car. She lost her footing at the last moment and started to slide down --

-- grabbed the gun from the policeman who barely threw himself out of the way before she brought it up, aiming at Chev.

No act this time. Chev saw the hatred in her face. He could hear others yelling at her to put the gun down. He backed up, but he could find no clear place as she pulled the trigger

Tomas moved and jerked in midstep and went down, taking Chev with him. Chev saw his wife crumpling, her shoulder bleeding. He hadn't heard the other gunfire.

"Damn! Tomas!"

Tomas rolled over and braced himself on one elbow. His side bled, and he'd gone sallow, but he cursed as he moved, and didn't look likely to die on the spot.

"Why the hell did you do that!" Chev demanded, hardly noting the others moving around them, except when Lee knelt.

"Damn, I thought that was what you paid me for," Tomas replied. "Don't tell me now that I misunderstood the job description."

"Ambulance on the way," Popovi said. He knelt, a first aid kit in hand. "She's going to survive, too, and spend a hell of a lot of time in prison."

Chev saw the way Lee looked at those words, and the nightmare came to his eyes for a blink before it disappeared.

As it turned out, Tomas was the only one who spent the night in the hospital this time.

CHAPTER THIRTY-SEVEN

Patrice and Perez arrived at the hotel room in the middle of the night. Lee answered the door, and she embraced him, looking both scared and angry.

"We stopped in Taos for food, and they had the news on. I can't let you two out of my sight, can I?"

Chev had been watching television. He'd said she was going to be arriving tonight, and there was no use trying to sleep before then. Lee had seen the worry in his eyes every time he spoke of Patrice, and the fear something might have happened to her as well.

Chev stood and crossed the room, limping badly as he used the cane. They embraced.

"You know, I could use a cup of coffee," Lee said to Perez. "Isn't there a Denny's out on Cerrillos?"

Perez looked over Lee's shoulder to the two who were moving back to the sofa. He nodded.

"Yeah. Great desserts, too. And you know, we should go to my place afterward, rather than drive all the way back here."

"Hey," Chev said, starting to protest.

"I'll see you in the morning," Lee replied, and walked out the door, pulling it closed.

They didn't try to follow and stop him. Good.

He didn't see the two again until the predawn hours of Friday morning when he, Perez and Father Tony showed up at the Desert Traditions Museum, ready for the next big step in their work.   Tomas had driven down to Albuquerque to pick up the group of archeologists who had flown in the night before and would arrive within the hour. Popovi, who had been lounging in Patrice's office, came and let them the three of them in.

"They're crazed," Popovi warned as they stepped inside. "The two of them have gone stark raving mad."

Lee looked down the hall past Patrice's office. "You know maybe we can --"

"Lee!"

"Too late," Perez said with a bright grin.

Patrice put him to work. Chev barely lifted his head from his computer to wave hello. Far too soon, the four archeologists arrived, and all of them looking intrigued. They also drew Jamie Manross, a photojournalist who knew Chev from some previous work. The strangers wandered around the still-closed museum while Lee and the others gathered the last of their supplies and paperwork for the day. Despite having had all this time to prepare, it still seemed frantic in the end.

And to be honest, Lee didn't care. By eight in the morning, they loaded up in two SUVs and headed off to the ruins. He felt like a kid on a vacation, hardly able to refrain from asking if they were there yet. They'd be out at the site for most of the day and probably into the night. Tomorrow the archeologists would get to see the olla at the same time Chev talked to reporters. This was going to be an interesting couple of days.

Lee rode in the larger vehicle with the five newcomers,

Chev, and Patrice, who drove. Tomas, Popovi, Father Tony, and Perez followed with supplies for the camp and extra rations for the day -- food, drinks, and more camera equipment.

Lee sat back and enjoyed the view. Creosote bushes blurred as they passed, and the distant mountains became a distinct dark blue tipped in white. He wanted to go hiking in the Sangre de Cristos this summer if the snow didn't melt away. Odd. He had not really thought about his future for a long time, but he would be here in the summer, and for years afterward, if all went well.

They turned off the road onto Rey's land, going past the ranch with a honk of the horn. Sheep scattered.

"We still have several miles to go, but now we're on land my Hispanic grandfather willed to me almost twenty years ago," Chev explained to the others. "It had passed through the family for generations. Worthless land, unless you really loved it. You can't grow two sheep here without importing food for them."

Patrice laughed and expertly navigated the dusty road, taking them beyond any other sign of civilization. Jackrabbits sometimes ran across in front of the car, and a herd of antelope raced away, quickly heading out of sight.

The others spoke quietly, still looking anxious. Lee smiled now and then, but he offered nothing. He put his right hand in his pocket, touching the small emerald bird Chev had given him to bring along.

"Hawk!" Rey said, pointing up into the sky. Lee craned his neck to see the bird as it drifted in a half circle over them. "That's a good sign!"

"Grandfather," Patrice said, slowing down. "An even better sign."

She pulled to a stop, and grandfather, still looking like

a natural part of the desert, came up to Chev's window and smiled benevolently at all of the passengers as he looked in.

"Here." He pushed a hand carved cane inside. "This will help you move better, Chev. Now go. You have wonders to show these people. Hey Lee, next time you go for a walk in the desert, maybe I'll go with you."

"I'd like that," Lee said, and he meant it, which made him feel odd. Despite the trouble he'd had, he loved this place.

They drove away, leaving Grandfather to his place. Lee opened his window and waved.

"How did he know you'd be here?" Jamie asked.

"The same way he knows everything else," Chev replied. "Personally, I'm beginning to think he has a cell phone, a laptop, and a wireless Internet connection. And probably a surveillance drone that watches my every move."

Patrice laughed -- but she also leaned forward to scan the sky.

When they finally hiked up to the camp, Lee watched the four new archeologists head straight to the sealed caves. The discussion immediately began on brick styles, meanings of the petroglyphs and pictographs on the rock face, and a dozen other esoteric subjects. Chev called them back to order. They ate out there by those sealed chambers, and Lee had the suspicion if they had stopped there, no one would have been displeased.

"We have more to show you," Chev said with a bright smile as he leaned on the cane. "Lee?"

Lee drew the green bird from his pocket, and the archeologists seemed to immediately forget the ruins that had intrigued them a moment before.

"There's more?" Alma Bissell asked, her hand brushing against the bird.

"Yes," Chev said. He still smiled. "This way."

The hike to the ruins went quickly, though Lee kept finding himself looking into the sky, watching for a Red Sun plane. Perez walked with him and didn't look any more assured than him, but they reached the ruins, where the newcomer's shock gave way to joy and excitement.

While the band of archeologists moved from one spot to the next, exclaiming over the various finds, Chev and his people looked on, grinning. After a couple moments, Chev drew their attention again.

"Excuse me," he shouted and drew all their attention. "I think you forgot something."

Lee held up the bird again. If there was ever a talisman of wonder, this was it.

"Where?" Louis Deel whispered.

"This way."

The group followed them to the back of the ruins -- and stopped again at the wall of history. The others had covered the opening with the original slabs. Chico, Lee, and Kitt slid them aside, and they went to the curve in the wall and the steps.

Jamie went in first with Chev, Lee, and Patrice next, and the others close behind. Battery operated lamps illuminated the area beyond the curve.

As they came to the little steps and could see the chamber, they stood in stunned silence.

"Oh dear God," Victor Giguere whispered, the first words after a dozen or more heartbeats of silence. He ran a hand through his gray hair, looking frantic. "Conquistador. Aztec. Oh please don't let this be a fraud!"

"It isn't," Professor Belinato said as she came in behind them, the others following as well. "We've already sent threads for analysis, as well as a tiny piece of parchment from the journal. It's been authenticated. Here's the paperwork."

She drew the papers out of her bag and gave them to him. Victor glanced at the words and handed them back. The others, faced with this wonder, didn't look at the offer of proof.

"This is not what we're trained to handle," Chev said. "But I wanted my colleagues here first before I brought in someone specializing in Aztec and Colonial Spanish history. By the way, there's another sealed door over there, and we have reason to believe there may be an Aztec burial on the other side."

"You've read his journal," Felicia Jacoby said, pointing at the small bound book on the board placed back by the body.

"Part of it. Lee, can you get it for me, please? Thank you. His name was Alejandro de Seville, and he was a cousin to Cortez who joined him late in the conquest after Cortez was already famous -- or infamous -- in Cuba."

Lee pulled on gloves Chico handed him, and lifted the book and board. Chev slipped on thin gloves as well before he carefully sat down on the stairs and took the book in hand. The rest of gathered close by.

*"This is from the first entry. It's written in an archaic Spanish, but I learned to translate the language back in college when I wanted to find material about my own family," Chev explained as he carefully turned the book to the first page. *Today I rode along the hills, where years ago my cousin Cortez and I rode before he sailed away. I thought he was mad to sail across that far ocean. But he has done well in this Cuba, despite the barbarians and the envy of his own people. He writes to say that this is the land of opportunity, a land where Midas must surely have lived, for everything is golden.*

Tomorrow I sail for the New World where, if God is kind, we'll find gold and fame. My cousin is so assured of his future that I fear he will annoy God himself with his egotism.

I am less certain, though not from the fear of God's wrath at my own egotism. Today when I rode above the city, I looked back and saw dark clouds on the horizon, rising between me and this far place of fame and fortune. Yet beneath me, bright still in the sunlight, lay all of Granada, like a jewel offered by God. How could we want to leave such a place?

I fear I will never return to this land that I love so well."*

Lee looked down at the body, little more than cloth and bones, and felt sorrow for the first time. How hard it must have been to sit down in this dark cave and know he would never go home.

"This second entry I'll read is about half way through the journal," Chev said, *carefully turning pages. "It explains what we have here in these words he wrote. *I am surrounded by barbarians and devils, and I can no longer tell which is which. God give us grace, for the Aztec will never forgive us now. Montezuma is dead, and the devil priests are calling for a Holy War. I warned Cortez, but he has denied me, and I know that he believes himself invincible.*

And maybe he is. Maybe God has given him the strength of Jesus and the blessing of the Saints, but I don't believe it is so. I have seen the children raped and the babies murdered. That is not God's work. The devil has my cousin's heart, and he sold it for gold, not glory.

He shall not have the gold. Not all of it. I will deny the devil that much of his tithe.

I have helped Mazatlcalli, one of Montezuma's younger bastard brothers, to get such wonders from the city as we could. Cortez doesn't trust me. I think he suspects that I have more knowledge of the language than I have let on, and he suspects conspiracies everywhere. That, of course, is why I haven't told him that I broke the language barrier months ago. He would think I was conspiring with the natives.

*And I have. I have conspired to save as many as I can. And even their gold -- because my people have become savages, and I would rather live with the true savages who are at least true to themselves."**

Silence still. Centuries divided them, but Lee knew Alejandro had been a man he could have liked and trusted. He had done the right thing in the face of injustice. It felt good to learn that such people had existed in all times.

*"And this is his last entry," Chev said, turning to the back of the journal. *"Ah, I have seen such wonders! I have walked in places that no one from Spain has ever seen, and I have lived with a simple people who are closer to God than those who pray each day in their Cathedrals. God has granted me a full life, and I know that I die in His Grace. There is peace at last.*

Though I miss the roses of home. I miss them still-- and the fine wines, and soft music. I wonder if there is a Spain in heaven, the Spain of my dreams where I still ride in the hills.

When someone of Spain finds me here and reads this journal, pray find a priest to bless my bones and assure my final passage to paradise. I know that my people will come. I have no doubt that they will spread far and wide, always searching for gold -- the curse of my cousin, Cortes -- when they should have searched for grace instead. God grant them the peace I have gained, and God grant them the love of this place that I have found.

And you, friend, who read this journal -- keep these treasures protected. I put them in your trust now. God keep you safe and go in His Grace.

And remember me.

*Alejandro De Seville, the 20th of May, in the Year of Our Lord, 1540.**

Chev closed the book and handed it back to Lee, who reverentially laid it back beside the man who had written it.

"You already brought him a priest," Jamie said,

nodding toward the body. "And a rose."

"Oh yes." He smiled again as he stood with Patrice's help. "This is Father Antonio's second trip. The one really good thing about Catholic Priests is they know how to keep secrets. But now the secret is given to you, and we'll share it with the world."

They didn't make it back to camp until sunset. The others cooked food for the group, and they talked about the find like children let into a toy factory.

"We have to be careful now that we're about to tell the world," Chev said, looking back up the trail. "But it was never meant to be a secret forever. Alejandro, writing in his journal, knew we would come here one day. We kept the site quiet this long because of the damn Red Sun people."

History in the making, Lee thought as he stared up at the stars -- the same stars Alejandro would have seen, almost the same place where he might have camped on his way to his tomb.

At dawn, he walked down the ravine and watched the sun come up. He'd never felt so alive. He'd never felt so happy.

Patrice and Chev came down and stood by him. She stretched and put her arm in Chev's when he offered.

"I know this might not be the right time yet," Chev said and shifted a little, then smiled. "Patrice, as soon as everything else is settled, will you marry me?"

Lee hadn't expected her to cry, or to embrace Chev as she gave her muffled her yes.

"Well," Lee said. "I'm glad to see that finally settled!"

They laughed and went back to celebrate with their friends.

CHAPTER THIRTY-EIGHT

Lee loved working at the site. In the six months since the official opening, people from around the world came to see the wonder, and he'd enjoyed meeting and talking with many. National Geographic had devoted almost an entire issue to the find as well as a television special.

Nothing seemed to be slowing down, either.

Lee had started taking classes a couple days a week, shuttling back and forth to Santa Fe, and once a week down to Albuquerque. However, what he really loved was being here, especially now since the weather had started to turn cooler again, with the hot days of summer past.

He had also started riding one of the horses, often with Leanne, who proved to be good company. He'd been afraid of her at first, but she gradually dissuaded him of his fear something would happen because of him. It was good. He liked having her for a friend, and it might go farther -- but they were both too busy right now to think beyond a ride now and then.

He loved the time, running free with the wind, watching the jackrabbits, coyotes, and sometimes an antelope, race off ahead of him. He'd found everything he'd ever dreamed of, and more, here.

The site kept getting better. In another month they were going to finally open the Aztec tomb. By then they'd have three new team members, specialists in the field. He'd met them all. They had to get free of their own projects to step in. So far he didn't think there would be any trouble with adding them. Chev had been very careful about whom he chose.

And it was still Chev's choice. The government talked about taking over the site, but they weren't talking very loudly after the fiasco with Red Sun's attempt to take Chev's land. It looked likely that Conquistador Ruins would stay in Chev's hands for the rest of his life. The government was happy to have it all privately funded, too.

Lee tried not to think about the Stillman trial coming up in the next week. He would have to be on the witness stand again, and thinking about it left a cold lump in his stomach. He only hoped there would be justice in the end.

Lee brushed at the sand along the edge of the wall in the Conquistador room where he and Kitt worked, listening as the tourists moved along behind the rail. Above them the relics of a different place glittered in the lights, they'd carefully set up in the corners. Lee had been self-conscious the first few days when he worked here, but he'd gotten used to it. He liked it when the occasional tourist asked him questions. They didn't get many people hiking up here, and those who came were genuinely interested in the site. Kitt could answer anything he couldn't -- but Lee surprised himself with his own knowledge sometimes.

He loved this place. Beneath the sand, he brushed away he could already see the tops of several jars. One, he thought, looked golden.

"Kitt -- come take a look."

"Hell, don't tell me you've found something else!" Kitt said. He came from his spot, leaping over the railing while a couple people laughed, watching him. "Good God, Lee. Look at this! Alicia -- get the camera and Chev!"

Kitt and Lee leaned over the work, brushing a little more away, examining the area. By the time Chev arrived they had found the edge of the sand pit and the stone floor. It had obviously been hand excavated. Chico came with a thin measuring stick, and Kitt pushed it down through the sand to the bottom. It looked about three feet deep.

"Nice find, Lee. I don't know how you do it," Chev said. He had a hand on Lee's shoulder. "Can you take a moment away so I can introduce you to someone?"

"Sure. No problem."

Chev helped him up. Lee still felt awkward with an arm in a brace. It didn't want to fully heal, but seemed to be doing better lately, and he hoped to have the brace off soon. It was hell when he got sand down in it, which happened every day.

Chev took him to a young man standing by the wall just inside the Conquistador's tomb. He looked nervous, and a glance at Chev showed a bit of uncertainty in him as well. The man nodded to Lee when he neared.

"I'm Andy Nuevel," he said. "Debra's second husband."

Lee started to back up. Chev put a hand on his shoulder. "Hear him out. I think you need to."

"We tried to find you after Debra talked to you," Andy said quickly. "It wasn't right, Leander. Gary is your son, and I told her it wasn't fair you never see him again. But... well, we don't want to upset his life, you understand?"

"Y-yeah."

Chev's fingers tightened on his shoulder. "Sorry to

throw this at you," Chev said. "But I didn't think taking the time to talk about it first was going to help."

Lee nodded. He took a deeper breath and looked back at Andy. Blonde hair cut short, muscular. Everything he wasn't.

"We'd like to introduce you to Gary as his uncle. We figure when he's older he'll need to know the truth, but for now, it allows you to come and visit him," Andy said, looking nervous and upset. Lee hadn't thought about how awkward this must be for him. "Debra feels really badly about what she said to you. Deb was scared after you got out, and then she realized you'd disappear, and she'd never have a chance to make it up. Reporters were bugging the hell out of her again, and she didn't think she could go through it another time. If you hadn't turned up on the news with all of this, I think she never would have forgiven herself. We'd have been paying detectives to find you. But we are, both of us, sorry. Really. It wasn't right, after everything else that had happened to you. She was scared."

"I understand," Lee said. He felt an odd little whisper of calm he hadn't expected. Everything Andy said made sense. It was not him she had really reacted against. And though he knew he couldn't have her back, it mattered less now. He had moved on, just as she had. "I really do understand. I hadn't thought about the reporters and all. They were hounding me as well."

"Can we work with his, Leander?"

"Lee," he said. He held out his hand. "I don't think we're going to have a problem."

"Good. Debra and Gary are outside. You ready to see them?"

"N-now?"

Andy looked worried. "We should have written -- but

Debra didn't know what to say." Andy sounded apologetic. "And we thought we'd like to just do it. I'm sorry. We can go back --"

"No!" Lee said, grabbing his arm. "Hell, no. I'd like to meet him. Bring them in."

Andy looked at him and then nodded. He hurried back out of the opening.

"Sorry, Lee. I didn't realize he had the wife and kid here with him," Chev said.

"It's all right," Lee said calmly. He surprised himself. But he barely had time for a deep breath before Debra walked in. She looked good. Older. Wiser. Happy, he thought. She had three kids with her, a girl she carried, another holding to her hand -- and Gary holding onto the girl's hand.

The boy looked a lot like his mother, but at that moment, with his eyes wide and staring around the room, taking in the statues, Lee only saw himself.

"Cool!" Gary cried out.

"Oh yes," Chev said softly. "That's your son."

And even Andy laughed.

The End
###

A FINAL NOTE

Once upon a time, I decided to try my hand at writing a romance novel.

I didn't start out with a very romantic setting: my hero released from prison, his wife remarried, and his former life gone. I sent him off to the American Southwest, an area I adore. I brought in his new boss (and his less than romantic problems with his wife).

Then I introduced him to Mary. Here, finally, I was moving into the romance part! They even had lunch together!

And then ... and then ...

There is a reason why I now outline books before I begin. At this point in the story, I got caught up in archeology, my love of ruins, and history research. Lee had quite an adventure. So did Chev, Patrice, and even Tomas.

Imagine my surprise when I finished the first draft and went back to read it. Oh, Mary. Right. I forgot all about Mary in my rush of historical fun. Mary didn't fit into that part of the book at all.

So I made what I thought was a logical decision. I had Mary murdered, and the death blamed on Lee.

And that was when I realized I am simply not cut out to write romance novels.

ABOUT THE AUTHOR:

Hello!

I am an eclectic and prolific author whose has published in a number of genres, including Young Adult Mystery, Contemporary Fantasy, Epic Fantasy, Science Fiction and numerous works on writing. While I started on the outer edges of traditional publication with sales to small press and magazines publishers, I have since moved most of my work to the Indie world and I am madly in love with the new world of publishing and the direct contact with readers.

I live in Nebraska with my husband, my cats and a small but entirely useless dog..

Connect with Zette:

Web Site: http://lazette.net

Twitter: http://twitter.com/lazetteg

Facebook:
http://www.facebook.com/lazette.gifford

Joyously Prolific Blog: http://zette.blogspot.com/

Smashwords:
http://www.smashwords.com/profile/view/Lazet
teG

FIND WORKS BY

LAZETTE GIFFORD

ON

CREATESPACE

SMASHWORDS

A CONSPIRACY OF AUTHORS

NOOK

AMAZON

AMAZONKINDLE

LAZETTE.NET

www.ingramcontent.com/pod-product-compliance
Lightning Source LLC
Chambersburg PA
CBHW071050250626
47159CB00002B/426